Praise for Georgia

"Complex and original . . . *Georgia* conveys O'Keeffe's joys and disappointments, rendering both the woman and the artist with keenness and consideration."

—*The New York Times Book Review*

"As magical and provocative as O'Keeffe's lush paintings of flowers that upended the art world in the 1920s . . . Tripp inhabits Georgia's psyche so deeply that the reader can practically feel the paintbrush in hand as she creates her abstract paintings and New Mexico landscapes. . . . Evocative from the first page to the last, Tripp's *Georgia* is a romantic yet realistic exploration of the sacrifices one of the foremost artists of the twentieth century made for love."

—*USA Today*

"Sexually charged . . . insightful . . . Dawn Tripp humanizes an artist who is seen in biographies as more icon than woman. Her sensuous novel is as finely rendered as an O'Keeffe painting."

—*The Denver Post*

"A vivid work forged from the actual events of O'Keeffe's life . . . [Tripp] imbues the novel with a protagonist who forces the reader to consider the breadth of O'Keeffe's talent, business savvy, courage and wanderlust. . . . It's this inquisitive spirit, one that is constantly seeking, exploring, learning and experimenting in both her personal and professional lives, that drives the novel. . . . O'Keeffe as a character is vividly alive as she grapples with success, fame, integrity, love and family."

—*Salon*

"*Georgia* is a uniquely American chronicle . . . and, in the end, a book about a talent so fierce it crushed pretty much everything in its path. . . . Tripp expertly makes drama of two traditional themes in the O'Keeffe story—the romance with Stieglitz and the development of her art—but it's the track about her art and his management of it and her struggle not to be dominated by him that makes her novel compelling. . . . In most first-person novels, the character talks to you. Here, she recollects with you—in her heart as well as her head. Which is to say that Dawn Tripp writes in much the same way as O'Keeffe painted: in vivid color and subtle shade. . . . a rare story of artistic triumph."

—*The Huffington Post*

"Dawn Tripp breaks new ground in this fictionalized account of the artist's years with photographer Alfred Stieglitz. . . . Tripp, making the bold choice to write in O'Keeffe's first-person point of view, succeeds brilliantly. The novel does not read like Tripp's version of O'Keeffe—this is the artist herself, whispering her secrets to the reader. . . . The novel is not so much a love story as the tale of a woman coming into her own. . . . The story of Georgia O'Keeffe burns a pure, bright flame."

—*The Providence Journal*

"Masterful . . . The book is a lovely portrayal of an iconic artist who is independent and multidimensional. Tripp's O'Keeffe is a woman hoping to break free of conventional definitions of art, life and gender, as well as a woman of deep passion and love."

—*Milwaukee Journal Sentinel*

"American artist Georgia O'Keeffe blazes across the pages in Tripp's tour de force. . . . The author manages to get inside O'Keeffe's mind to such an extent that readers experience her transformation . . . they will feel the passion that infused her work and love life that emboldened her canvases. . . . The relationship between Stieglitz and O'Keeffe, and her metamorphosis from lover to wife to jilted partner, is poignantly drawn. Tripp has hit her stride here, bringing to life one of the most remarkable artists of the twentieth century with veracity, heart, and panache."

—*Publishers Weekly* (starred review)

"Tripp's best work yet . . . she takes a household-name artist, one whom most people know next to nothing about in terms of personal or love life, and paints a vivid portrait of the artist, using a palette of passion, temper, ego, jealousy, desire, selfishness—all the hallmarks of artistic genius—so believable, so cinematic, it's hard to tell fact from fiction. . . . O'Keeffe is fully formed and complex, breathing right there on the page."

—*SouthCoast Today*

"A dazzling exploration of Georgia O'Keeffe's artistic career and the deeply human woman behind the cultural icon . . . Tripp's writing is the linguistic equivalent of O'Keeffe's art: bold, luminous, full of unusual juxtapositions. . . . While it will appeal to fans of O'Keeffe's work, *Georgia* will also draw readers who love a compelling story. By exploring one woman's struggle to be seen and valued for herself, Tripp asks important questions about gender, love and the roles of criticism and public image in art."

—*Shelf Awareness*

"A smart, immersive read . . . Tripp has done a brilliant job of capturing these two larger-than-life personalities and their circle. She does not flinch as she details the struggle and many costs (personal and professional) this 'woman painter' paid to achieve her autonomy and agency. . . . Strong, frank eroticism, elegant writing, and lots of delicious art-world detail will make you want to put this on the very top of the books on your nightstand."

—*Library Journal*

By Dawn Tripp

Moon Tide
The Season of Open Water
Game of Secrets
Georgia

Georgia

Georgia

A NOVEL OF GEORGIA O'KEEFFE

DAWN TRIPP

RANDOM HOUSE · NEW YORK

Published in the United States by Random House, an imprint and division
of Penguin Random House LLC, New York.

RANDOM HOUSE and the HOUSE colophon are registered trademarks
of Penguin Random House LLC.

RANDOM HOUSE READER'S CIRCLE & Design is a registered trademark
of Penguin Random House LLC.

Originally published in hardcover in the United States by Random House,
an imprint and division of Penguin Random House LLC, in 2016.

LIBRARY OF CONGRESS CATALOGING-IN-PUBLICATION DATA

Tripp, Dawn
Georgia: a novel of Georgia O'Keeffe/Dawn Tripp.
pages; cm
ISBN 978-0-8129-8186-5
eBook ISBN 978-0-679-60427-3
I. Title.
PS3620.R57G46 2015
813'.6—dc23
2015012643

Printed in the United States of America on acid-free paper

randomhousebooks.com
randomhousereaderscircle.com

9 8 7 6 5 4

Book design by Simon M. Sullivan

For Kate Medina

Georgia is a novel, a work of fiction inspired by the life of the American artist Georgia O'Keeffe and, in particular, her relationship with Alfred Stieglitz.

I came to O'Keeffe's story through her art, specifically a show of her abstractions held at the Whitney Museum of American Art in 2009. That show was a revelation. I have always admired O'Keeffe's work but, like many, I knew her as a representational artist. I knew her giant flowers, her cow skulls, her Southwest landscapes. That day at the Whitney, as I moved from piece to piece, I began to draw together an entirely new understanding of O'Keeffe and her art. As early as the fall of 1915, at twenty-seven years old, she was creating radical abstract forms when only a handful of artists were bold enough to explore this new language of modern art. Her abstractions of that time—and those she continued to create throughout her life—were ambitious, gorgeous shapes of color and form designed to express and evoke emotion, and they were stunningly original. I was overturned. Who was the woman, the artist, who made these works? And why was she not recognized for the sheer visionary power of these abstractions during her lifetime?

In the Whitney show, O'Keeffe's art was shown alongside photographs Alfred Stieglitz had taken of her as part of a portrait that spanned twenty years: images of O'Keeffe's hands, face, body— some clothed, others nude. There were also excerpts from letters O'Keeffe and Stieglitz exchanged over the course of their relationship, from 1916 to 1946. The language of those letters was sharply intimate, vulnerable, complex. O'Keeffe's letters revealed a woman of exceptional passion, a rigorous intelligence, and a strong creative drive. Her letters had a raw heat that felt deeply aligned with the abstract pictures I was seeing on the walls, but at odds with the image of O'Keeffe I'd grown up with: the aged doyenne of the Southwest, poised and cool, holding the world at arm's length.

In the weeks after the show, I read several biographies on O'Keeffe, and what struck me is that while each hewed to the core events of her life, there were curious discrepancies in fact as well as varied interpretations of the woman behind the icon. This fascinated me.

In my early research, I gleaned that a central struggle in O'Keeffe's relationship with Stieglitz was the battle over her image as an artist and the "branding" of her work. While O'Keeffe allowed passion— creative and sexual—to be a key inspiration for her art, she would explicitly come to resist and ultimately refuse to allow her art to be cast in gendered terms. In time, she worked to redefine herself as an artist according to her own vision. While O'Keeffe would continue to use abstract forms as a vocabulary in her art throughout her life, the critical reception and initial public reduction of her work into gendered terms had a profound effect on her willingness to show the purely abstract pieces, which are arguably some of the most innovative and original works produced in the twentieth century by any artist—male or female.

The critical language repeatedly used to describe and define

O'Keeffe's work by (mostly) male art critics during her lifetime was an important inspiration for this novel. This language frames her works in gendered terms—and continues to limit our perception of her art and influence today. For me, the pull to write this novel was not just to explore O'Keeffe's life and art but also the challenges faced by women at the forefront of any discipline.

These themes became the bones of my story.

Along with O'Keeffe's art and Stieglitz's photographs, several additional sources were critical to me in the early stages of writing this novel: Roxana Robinson's biography *Georgia O'Keeffe;* Hunter Drohojowska-Philp's *Full Bloom: The Art and Life of Georgia O'Keeffe;* and Benita Eisler's *O'Keeffe and Stieglitz.*

Barbara Buhler Lynes, an art historian, professor, and a founding curator of the Georgia O'Keeffe Museum in New Mexico, is widely recognized as the preeminent scholar on O'Keeffe's art and life. Lynes's work, perspective, and insights have been invaluable. While I recommend all of her writings on O'Keeffe, the three works that were most vital to my process were: *Georgia O'Keeffe: Catalogue Raisonné; O'Keeffe's O'Keeffes;* and *O'Keeffe, Stieglitz, and the Critics, 1916–1929.* In this last book, Lynes comprehensively maps how critical reviews of O'Keeffe's early work influenced the way she would choose to portray herself and her art.

I was in my third draft of this novel when the correspondence of O'Keeffe and Stieglitz was published, having been sealed for twenty-five years after her death: *My Faraway One: Selected Letters of Georgia O'Keeffe and Alfred Stieglitz: Volume One, 1915–1933,* edited by Sarah Greenough. These letters were very useful in terms of clarifying the timing of events and revealing certain key dynamics of their artistic and marital partnership: the powerful bond between them, the flow of ideas, as well as the storms, politics, and, at times, untenable emotion that marked their relationship.

In this novel, I've attempted to capture the spirit of two extraordinary artists by imagining dialogue between the two of them and others in their circle of friends, family, and acquaintances. The letters, dialogue, and scenes in my book are invented. Since this is a work of historical fiction, I took inspiration from actual events and letters that O'Keeffe and Stieglitz exchanged, as well as biographies about both artists, published interviews of O'Keeffe, speeches she gave, and catalogs and other writings by both O'Keeffe and Stieglitz. On occasion, some of O'Keeffe's and Stieglitz's actual words from these sources are used in dialogue exchanges or in Georgia's thoughts within this novel. Less frequently, short phrases from other letters and sources are embedded in the dialogue or in other parts of the narrative. Where snippets from reviews of O'Keeffe's art appear in quotes, the quoted language is the exact language used in the referenced review. My use of statements that the historical record tell me were made and my reference to incidents or events that did happen are not intended to change the entirely fictional nature of this work.

In addition to the works listed above, I found the following texts useful in my research: *Georgia O'Keeffe* by Georgia O'Keeffe; *Georgia O'Keeffe: Some Memories of Drawings* by Georgia O'Keeffe; *Georgia O'Keeffe: Circling Around Abstraction* by Jonathan Stuhlman and Barbara Buhler Lynes; *Georgia O'Keeffe: Art and Letters* by Jack Cowart, Sarah Greenough, and Juan Hamilton; *Georgia O'Keeffe: Abstraction* (Whitney Museum of American Art), edited by Barbara Haskell; *Stieglitz: A Memoir/Biography* by Sue Davidson Lowe; *America and Alfred Stieglitz: A Collective Portrait*, edited by Waldo Frank et al; *Lovingly, Georgia: The Complete Correspondence of Georgia O'Keeffe and Anita Pollitzer*, edited by Clive Giboire; *How Georgia Became O'Keeffe: Lessons on the Art of Living* by Karen Karbo; *Alfred Stieglitz* by Richard Whelan; *Portrait of an Artist: A Biography of Georgia O'Keeffe* by Laurie Lisle; *Georgia O'Keeffe: The Poetry of Things* by Elizabeth Hutton Turner; *Georgia O'Keeffe* by Lisa Mintz Messinger; *Two Lives, Georgia O'Keeffe & Alfred Stieglitz: A Conversation in Paintings and Photographs* by Belinda Rathbone, Roger Shattuck, and Elizabeth Hutton Turner; *Georgia O'Keeffe: A Portrait* by Alfred

Stieglitz; *Georgia O'Keeffe and the Camera: The Art of Identity* by Susan Danly; *A Jean Toomer Reader: Selected Unpublished Writings,* edited by Frederick L. Rusch; *A Painter's Kitchen: Recipes from the Kitchen of Georgia O'Keeffe* by Margaret Wood; *The Book Room: Georgia O'Keeffe's Library in Abiquiu* by Ruth E. Fine; *O'Keeffe: Days in a Life* by C. S. Merrill; "The Rose in the Eye Looked Pretty Fine," a profile of O'Keeffe by Calvin Tomkins published in *The New Yorker* in March 1974.

PART I

I NO LONGER LOVE YOU *as I once did, in the dazzling rush of those early days. Time itself was feverish then, our bodies filled with fire. Your fingers inside me, mouth grazing my throat, breast, thigh—the metallic scent of the darkroom, smells of sweat and linseed oil, a stain of cocoa on the dining table. It was all smashed together back then—art, sex, life—mixed into the perfect color, every shadow had a substance, shape, and tone. Your bowler hat, the lead-rolled gleaming whiteness of an empty canvas, tubes of paint lined up, my dressing gown on the floor, and you above me, light moving on your shoulders. Your eyes did not leave my face. When you touched me then, you moved so close to me—so close and hot and fast and deep.*

I no longer love you that way. My hands are cool now, the past remade and packed away. Sometimes, though, late at night the air lifts and I feel it—the faint burn of your eyes on my closed lids. Still. That sense of you rushing back in.

I

1979, Abiquiu, New Mexico

I BOUGHT THIS house for the door. The house itself was a ruin, but I had to have that door. Over the years, I've painted it many times, all different ways: abstract, representational, blue, black, brown. I've painted it in the hot green of summer, in the dead of winter, clouds rushing past it, a lone yellow leaf drifting down. I painted the door open only once. Just before he died. In every picture after, it was closed.

This is not a love story. If it were, we would have the same story. But he has his, and I have mine. He used to say it all began with the charcoal abstractions I made in 1915 before I met him. I was twenty-seven, a schoolteacher, poor, driven only by a singular, relentless passion for my art. One night, I turned my back on everything I'd learned about what art should be, I locked the door of my room and got down on the floor with large sheets of paper and charcoal. I remember the cool hush of the night through the window as shapes poured out of the nub of charcoal in my hand.

Finished, I rolled up the drawings and sent them to my friend

Anita Pollitzer in New York. She brought them to Stieglitz at his gallery. When he saw them, he told her, "These are the purest, fairest, sincerest things that have entered 291 in a long while."

I knew who he was—everyone did. I'd met him once before though he would not remember. The father of modern photography. An icon of American art. In groundbreaking shows at 291, Alfred Stieglitz had introduced New York to the work of Picasso and Matisse. A brilliant photographer in his own right, he was known more for the careers of the artists he'd "made."

I wrote to him at 291 and asked him to tell me what he saw in my charcoal drawings. He wrote back to say he wanted to show my work, I should send him more. We exchanged letters back and forth across the country. I spent every extra dollar on brushes, paper, paint.

Over the years, this would be the story he told, again and again, until it became The Story: those charcoals; his discovery of me; our correspondence that began shortly after. He would say I was what he had been waiting for. What he had always known was meant to exist.

Because Stieglitz used words with a certain unique force, his version of our story prevailed.

"You will be a legend," he said to me once.

I laughed.

"No," he said. "I see it. It's already in you."

Legend. A word he would use again and again.

He had faith in me. He did not give me greatness, but his faith in my early work gave me the space to achieve it. He knew this then, and perhaps on some level he also knew that for me to fully become the legend he saw, I would have to leave him.

Tonight in New Mexico, so many years later, the air is clear. My sight is gone, but I know this view by heart. The ropy silvered turns of the road passing below my window, the shrubby heads of the cottonwoods, the river valley, the distant line of hills. The shapes of the world out there are shadowy. Lean and contoured strokes, they glow. The moon shines and cuts the night open.

THERE'S A GRAIN of truth to Stieglitz's version of things: The story of my art in his life did begin the moment he unrolled those charcoals. But to my mind, our story began more than a year later. I was still teaching, at a small college in Texas, sending him my pictures as I made them. A curious intimacy had begun to evolve in our letters.

It was late May 1917 when Stieglitz wrote to say he had hung a small show of my watercolors and charcoals. My first show. It would be 291's last. He was closing the gallery. The war. I felt my heart skip as I read those lines. What I'd give to see my things on those walls.

For three days, I walked around with his letter in my pocket. Then I went to the bank manager's house on a Sunday and begged him to open, so I could withdraw the last two hundred dollars I had to buy a train ticket from Texas to New York.

I did not tell Stieglitz I was coming.

II

May 1917, New York

291. THE WALLS are bare, already stripped. He looks up and when he sees me standing in the doorway, his face changes, softens to a simple pleasure, lit. "Georgia."

He dismisses the two fellows he was speaking with.

"You've come all this way," he says. "I had no idea you were coming to New York."

"I know, I should have told you."

"Your show was taken down two days ago. I'm sorry."

His eyes are dark, piercing through his bent spectacles, a kind of deep-set fire in them; his hair thick and wild, turning steel gray. He is in his mid-fifties, nearly twice my age.

"Where are you staying?" he says.

"With a friend. Near Teachers College."

His eyes have not left my face. "Wait," he says. He goes into the back room and reappears with two of my pictures.

"Sit down." He gestures to a chair.

I shake my head. "I'd rather stand."

He pauses. "You aren't going to leave?"

"Not yet."

"Good."

He begins to hang my art, piece after piece. My watercolor skies, my charcoal landscapes of the canyon with the humped shapes of cows, my numbered blues. He hangs them exactly as he'd placed them for the show. A sureness in how he handles them. Prophet. Seer. Giant of the art world. Iconoclast. The small room is hot. I can feel threads of sweat moving down my body, heat in my throat, in my hands.

He is married, I tell myself. A wife. A daughter. You're his artist. Nothing more.

I think back to a day in February, his letters were piling up—sometimes five in a week—I had begun to dread their coming. Began to dread even more the impatient hunger I felt for them to come. And on that day, in the one free hour I had between classes, instead of going to the post office to see what he had sent, I made myself not go. I bought a box of bullets instead, took my gun and some old tin cans, walked out across the plains, threw the cans onto the ground, and shot at them like I could blow that hunger right apart—

Now, at 291, he strides past me. The gallery walls are no longer empty, as they were when I arrived. The room has sparked to life.

One piece does not hang straight. He crosses back to it and gently shifts the frame's edge to be just as he wants it. Then it is done. The room is very still. Light filters through the skylight to the floor.

He turns to me. "Look," he says. My eyes flow slowly over the walls, over my art. "You should have been here to see the whole show," he says. "You would have seen how it stunned them. I can't tell you how many times I had that thought: If only she were here." His voice drops. A nameless, burning thing between us. I laugh, an awkward laugh, but it breaks the spell and things are light again. I am light, and he is just a man. I walk with him through the room, looking at my pictures. We pause at a painting of the Palo Duro canyon—the golden sloped walls, rimmed with fleecy clouds, wet blue sky in the upper right corner.

"That country out there is entirely unlike New York, isn't it?" he says. "And you love it, don't you?"

"The sky is just so big. The distances. It's hard to describe. It reminds me of Sun Prairie."

"In Wisconsin?"

"Yes. Where I grew up."

Farmland rolling away, fields of grain and wheat. But it was the sky I loved most, its gorgeous, blazing moods. When chores on the farm were done, there was nothing to do but wander out into that sky.

We are still facing the picture of the canyon, standing near enough that I realize I could stretch my fingers and touch the point at his sleeve where the wrist disappears at the cuff.

"It's important that you work more in oil," he says. "You'll have to—you know."

"Oil is stubborn. I don't always like it."

He laughs. "You will learn to."

It is the future he is speaking of.

He quotes from the critics, some of the reviews. I have already seen them. He sent them to me and, though I could not quite bear to read them, I notice the words live on his tongue: *exile, privation, flowing, rise, mystical,* in a *sensitized line.*

I am aware of him standing near me—so near, it feels almost unsafe.

"I want to photograph you with your pictures," he suddenly says. "May I?"

I nod. He goes into the back room and returns with the camera and tripod.

"Stand there," he says, pointing to one of my blues. "In front of that. No, not to the side, put it behind you. Make it the background of you."

Inch to the left, three inches forward, half an inch back. He knows what he wants. "No, less. Turn your chin. Yes. That's it." He disappears behind the camera under the worn black cloth.

"Look directly here." His voice snakes into the room like it is not his voice, but another—softer, lower, streaming from the lens.

I can feel him, watching me, waiting, the other side of the camera, the silence of the room charged now as he waits for the light to shift and fall a certain way, an expression on my face that he is waiting for, he will wait until he has it.

"There," he says. "Now. Whatever you are thinking, don't lose it. Don't move. Don't blink. Nothing."

The shutter clicks. I am counting. Counting. It takes so long—but there's a kind of raw pleasure in holding still, like I am stone on the outside, my heart beating through my skin so deep and loud I'm sure he will hear it. I'm aware of his eyes behind the camera, the hot dark work of them, and I feel my body rise.

"Don't move," he whispers. "Georgia."

III

I STAY IN New York for ten days. He invites me to lunch and we walk the streets, laughing, talking. The buildings seem to shimmer, spring sun striking off them. He tells me about Oaklawn, his family's summer home at Lake George—how he always starts to feel the pull of it this time of year, in spring when the buds swell and the world is busting open.

"I love the Lake the way you love your plains and sky."

I glance at him. A small white dog runs across the path in front of us, a child running after, long spindling legs churning. He talks about his daughter, Kitty, who will enter Smith College in the fall. He calls his wife Mrs. Stieglitz, a strain in the silence that follows.

He asks about my family. I talk about my four sisters: Catherine and Anita are married, Ida's a nurse; Claudie, the youngest, still in school, lives out in Texas with me. I don't talk about our father who turned to drink and disappeared. I don't mention my mother who died last spring.

We come to a man selling oranges and stop for one. I peel it as we walk, my fingers tacky with the juice.

"Do you miss Texas when you're here?" he asks.

"Right now?" I say lightly and smile. "No."

There is a push in the silence between us. I am keenly aware of the stink of the horses, the blare of the cars, voices passing, trees like green shadows. A carriage passes by.

"You must continue to send me your things," he says.

"Even with no gallery?"

"I'll find a way to show them. And you must send them carefully—better packaging, more postage. They must arrive safe."

"It's hard to imagine there will be no 291."

I see him frown. "There was no choice anymore. The war. The expense."

"It just feels wrong that something with such meaning would not exist."

"It will exist somewhere else. Just keep making your pictures and send them to me." He smiles then. "You, Great Woman Child."

He has called me crazy things like this in his letters. "How can I be both?" I say. "Both Great Woman and Child. Tell me. I've wondered this."

I expect him to laugh, but he doesn't.

"That's what gives your art greatness," he says simply. "You have what a child has—a pure unpolluted instinct. What I call Whiteness. And you are a woman."

So casual—how he uses that word, *Greatness*—as if he's unfolding something I already know.

BACK AT 291, he introduces me to a few of his circle—the men. There's the collector Jacob Dewald, the inventor Henry Gaisman, the painter Arthur Dove. They have already seen my pictures—and are full of compliments and praise. I briefly meet John Marin, the best-known of Stieglitz's artists. He'll render smashed sunlight on a coast in forked block lines. When I first saw his work, it reminded me of Kandinsky.

Stiegtliz's newest protégé, Paul Strand, is also there. He has a work apron on, a hammer in his hand. He looks like a boy dressed up in someone else's costume. A solemn round face, blue eyes. He shows me one of his photographs of bowls—four very ordinary kitchen bowls—but cropped close up, disorienting.

"So beautiful!" I say. And it is—how the curve of one bowl falls into the curve of the next—a definite, near-perfect balance in resolute asymmetry.

"A similar sense of feeling to your blue spiral, Georgia," Stieglitz says, coming over.

"Different, though," I say.

"How?"

"Here, in the bowls, the movement is happening in many directions at once. Not only one. The cropping intensifies that. It magnifies the motion and makes us believe it continues." I point at a shadow in the shape of a blade, sharply cropped, at the print's edge.

"Exactly right," Stieglitz says, a beat of triumph in his voice, "although I have to admit I myself didn't see it quite that way before." He looks at Strand, then at the others. They nod assent, his admiration echoed in their eyes, and in that moment I understand: There are things this man values in me, things he wants. He treats me as an equal, more than equal, and for that reason alone, others will see me that way.

ON JUNE 1, there is only rain, as if the city itself will pour away. I wake at dawn and watch the world outside slide down the window glass.

At the train station, Gaisman goes off to check the schedule. Stieglitz and I are alone on the platform. The ache is almost unbearable. A strand of hair falls across my eyes. He moves it.

"Lovely, You," he says.

I kiss him then, his face in my hands, drawing his mouth onto mine. I press my body into him, my breasts against his chest through my shirt, his hand moves into the small of my back, the touch electric, wild—his breath mixed with mine, skin raw, my mouth opening, hungry, like I could draw every trace of him into me.

He pulls away, just slightly, still holding me. Shadows pass around us. His hand slips under my coat up my ribs, that fresh strong smell of him so near.

"Now, it's everything, isn't it?" he whispers.

Later, he will swear he never said it—that it was my imagining.

SEVERAL WEEKS AFTER I have left New York, the photographs he took at 291 arrive at the Canyon post office. When I cut the string, slip them out, and see the woman there, the strong-cut angles of her face, for a moment I will not recognize her, but I will fall in love. Not with him. Not yet. But with the woman in the photographs—that quizzical, almost feral expression in her eyes—a restless ambition fused with desire.

I will never tell him this. Not as sharply as I feel it in that moment. Years from now, I will tell a version of it. I'll strip out what I need, small glittering pieces that shed light a certain way. It does not matter. A life is built of lies and magic, illusions bedded down with dreams. And in the end what haunts us most is the recollection of what we failed to see.

IV

1917, Canyon, Texas

HIS LETTERS COME—LIKE food, water, breath. The days bleed together until it's only his letters that mark out time. Five, ten, sometimes fifteen pages. He writes of daily things, some appointment he had, the new office he has rented at the Anderson Galleries, an auction house on Park Avenue. He writes of the war—his sudden despair when he learned that American troops had landed in France. *But then I think of you,* he writes, *and wonder what you are doing out there in your country. It's nearly real to me—that place I've never seen—because of how you describe it. When you've painted more, send them to me.*

One evening when my sister Claudia and I are out on the front porch of the boardinghouse, heavy footsteps come down the hall, growing louder. The screen door opens, and our landlord steps outside. He is a big man, hands like slabs of meat, a ruddy face. As he is walking by me, I shift on the step to make room so he can pass.

"What's that you got there?" he says.

"A painting of the canyon."

"Don't much look like the canyon." He laughs then, hearty and rude. "You must have had a bad stomachache when you painted it."

"Maybe next time I've got a stomachache, I'll make a picture of you."

This stops him. On the last step, he turns and looks back at me.

"You do your teaching work, Miss O'Keeffe, and pay your rent."

"You have it mixed up," I say. I point to my painting. "This here is my work. The teaching—that's just my job."

AFTER HE'S GONE, Claudia remarks in a low voice that I shouldn't talk back like that.

"It's a good place where we live, Georgia."

"There are plenty of places to live."

She frowns. A cheap place is what she means. Before I went to New York, I might have cared a sliver for what people thought. Now not at all.

I study my watercolor, the canyon with crows, made in a dizzying rush. Orange and green hues intense, the water, how fast it moved and leaked and dried.

"I almost caught it here, Claudie. Almost."

"I completely forgot," she says. "Ted Reid came by. He was asking for you."

"How forgettable."

"You seemed to like him well enough before you left for New York."

"Ted's very nice."

"What then?"

"He's just not what I want."

"And what is it that you want?" she says slowly.

There's a loose splinter of wood on the step beneath me. I pick it free. "Spit out whatever it is you want to say, Claudie."

"Mr. Stieglitz is married."

"I'm entirely aware of that. What exists between Mr. Stieglitz and me is what would exist between any two people who share a passion for art. I don't expect you to completely understand, but don't judge it as something it's not."

She looks stung. I close the thought of the kiss at the train station out of my mind.

"He's held a show for me," I say. "He's sold three pieces of my work. Does that matter? Yes. He sees me. He sees what my art can be—risks I haven't taken yet, things I can still do to improve. He's different from other people, and sometimes I feel New York's the only place to be if I want my art to amount to anything."

She considers this. "You must compare it constantly, what you felt there and what's here."

"There's not much here."

She laughs.

"I do love that nothingness here," I say. "The nowhereness. It makes the sky feel big. Plus, you are here, which makes it so much nicer. But I can't begin to describe what it felt like seeing my art on those walls. Like my future was right in that room."

She comes to sit on the step beside me and reaches for my hand, my lovely youngest sister, Claudie's sweet open face—eyes still questioning, though. She's sensed that while everything I am saying is true, something is not quite as it should be.

A few days later, I choose the best among my paintings of the canyon, along with a series I did—Light Coming on the Plains. Three different pictures of an early-morning sky.

I am curious to know what Stieglitz thinks of each, which speaks to him and why. They have a certain livingness—these pictures—that feels true. At the post office, though, I almost fail: They aren't perfect. They could be better. What if he doesn't like them? What if he feels they don't have the greatness he saw in my charcoals and numbered blues? What if those days in New York that I've not been able to shake out of me since did not mean to him what they meant to me? That kiss.

Leaving the post office, I bump into Ted Reid.

"Georgia, I've been looking for you everywhere."

"I'm at school every morning at eight to teach. You know where I live. You couldn't have been looking too hard."

On his face, a pink flush. "I told Claudia to tell you I'd come around."

"Yes, she said that."

He walks me back to the house, saying funny things and making me laugh. Then he gets a little serious and says there are some other things he wants to talk over with me. He digs the toe of his boot into the road. He is a fine young man, a star athlete, one of the town's favorites.

He invites me to go for a walk out to the Palo Duro canyon. I say no at first, but he looks so crestfallen that finally I agree. And that evening as we sit there on the canyon rim, his strong arm comes around my shoulders in the moonlight, and he kisses me, a long slow kiss, and I let him, like I could wash that other kiss out of my mind. Then he asks me to marry him, and I throw my head back and laugh. He gets all befuddled, and asks again. I shrug loose from his hand around my shoulder.

I know what Ted likes about me. My drive. So different from any other girl he knows. He's said this before, and I've explained to him that living with me for half an instant would shred him to bits.

"I'm planning to enlist," he says.

"You should stick around and graduate first."

"I'd stick around for you."

Something in me shrinks. "Don't be stupid," I say, snipping the last bit of closeness between us.

I have seen into the future, I could tell him. In that future I am always alone.

I PAINT AND teach. I poke desert flowers into jars to make still-life models for the older students. I bring small rocks and bones back from my night walks and arrange them on the desk in the classroom. Two young boys draw submarines. One draws a soldier with big orange clouds. War clouds, he explains. Always war. There is one other little boy, though, who paints a landscape with a purple star, and a house on each side, and trees. It's a funny picture, not as well done as the rest, but I tell him I love it, because it is free.

"It isn't for sale," he says solemnly.

I laugh. "That's not what I meant."

Then he tells me he made it for me.

CLAUDIA BRINGS THE afternoon mail. A letter from Stieglitz. The one I've been waiting for. He has received the paintings, the series and the others. He loves them. He loves them.

Georgia O'Keeffe! I want to crawl inside that world. Lie down under that same sky. Let the same dark night soak into me.

It seems like ages since I've seen your face, heard you laugh—your lips on mine.

There, I've written it. Something happened in that kiss, didn't it? I think about that when I look at these pictures you send.

I turn the page and see a few sentences he has written across the top, in small-print letters almost like an afterthought—*I wonder what kind of child I would give you. Would you let me?*

I let out a short cry.

Claudie's head snaps around. "What's wrong, Georgia?"

My hand covers my mouth and I stifle a laugh. "Oh, nothing," I say. "Nothing."

She glances at the letter in my hand. I fold it and go upstairs. I just need to be alone, to read his letter again—what he said about my pictures and his question. Through the wide middle window, the sun has begun to sink, the dark shape of a horse walking across the plains.

I take out the cardboard box of photographs he took over a month ago, in 291.

I prefer the one with her hands to those of her face. The gesture of her hands echoes the spiral form of my painting on the wall behind.

There was a moment that day, in 291, when he set down the camera, came near me, touched my cheek and turned it with his hand. A tremor under his finger. Like a sled going fast downhill.

She has a certain poise, that woman in the photographs. She is me and, at the same time, not. I've always thought of my face as round, but in the prints there are angles—cheekbones, jaw. Beautiful. She knows exactly who she is, and there is something so breathtaking in it all, not just in her, but in the inviolate space of this exchange. In my letters, I've begun to write to him things I can't say to anyone else: my ideas about art—how sometimes I'm so full of shapes and colors, my mind can't hold it all in. It's become clear to me, though, that if anyone were to understand the particular language of my pictures of light on the plains or the flow of an abstract shape, it would be him.

I look up. It is dusk. The evening star hangs just there through the window above the stick limbs of a windmill. Far off, cows move like tiny black chains, slowly at the sky's hem. The wind blows the sound of their lowing around so it seems to come from everywhere.

I walk out into the falling daylight across the plains, past the ugly white houses, black windows, his letter folded in the pocket of my skirt. I can feel its edges against my thigh. When the town is a pebble far behind, I lie down on the hard dry earth and let my head fall back. The evening star, unearthly, and the feeling, to be enthralled by nothingness. The sky, so wonderful and big, I breathe it in so deeply. I lie there in the cold quiet, a small thought moving at the edges of my mind—the possibility that he is like that open space, vast like these plains, this night, vast enough it seems sometimes to hold me.

THE NEXT DAY after I teach my class, I close the door, pull out a sheet of paper, and lay it on the table with my paints. Water on my brush. A pale wash of sky, orange-yellow. A slight resistance in the woven surface of the paper. I add a line of deeper red, blazing into the light, more energy, more life, quickening—a faint electric thrill in my fingertips as the brush sweeps back and forth, the loss of time, of self, as the feeling of that shape in my mind drives through my hand. The colors seep, sky almost to the edges, just a scrap of whiteness toward the top—my star.

I finish the painting and leave it, rinse my brush, lay it down. I change the water in the bowl. The air in the room is stifling. I crack the window open.

I take a clean sheet and start again, leaving a spot of white for the star in the same place, high up, off center to the left. A yellow glow around it, then rings of darker yellow-orange, red—the colors bolder now, a braver slope in the line, less control. One dark thick stroke below—the weight of land to balance the pure driving radiance of the star.

The pictures, startling. A humming in my body.

I make it again, letting go of the edges even more this time, past where I think they should be, I push them farther, letting that burning light become the night sky, the colors strike into one another, bleed. Each different evocation of that star—luminous, abstract—an answer to the dark hot work of his eyes moving over me that day in 291. As perhaps almost every picture I've made since has been.

V

As the summer passes, I spend more and more time alone. On an evening when Claudia goes out, I sit on the steps with one of his letters. He writes of the July offensive in Ypres, stunning casualties, so tragic and unnecessary—he writes how the war has completely dismantled America's young fascination with modern art. *They distrust everything foreign now, Europeans in particular. And The Marriage, I'm sad to admit, is a shambles. Mrs. Stieglitz has never understood me. There's nothing between us except for Kitty, and I would not break my daughter's heart. I took her to college last week, now she's gone. So much, it seems, is gone. Prewar hopes,* Camera Work, *291, gone. But you are the lamp. The spirit of 291 continues in your art—*

Against the vastness of his letters, the town has begun to feel so small. I am some snapping lunatic fire stuck in this wound of a town. The women laugh behind my back because I wear men's shoes and long straight black dresses, because I am almost thirty, unmarried and not looking to be, and because I do not believe in the warmongering posters slapped up on the walls of the general store, charging us to slaughter every German. Such ignorance. I call it that. And they shun me for it—for how I speak my mind and for how I go tramping about in the dusk like a crazy person shooting at small game and tin cans.

A RAW SCRATCHING in my throat and a cough I can't seem to shake. I've not been feeling well. I've blamed it—jokingly to Claudia—on the town, how I am choked by its backwater stupidity, the hostile looks. But the cough grows worse. There are days where I have trouble speaking.

Claudia is preparing to leave for a job student-teaching in Spur. It's good work, but I can't quite make sense of a life in Canyon without her. She's been my charge since our mother died. Two days before she is to go, I sit on the bed as she packs her things.

"You need to see the doctor for that cough," she says, tucking a ball of stockings into a pair of shoes.

"It's getting better," I say.

"It doesn't seem to be. What if it gets into your chest?"

"It won't." But my breath catches, and I cough, hard, my body doubled over.

"I'm not going to leave you like this," she says.

"You will go, Claudie. I'll be all right." My voice calm again, controlled, the oldest sister's voice she knows—the levelheaded strong one, the one who is in charge, who will not be argued with, the one who does not break.

THE AIR GROWS cold. Brutal November winds tear through what's left of the leaves on the locust trees. I have to stuff paper down the front of my dress to block the winds as I walk back and forth to class. I go to the doctor and he mops out my throat with long metal instruments, and tells me I must be more careful. He's heard I take long walks at night on the plains. I must stay inside. Stay quiet. Keep the cold air out of my throat. He asks about my family history. "Consumption?" I shake my head no. Silent. Lie.

He sticks a needle into my arm, it goes in deep.

———

A BATCH OF my things arrived in New York crushed. Stieglitz has salvaged them but is angry with me. *Such rare & glorious things, these works of yours, packed in nothing but a flimsy cheap tube and sent unregistered mail,* he scolds. He proceeds to lay out explicit instructions on how to package in the future what I send.

Tears spring to my eyes, a sting of shame for what he does not understand and what I am too proud to explain—how careful I have to be with money. I haven't much. Nothing left over to save. My throat hurts, the pain growing sharper, more intense.

A savage and futile desire. I miss him. I wish he were here with me. I can't paint. I seem to have nothing to say.

IN NOVEMBER, THE school invites me to speak at a faculty meeting about theories of modern art. When the invitation comes, at first I think it's a joke—they despise me—but I accept, what choice do I have? I pore over my books—arguments about art and the human body. Arthur Jerome Eddy's theory that, in painting, one should strive for a higher abstract language—spiritual, pristine. These are theories that meant something to me once. I find myself tearing holes in them now.

When someone looks at something I have painted, I want them to feel what moved me to paint it in the first place. I paint as I feel it. Light, sky, air. As I want it to be felt.

In my speech, I stand up and talk about how when you make a picture—whether that picture is of a chair or a bird or a canyon— you have the chance to say something about what life is, and what it means to you. A picture might be beautiful but if there's no life in it, it's no good at all. Then I take them all apart, the entire faculty, and how they teach, the men most of all, because they are the ones who are always so convinced they have a corner on what's right. I tell them that their program is essentially useless, crammed too full of rattly ideas that have no basis in human emotion, sensation, or need.

I am quite convinced they'll stone me but they don't. Afterward, some of the women come up and seem almost pleased, giddy that I could have gone on like that—out loud. I shake their hands and leave and go to bed.

STIEGLITZ WRITES, *I am worried about you, the cough, the illness.* He seems so far away. *I'm afraid it's worse than you're letting on. Your handwriting has changed. The letters are very small. You must get well.*

I FALL TOO ill to teach. The cough has moved into my lungs, and the doctor tells me I'm as close to having TB without actually having it as anyone he has ever seen. He says the word so evenly it almost slips past me. My head spins. "You'll need to go south," he says gravely, "to a warmer climate. Or else." He rubs those last two words in hard, like salt in a cut—but his eyes are gentle and sincere. He is someone I can trust. I feel a sudden bolt of fear. This cough—this stupid, nagging cough—it is not nothing. *If you are not careful. Take care. Go south. Or else.* My mind a thousand glittery pieces. Everything I want—the vast hope and the magic—his letters, my art, that kiss— lost.

The doctor is looking at me still. "Do you understand?" he says.

I tell him then.

VI

Before

THEY FELL LIKE trees, the males of my father's family. First the gritty flush, then the telltale, hectic cough. Consumption. It got into their lungs and shredded them.

My father had left school to pour himself into the fields when his own father died of it. Then it took his two older brothers. His last brother, the youngest, Bernard, died in my mother's arms. She had brought him into our farmhouse to nurse him because there was no one else. I remember her stern and regal face bent over him—her lovely aquiline features, residual traces of the royal lineage she had descended from to this. She would place her hand under his neck to lift his head, a glass of water to his lips, blood in their cracked seams. The light did not quite reach him, but fell just to the side—as if it had made its choice—and when he passed, he left the last share of land to my father "for one dollar with love and affection bestowed."

We had two dresses each. One to wear while the other was washed. My sisters wore bright-colored sashes to cinch their waists with a lean splash of color, but I preferred mine loose and straight and plain. Our mother was cool but not unkind. Her eyes luminous, austere, held a sort of distance we did not belong to, like the line at the end of the sky—that silent point of reference that held everything tethered, the line that seemed to meet the land but never did. She was educated, mannered, intelligent, she'd wanted to be a doctor once but was married off to my father to merge the farms of their two families. She read to us in the evenings and on rainy days, and my brothers and sisters and I would listen, rapt and silent always, sitting on the great skin of the buffalo our father had shot once in the Dakotas.

After Bernard was gone, and the room where his red-flecked sputum stained the floor had been scrubbed and tidied, linens burned—we never spoke of him by name. There was a day, though, I remember, not long after. Late summer, the warm breeze pressed through the open window, I came upon my mother sitting in her bedroom. On the table beside her were a pair of gold-and-emerald earrings, an exquisite gift her father, George Totto, had made to his wife, Isabelle, before he sailed home to Hungary to claim a lost inheritance and never returned. Those earrings were my mother's most prized possession. She pinned them to her ears when she entertained ladies from town for tea—a token of wealth and exile, of exotic splendor and the quiet stain of betrayal. The day I found her in her bedroom, the earrings laid out on the table near her, she was sitting very still, and I stayed more still in the doorway so she wouldn't know I was there. It frightened me, her broken face, grief pouring through it. It was not Bernard she was mourning—I was eleven and old enough to understand—but her own relinquished life.

Everything changed. Our father grew solemn, skittish. No longer the fiddle-playing, laughing, lighthearted man that I adored. Fear of the white plague dogged him. Every cough or fever made him jump. He drank heavily. There were rumors of horse theft, gambling, fights, a woman he kept in town. Our pact was a common silence. That was understood. We never spoke of any of it.

The following winter, the mercury dropped to thirty below. Snow piled up ten feet.

Drawing classes began for us that winter. I did not have the talent my younger sisters had. We were taught to copy shaded cubes and chromos from the Prang drawing book. We drew sprays of oats and twigs, painful imitations of still lifes, inflated red roses, a pharaoh's horse—failed paintings that my mother framed and hung.

One night on my way upstairs, passing by the window on the landing, I caught a glimpse of something fleeting on the snow. I took a step closer. Just moonlight on the field. That's all it was. Trees bare and dark against the snow. Across the field, a pale lean strip of sky lay like a long thin door.

I made a picture of it—the first picture I made that said something to me—trees, shadows, moonlight—and not moonlight as I saw it but the feeling I had looking out at that field—the soft work of night, how it skinned the world open.

For the snow, I left the paper bare, but it looked too honest, too desolate and familiar, and I scratched thin gray marks to cover it with the impression of a road.

I destroyed that picture soon after, but from that moment on art would become this for me—singular, indissoluble—the one thing that could rein in the chaos and fear to transmute an untenable world to some form of beauty even as that world fell away.

MY PARENTS SOLD the farm and left. My mother was just beginning to show the early signs of illness, but still we knew. We headed east. My parents had sold most of what we owned, like they could rinse themselves of the soiled fate the farm had come to stand for. They took the money, the Irish silver, a favorite carriage horse. My mother packed the gold-and-emerald earrings and the framed copies of paintings that I hated. I packed the moonlight on the field.

VII

1918, Waring, Texas

ON THE DOCTOR's orders, I take the train south to my friend Leah's farm in Waring, near San Antonio, where the air is warmer, more gentle and refined, a sparkly mist that drapes the houses.

My strength returns. I begin to make a few things: sketches with graphite on cream paper—one of Leah, another of a bowl of fruit—then some watercolors of the house next door at night, the big tree looming over it, and the moon peeking through. I make the sky in squiggling light bursts—the way the shimmer of the night breeze feels on my face.

Stieglitz's letters take a new turn. *What if you came to New York? I could look after you. I could make sure you got the rest and care you need. It's on my mind these days. What if she came?*

He tells me that the painter Wright stopped by his office at the Anderson Galleries just as a few of my things arrived from Texas. They looked at them together. Wright remarked on my use of color, then said, "O'Keeffe isn't painting—it's the beginning of a new art."

My heart turns over. I look up and everything seems different—

naked changing colors of the late afternoon, blue rolling hills and how the sun soaks the little yellow house across the way, light splashing over the red tiled roof.

What if I did go?

I SLEEP WITH Leah in her bed, her body warm and soft near mine. I wake up early and sketch her sleeping, her dark head thrown against the pillow, lips parted, long hair streaming out in tangled waves. It's a simple, abstract drawing—the tumble of hair, the impression of a face.

The lilac bushes in the backyard throw their wild scent. The world at dawn feels soft and kind. I gather wood and carry it back into the house for the fire. And Leah is up, stalking around the kitchen in her man's coat, her slender feet poking out underneath.

"It's so different when you're here," she says. "You're so still it makes me still."

"I'm only still because I've been sick."

"No, it's deeper than that—the way you always know *exactly* what you want."

It's the slightest thing—the emphasis she places on the word *exactly*. Innocent. And wrong. I don't answer. Silence is the easiest way to wrap in what I feel. I sip my tea and with my napkin wipe away the wet ring the mug has left.

LATER THAT MORNING, I write to him what I have been afraid to write. "I love you very much today." It seems suddenly very simple, and straightforward.

I tell him I am better, but I know he won't quite trust it.

I want you here, he writes back. *Nothing must happen to you. Could you be happy here?*

He tells me that Paul Strand is coming out this way, and in the middle of May, Paul arrives. At first he tries to deny that Stieglitz sent him. I laugh.

"Do you think I don't see through that ruse?"

He gets all flustered then, his blue eyes uncertain, like he is trying to discern if I am laughing with him, or at him. Paul is so easily thrown.

"Oh come on," I say. "Did you bring any of your prints along? I want to show Leah." That evens things out, and he shows us some of his new photographs, and I feel happy, looking at them. It's like having a shred of Stieglitz's world out here in the wide-open nothing of Texas.

A wife, I remind myself. That bony reprimand. Don't toss your future over for a man. He has a wife. How many times have I said these four words to myself over the last months—words that should matter, that did seem to matter once, and somehow now do not.

June 1. A year ago today I left New York. He brought me to the train station. I kissed him.

On the dresser is a short stack of the books he has given me: *The Letters of Van Gogh,* Clive Bell's *Art,* Eddy's book on cubism, and a copy of Goethe's *Faust,* which was the first book he ever sent to me. It is his favorite, he has told me, he was nine when he first discovered it. He rereads it every summer. He swears it settles something in him—oddly enough—that tragic story of the unsatisfied romantic hero who will swap his soul for one transcendent glimpse of the unknown. There's a brown thread loose at the binding. I pick up a pair of nail scissors and snip it at the root.

He is my future. That is that.

I send off the telegram.

Yes.

VIII

New York

THE WHEELS OF the train knock over the tracks hurtling north. Paul touches my arm. "We are almost there."

Through the window, I see the city rising toward us in the dawn. Gray geometric shapes, angles turned every which way, the river a ring of wide-hammered silver. The fever has come back again, a low grinding pressure in my chest.

WHEN WE ARRIVE, Stieglitz is on the platform waiting in a porkpie hat, a loden cape. Strand holds my arm as we step from the train. My body feels weak, but I feel a surge of joy as Stieglitz takes a step toward us. His arm comes around me as his cloak sweeps against my cheek. He holds me tightly—the strength in his arm around my shoulders—everything in me turns suddenly soft. "I could not believe you would come," he whispers. "I read that telegram over and over and still did not believe that you would come."

He steers me through the great arched hall, dusty violent sunlight pouring through the upper windows. We move slowly, as through a dream. I can feel my body shaking, chills working through me.

The city hits my skin—noise and smells, a street sweeper at his work just outside the door swush-swushing his broom across the sidewalk as we step out.

"My niece Elizabeth, Dove, and the men—all are so glad that you've come." He has slowed his pace to keep his steps in sync with mine. I raise my eyes, the worry on his face so lovely.

Strand raises his arm and hails a taxi for us, then with a farewell he heads off walking down the street. Stieglitz bundles me into the cab like he knows I'm a million tiny feverish pieces, all in disarray. My things are loaded in. The driver slams the door—such a final sound—for a moment I am sure I've made a mistake. But then his voice brushes near my ear.

"There's so much to say," he says as we move out into traffic, the queer rush of the city moving by—so different from the country I've just come from. He draws me more tightly against him.

"You're still unwell," he says. "You didn't tell me."

"It only just came on me again."

There's a dim triangle of sky visible through the upper edge of the taxi window, very high up above the buildings. My breath catches, too sudden, and I cough, leaning forward, my head against the seat, that awful taste in my mouth. He holds me until I am done. My head is light, airless. When the cab makes a sharp turn, I fall back into him. I can feel the coolness of his skin near my face, light kisses through the sweat and the fever, the coolness of him like clear water.

"Darling," he says. I think he says. His voice is an echo, and I have the sense that this has already happened, for years I've been traveling toward this moment, the back of this taxi, this exact course.

"Four flights," he says, when we arrive at his niece's building on 59th Street.

"It is more than four," I say under my breath as we climb. A thou-

sand stairs. The cough flares again at the landing partway up. I have
to stop. He waits with me. I gather myself, he holds my arm, and we
continue slowly up the stairs. He has cleaned the studio. Had new
keys made.

The room is filled with sunshine, it streams through the windows
and the skylight. Pale lemon-colored walls. The floor painted orange,
so ridiculously orange it makes me laugh. I see how it startles him, the
sound of my laughter. After the wild intimacy between us in those
letters we hurled back and forth across the country, now suddenly
here we find ourselves, our slighter, imperfect human selves, in this
lovely shoe-box room.

"There's a bathroom down the hall, a second room, smaller, where
I've stored some of my camera things," he says, "books, some art."

In the corner the bed has been made—a simple cot—the sheets
crisp, evenly lined. There are a few chairs, a table.

I lie down on the bed, springs creak.

"You must not sleep yet. Have something to eat."

"I'm so tired." I slip out of my shoes and crawl under the covers. I
hear him by the sink, filling a glass of water. The walls of the room
soften.

When I wake, it is night, he sits in a chair beside my bed, his face
in the lamplight, his eyes dark and solemn behind the pince-nez, the
bronze rim. I love his broad nose, the mustache, the slight uneven-
ness of his teeth when he smiles, how his hair creeps from the temples.
It was his hand that woke me, his hand on my forehead slipping down
my face, cradling my cheek in his palm.

I remember the train station—a year ago—his hand in the small of
my back, my body against him. It feels so distant now. Another life.

"I'll let you sleep," he says.

He leans over. His lips graze my forehead. Then he's gone.

IX

His face lights the next morning when he sees me sitting up in bed. "You look better. Rested." He's brought fresh eggs from Arthur Dove's farm in Westport. He cooks them on the stovetop, pronounces them "coddled," and brings them to me.

He has brought me oil paints, smug in their small tubes. They lie at the end of the table, along with a book, some paper, and a brown wrapped package of other supplies.

"I didn't bring these things to suggest you start today. I just don't want you to be bored."

"I am never bored. I like this space."

"You seem better today."

"I feel better."

"Read, write letters, stay in bed until you are well."

I nod to the package. "Are there watercolors?" I ask.

He nods. He knows that I love the transient wash of thin colors moving—how quickly you have to work, unlike the sluggish, pretentious oils.

He is studying me.

"What?" I say.

"Nothing," he answers.

I smile and point my knife at his plate. "You haven't touched your food."

WHEN HE LEAVES, I am aware of his absence. I can't sit still. I wash the dishes, take other dishes out of the shelf near the sink, and wash those as well. Tiny demons surface in my thoughts: How have you managed to find yourself in these circumstances? It can't go on, you know. Absurd. He is married. A daughter, a wife. Look at you. Practically tied up and owned by a man you can't have. For shame.

I prowl the apartment. The hall bathroom is armed with several bottles of Synol soap. I find his camera things in the back room: funnels, pans, developing trays, a white umbrella, two tripods, boxes of books, negatives, prints, and mounting paper. I feel like an interloper. I sift through the art things he has left on the table for me: a book, watercolor paper with a heavy weave, paints, brushes, primer, boards. A new palette, so smooth and unpolluted.

My head is beginning to ache. I take a pen and paper and crawl into the bed to write to my sisters. I leave the other things on the table, untouched. *Dearest Ida*, I begin. How to explain it? That I am living in a studio apartment that belongs to a man who has committed himself, his passion, finances, and faith to my career. It all sounds like a foolish sham.

IT'S DUSK WHEN he returns. He sets his satchel on the chair.

"How are you feeling?" he asks.

I don't want to tell him. They hounded me all day—the thoughts, the doubts, the way this must look to anyone else who isn't us. He asks what he can fix me for dinner.

"I'm not hungry."

"You should eat."

"I had some crackers."

He comes over to the bed and sits in the chair. An awkward silence. He goes to touch my chin, I draw back, the slightest movement, his hand falls.

"I am sorry—" he says, glancing away. I touch his hair, gently at first, then push my fingers deeper into it. He raises his eyes. Such sadness in them. Such desire. It takes my breath.

"Will you trust me?" he says. "Will you trust that I'll do nothing to hurt you?"

Something in me softens. "I will."

HE COMES EVERY morning and every evening. He cuts up fruit, slices ham. He makes me oatmeal, toast, and juice. He tells me stories of his day—who he saw, his niece, his mother, some other artist, what thing of mine he showed to someone else and how they loved it, how all of them love me already and cannot wait until I'm well. By early evening I am tired. We have dinner together. Then he leaves and walks the streets, because he can't bear to go home to the Madison Avenue apartment he shares with his wife. He recruits Walkowitz or Zoler to go off and tramp around with him, or he goes alone to an inexpensive restaurant open late and writes letters until midnight when he can slip back to 1111 Madison, sure that the rest of the house is asleep. A vagabond, he describes himself, practically homeless, and I tease him saying he's got no inkling what that word truly means.

During the day, bright light floods the room. I drag the table and stool under the skylight and begin to paint. The paper feels vast and unbound, full of possibility. I begin to clean up an hour before I know he will arrive. I move the table back into its place and climb into the bed as if I have been at nothing all day. If I've done something decent, I show him. More often, though, I tear up what I've made.

In every moment he is there, in every word, every tentative gesture, I feel a thrill. I see how his eyes study my face, the lines of my body, that quiet, particular hunger—then he'll catch himself and look away. We talk for hours. He tells me how they used to call him Hamlet as a child.

"Because you were dramatic?"

"Philosophic."

I laugh. "Philosophically moody perhaps?"

He tells me how he loved horses, loved the races, loved to bet. He could beat his father at billiards by the time he was nine. One evening, ten days after I've arrived, he tells me how he lived in Berlin when he was around twenty. It was his first taste of freedom, and he was bored with his studies at engineering school. He could afford to be bored with a twelve-hundred-dollar-a-month allowance from his father. Then he met Professor Vogel, who taught photography, and he bought his first view camera that used dry plates. He fell in love with an older woman, a prostitute named Paula, and he lived with her there, in an apartment in Berlin's red-light district.

"There were caged birds hung in every window, their cries pierced the streets. Someday," he says, "I will show you the photograph I made of Paula. She was my first love. There were many photographs I took, but I kept only one from that time."

I feel a chill pass through me. When he tells me these things, it strikes me how much life he has already lived. My past feels threadbare in comparison.

"Soon you will come to Lake George," he says. "You will love the Lake—there's no place I love more."

"I've been there once," I say, avoiding the question of how I can go there when he has a wife, named Emmeline, Emmy. She is a brewery heiress. It was her small fortune that bought 1111 Madison. She is the invisible piece of furniture we step around.

"You were at Lake George?" he says.

"I won a scholarship to the art colony there."

"Amitola?"

"Yes."

"Which building did you stay in?" It turns out that twenty-eight years apart, we slept in the same room. "A magical coincidence," he says.

I laugh. "All for my painting of a dead rabbit and a copper pot. That same summer, there was another art contest, do you remember? Your father judged it and the painting he chose was done by a young male student at the League. It was a portrait of a certain dark-haired girl who happened to be me."

He is elated. "I remember that painting!" he cries. "And it was not my father who chose it. He asked for my opinion, and I told him it could only be that painting. There was no other choice. I have never forgotten that face." He squeezes my hand. "This was meant to exist. You. Me. Here together in this studio. Down to this unforgivable orange floor."

WHEN I WAS twenty years old, in 1907, I had shown enough talent that my mother decided that with a proper education I might be able to make a living as an art teacher, and paint in my spare time. She scrimped and saved enough money to enroll me at the Art Students League in New York. I had short black curls the boys loved. They reached out to pat the bounce of my hair so often that they and everyone else came to call me Patsy. I lived in a boardinghouse on 57th, the room was a few dollars a week, and I took five-month courses, instead of eight, to save an extra thirty dollars. I dressed up as Peter Pan for the League Ball. I took classes with Luis Mora, who always drew his wife's head and hands in the margins of his students' work. The teacher I loved best there was William Merritt Chase—so madly flamboyant, with his ostentatious dress, his monocle, suede spats, and silk top hat. He was the only one of any of them who seemed to be doing something different in art, something of his own. He ordered us to do a painting a day—to work quickly, without thought, using bold, instinctual strokes of loaded color.

One morning in early January, I was on the way up the stairs to my life-drawing class when a shadow fell across the steps ahead of me. I looked up. Eugene Speicher, an older student, tall and handsome, stood several steps above. I went to go around him, but he stepped in front of me, blocking my way.

"I have a request, Patsy."

"I'm late to class."

"I want you to sit for me."

"I won't make a good model."

"I think you will."

His eyes were striking, very light. An amused smile played over his mouth.

"Let me pass," I demanded.

"Say yes."

I looked up at him, angry now. "I have class."

"Come on!" He laughed, his eyes teasing. "You know well enough it doesn't matter what you do. I'm going to be a famous artist. You'll wind up teaching in some girls' school. Just sit for me."

My face burned. Furious, I pushed past him, walked quickly down the hall, and slid into my seat, in the back row of the life-drawing class. It was a class I disliked, second only to anatomy, so tedious. I'd never been good at human forms. Less than a quarter of an hour later, I left and found Speicher in a room upstairs.

"What are you doing here, Patsy?"

"I changed my mind." I dropped my things and sat down on the stool at the front of the room. I was curious to see how he would paint me. As he began to sketch lines on the canvas, a thought struck me. There was nothing I had to do. No effort or decision to make. I only had to sit there and be still.

When he finished, I looked at what he had done.

"It came out well," he said.

"Well enough, I guess. I'm not convinced I see *famous artist* in your future, either." A group of boys burst in just then. Friends of ours, they were on their way down to see the Rodin drawings at 291.

They wanted to go and bait the famous Stieglitz. Rumor had it he loved to argue. They wanted to get a rise out of him and see what he would do.

It was winter. Snow covered everything, white and glistening on the trees, as the raucous gang of us flowed down Fifth Avenue to 291. Climbing the steps, I brushed my hand through the snow on the railing. It fell with a thud and made blue shadows. We crunched into the frail cage of the elevator and swayed up to the second floor.

Stieglitz stepped from the back as we came in, surveying us coolly over the pince-nez, a print dripping from his hand. It was the first time I'd laid eyes on him, though his reputation was known by every art student in the city. The boys got into it with him right away over the Rodins—*What makes them art? Some squiggled lines a child could have drawn, how could that be art?* He railed at them for posing such questions, shaking his fist at their ignorance. His nostrils quivered, dark fire snapping from his eyes. Their voices rose, strident, tense. He spat back, "Art is life. Not reiterative. Not imitative, ever. It's always new. Otherwise, it is not Art."

As they argued, I slipped away into the second room, a quiet alcove, and found myself alone, no chair to sit on, only the lines of Rodin's women on the wall. I didn't think much of them. But as I stayed with them, my eyes passing over them, I could feel something, some suggestion of raw power in the crude lines. *Life,* Stieglitz had called it. The drawings unsettled me, but I could not tear my eyes away—something about the bend of a leg, a back arched, the suggestion of breasts falling back, the smudge of shadow between the legs, not careless at all, but seeming so. Then the boys came and found me, and we tumbled out of the studio. Stieglitz threw us out, really.

Several weeks later, walking one night with some friends down Riverside Drive, I saw the trees, their limbs so deeply black, under the frail sheen of the sky. A shiver ran through me. I stopped and stood there, my booted feet cold in the snow, and felt it—that curious rapture, my body blown open to those shapes.

"Georgia, come on!"

"No, I have to go." I said.

The light beat like silver dust on those trees—touching them, shaping them—I turned and walked away—I had to keep it—the intensity of that moment—and then I was home and the brush was in my hands, and I let the feeling hone to a sane, cool edge—no time, no thought, only that clear intent, my fingers taut on the brush, the colors like dark water, that mood passing right through my hand into the lean black forms of those trees.

I stepped back. It was good. It was good, the painting. Nothing I had ever been taught. Nothing, either, like the Rodin drawings. And yet.

The next day, I showed it to another student at the League. "Very nice, Georgia!" he said. "But you put no color in those trees. You can't just have black. Think about the impressionists. It won't take much to improve it. Here, let me show you." He took a brush, dabbed some paint on the end, and made one mark after another, bits of color through my trees. Afterward, I stared and felt a kind of fascinated horror. Not that he had done it. But that I had not stopped him.

I kept that painting for a very long time after, to remind me.

I ASK STIEGLITZ now if he remembers how that group of boys came in to challenge him to explain how those raw lines of Rodin were art—and how he tore them up.

"There were so many days like that," he says. "Many people look at work like Rodin's and don't see it."

"I'm sure you never noticed me."

"I did. I barely remember those boys—they were just anyone else. But I remember you, the quiet one, standing alone in the corner."

I laugh. Of course he does not remember. "Actually, I fled to the other room, you were so enraged."

He shakes his head. "How could anyone not *feel* the life in those drawings?"

"I wasn't sure I liked you that day." I say this lightly—almost teasing—but his face falls.

"Do you care for me?" he says.

The air sharpens.

"Of course," I say.

He leans toward me, takes my face between his hands, and kisses me. First once on each eyelid, then on each cheek. It is different now, the kiss—the pressure of his lips, the heat of his breath. My lips part, his tongue moves into my mouth.

I draw him onto the small bed with me, his body on mine, he's hard against my thigh, and I kiss him, I want to pull it all inside me—the lives that he has lived, what he has known and learned and seen and felt and wondered, the places he has traveled, the women he's loved, the art he's seen and worshipped, defended and despised, the genius, the revelation, the full sweeping range of his life.

He draws away, still holding my face in his hands. The room is dark now. He's turned down the lamp. His eyes glow in the lean wicked beautiful night.

"What do you want, Georgia?" he says.

I want what I have no right to want. He knows.

His hand drops, his fingers touch my throat, my neck. A finger moving along the edge of the dressing gown, his eyes following his hand. "Not such a little girl," he murmurs. He draws the edge of the neckline back. My breast shines, the skin very pale in the dark. He squeezes it, then drops his head, I feel his mouth hot and wet on me. I grip his head and push my fingers through his hair, my body rising to meet him.

It's almost unbearable when it ends. He stops and pulls away. I go to reach for him, but he catches my hand and sets it on the bed.

"No, Love. Not yet." He draws my dressing gown closed. "What I want of you is much more."

X

My body glitters as I walk to meet him for lunch. I pick him up at his office, a few small rooms he has rented at the Anderson Galleries since 291 closed. My watercolor *Blue Lines* hangs on the wall by the office door. Some of the men are there—John Marin, whose puritan features collide so imperfectly with a quiet roguish smile; the painter Arthur Dove, visiting from his farm in Connecticut; the critic Paul Rosenfeld, who writes for *The New Republic* and *Vanity Fair*. They've already accepted me. I am one of the artists, and no one, for instance, takes a second glance at my unconventional clothes: flat simple shoes, straight black skirts.

Stieglitz and I eat together at a simple restaurant, the open secret of us just sitting there at a small table. With silverware and glasses and red napkins, it all feels so ordinary—the patron with his artist.

"When did you first paint something that you loved?" he asks as we wait for our meals. I tell him about the crude pencil drawing I made when I was twelve, of the moonlight, the snow-filled field. I don't know that I loved it, I say. But everything around us was falling apart—the farm, our family, my childhood—everything seemed to be washing right away—and I remember feeling happy as I scratched those funny pencil marks to make a road, because I understood then that there would always be a new blank sheet of paper I could pour myself into. No matter what happened, my art would be the one thing that remained.

The waitress brings our food. He's ordered spaghetti with fresh tomato sauce.

"You like to order spaghetti," I say.

"I order what's cheap."

"Not true. That chicken you ordered two days ago was not so cheap."

"My glasses were not working well that day. I mixed up an 8 with a 3."

I laugh.

I lean slightly across the table and whisper. "I like it when you do that—when I don't quite know if I can trust what you say."

"You can always trust what I say," he insists with an odd solemnity. "I want you to believe that." It's desperate and intimate, the way he says this, and I feel my breath catch.

HE BEGINS TO photograph me in the apartment in the afternoons when the light is full. He mounts his camera on the rickety tripod covered in a worn black cloth, a white umbrella to throw light into the shadows. He brings props—a bowler hat, a thimble, a tailored black jacket with a crisp white collar—he brings my early work, my watercolors and the charcoal drawings. He pins them to the wall and poses me in front of them.

THE ROOM IS tense in the late-June heat. "Not quite right," he says, lifting his face from the camera.

"Too hot today," I complain.

"You're not always a cooperative model," he says, removing the bowler hat. My hair tumbles to my shoulders. "Are you, Georgia?" He touches my throat.

"Do you always get exactly what you want when you want it?" I ask playfully.

In one fierce movement, he pushes me back against the wall, his body pinned on mine, his hand between my legs. I gasp.

"Often." He kisses me hard. He begins to peel the clothes from my body. Unfurling my black stockings, he leaves them on the floor. He draws me to the bed and spreads my legs apart. His fingers move up into me. It feels like I am turning inside out under the moving pressure of his hand. The room is unthinkably bright. A sheen of heat and sunlight washes through my mind. He lies with me, fully clothed, and his fingers move more quickly now, my hips press up against his hand as he touches me. His teeth graze my breast, the nipple hard in his mouth. I stretch my arm over my head and clutch the edge of the bed. My head explodes with light.

I lie there, breathless, undone.

"You are beautiful," he says.

"Do everything to me."

"Soon." He takes my chin and turns it slightly to the right. "Look there." He points to the wall across the room. "Eyes a touch lower. There."

He walks back to the camera. From the corner of my eye, I see him studying me, the composition of the image of my body, the rumpled bed.

"Better?" I say without moving my face.

"Much." His head disappears under the black cloth. "Don't move," he says. And I am still. Counting. Counting. My body has begun to cool, my mind softens and drains, a familiar thoughtless pleasure coming over me like sleep.

AFTER THAT, ON the afternoons when he photographs me, I tease him, "If you want me to be cooperative today, you must do that thing to me first." And he does. He explores every inch of me, his lips graze my shoulders, my stomach, my knees.

"Make love to me," I whisper, more insistently.

"Not until things are settled," he says, and I feel my face flush, remembering—the wife, the daughter, his other life.

IN JULY WHEN Kitty is away at camp, he picks me up one day along with his camera things, and takes me to the apartment at 1111 Madison Avenue. Emmy is out, he explains, on a shopping excursion all day. I am too curious to resist. Tall doors. Gilt mirrors, high ceilings, windows hung with drapes, ornate lamps, heavy dark Victorian furniture. I stay close to him as he leads me through the apartment—everything untouched, like rooms that were left years ago, and have remained uninhabited since. I don't belong here. I feel her presence in the luxury, the crowded perfection of so many things.

"It seems so unlike you," I say.

"It is."

His photographs, though, are on the wall, and symbolist prints, one of a naked Eve with a large snake.

"Who made that?" I ask.

"Von Stuck. It's called *Sin*."

"I wish you hadn't told me that."

A smile plays around his mouth. "I've not committed the actual act of sin. I am guilty of nothing."

"I would say you're worse than guilty because you deny it," I say, laughing. It seems essential to make a joke of it all and pretend it doesn't mean what it does. What he is saying. Doing. That we are not where we are.

"It's just a photograph," he says, unbuttoning my shirt. He poses me against the wall. He's shot three times when I freeze. Voices outside the front door, then the door opens and a woman is in the apartment, somewhere, calling him—I've never heard her voice.

I am still fumbling with my shirt when she walks into the room. Her eyes flare when she sees me, so wide like they will overspill their edges, understandably so.

"*What* are you doing home?" Stieglitz demands sharply. She turns to him, the room falls silent, a precipice.

"What are *you* doing here?"

"What does it look like I'm doing? Camera. Tripod. Wouldn't it be reasonable to assume I'm working?"

She is carrying a shopping bag. It drops to the floor, wavers, then falls over. A piece of ivory silk slips out. She is small, but thickly built. She might have been lovely once, in a distinctly feminine way. Her fingers are shaking—I can see the light tremble of them near the peplum waist of her overskirt.

She waves her hand in my vague direction. "Your model?"

"Miss O'Keeffe has generously agreed to serve that role today."

"Miss O'Keeffe."

"If you would rein in your assumptions, I will introduce you."

She turns and looks at me, as if now, armed with my name in hand, it is possible to do so. I feel the seconds skip—the awful claustrophobic dimness of these rooms, this marriage.

I stand still and stare back at her. No other choice but to stand here and play my crooked part in this exchange. I try to keep the waves of nausea down as outrage washes through her eyes—it's poison, the way she is looking at me. It does not matter that we've never fully made love, I see that now. Why would she care, given what we appear to be? She's a woman of appearances, and the house of appearances is falling now.

But as she stares, I slowly realize that for her, it is not quite so simple; it is not only the sense of being betrayed, but a furious disbelief that he would have let a woman like me—plainly dressed, common—into her space.

"Be civil, Emmeline," Stieglitz says. It's a shock to both of us—

his voice, the evident scorn, and as those words hit the glass silence of the room, her face contorts into something monstrous, and she begins to yell—betray, filth, nothing, whore.

I slip my last shoe on and stride past them, my knee hits the leg of the desk, the pain sudden, intense, but I keep going. I find the front door, and then I am through it. I slam the switch for the lift and wait in the hallway, their voices coming nearer, a sudden pause, a choked sob, then her wail—the sound is horrible, broken and strange— nothing I want to ever hear again.

XI

THE STUDIO DOES not feel like home. I walk in and sit down at the table, then can't sit, the chair feels too hard. I have to leave. It's a horrible thing we've done, and I've allowed it. I must go somewhere. Back to Texas. Or to my sister Anita's house. Crawl in on my knees and beg for one of her spare bedrooms until I get my bearings, find work, figure out where to go.

I pull my things from the closet and the drawers. My dresses, my shoes. I pack the books I brought with me. Letters from my sisters. I hesitate at the art supplies. Are they mine? Not after today. Nothing here apart from what I brought into this room is mine to take from it. Remember that, I tell myself harshly, and feel a slight tearing in my heart. The walls look dirty, grim, the yellow a sad jest of itself— chipped paint on the ridges of the radiator under the window. These flaws. I never noticed them before.

How I've loved it here. In our shoe-box room. Only twelve hours ago, I was lying on the little bed alone, the green night washing over these same walls, the skylight held the stars like a net, and I looked up into the night pouring down, missing him, loving him, and thinking that these four walls made the loveliest room in the world.

I cannot stay. I don't want to go to Anita's—she'll ask too many questions and the thought of explaining makes me cringe. No mother to go home to. And my father working somewhere in Virginia—it's been months since we've spoken. I could find him, though. He would not demand to know the story of how his eldest daughter, the strong one, the proud and capable one, has gone and made such a wreck of things.

The charcoal drawing catches my eye. He left it on the desk beside his black folder holding other works of mine. I touch the edge of the paper—such cheap paper—all I could afford.

I set the drawing with my things and lie down on the bed, my face in my hands, hot tears.

HE COMES THAT evening, his face haggard. He carries his satchel and a valise. She gave him an ultimatum: Stop seeing me or stop coming home.

"It took me less than ten minutes to pack," he says. I stare at him. He seems almost proud. Then his eyes fall on my clothes, still laid out on the bed, the stack of books, the charcoal drawing.

"What's this?" he says.

"I can't stay."

He looks from the open bag on the floor to me.

"No," he says. It's a slight word, *no*, it can mean so many things, but in this moment, in this room swept through with blue dusk, I hear the crush of his heart in that tiny nothing. Just that one word. *No.*

I go to him, and slip my arms around him. He holds me tightly.

"I don't want to break up your family. I don't want to hurt you," I say.

"You could never hurt me unless you left." His voice quiet. "I'll give up anything or anyone that cannot understand that." I push back from him. I need to see his face. His eyes are tired, forked lines at the edges. In the dim light, they look deeper than they are.

"What of Kitty?" I say.

"I don't know."

"You've stayed this long for her. You know she'll suffer. This will not be easy for her, and that will make you suffer. I understand that— she's your daughter."

Still holding my arms, his grip tightens. "But you are my life."

OVER THE NEXT few days, the aftershocks of the drama unfold: the onslaught of recriminations, tearful phone calls, letters from Kitty hand-delivered by messenger. Her grief and fury at her father for what he's done. It feels hollow, almost scripted.

"It's her mother feeding this rot to her," Stieglitz says.

"We are partly responsible."

He turns. "You have no idea what you're talking about. This marriage was over long before you came." I feel myself shrink, something darkly out of place. Then he reaches for me, contrite, tears spring to his eyes, but it takes a moment before I can let him hold me again.

The next day, he phones his sister's husband, George Engelhard, to start divorce proceedings. Boxes and crates of personal items appear at the studio. Books, pictures, dishes, pans, funnels, cameras, prints and printing frames. He moves the rest of his things from 1111 Madison into storage in the basement of the Anderson Galleries. He has another small bed brought in and sets it across the room from mine. He hangs a blanket on a string between them.

XII

In August, his mother summons us to Lake George. She wants to
meet the cause of all the upset—the dark-haired creature her favorite
son is overturning every applecart for.

"I am not always keen on families," I tell him on the train.

"They'll love you," he insists. "And you will love the Lake."

I smile. "That's not what I said."

At the station, we're met by Fred Varnum, the man from the house,
who loads our things into the carriage and drives us the short distance to Oaklawn. The house is at the edge of the lake—a sprawling
Victorian with a hodgepodge of gables, turrets, and porches. The
furniture is old, all sorts of somber atrocities jumbled together—
hangings, statuary, lamps—gold-framed paintings mask the walls.
Every window is bound by heavy draperies as if light is forbidden
here. His mother, Hedwig, is warm—plump and apple-cheeked—
when we meet, she smiles and presses my hand tightly. My anxiety
lifts.

She puts us in separate bedrooms, as he had told me she would.

She seats me beside her at every meal—three meals a day, plus tea with cakes every afternoon at four o'clock. Everyone assembles. Nearly the entire clan is there—more names than I can easily remember—siblings and children and spouses and nieces and nephews, cousins and brothers- and sisters-in-law. Stieglitzes coming and going—his sister Agnes; his other sister Selma, overflowing in chiffon—as high-pitched and imperious as he'd warned; his niece Elizabeth, the most grounded and sensible among them. I'm so used to solitude and this is anything but. I've never seen so many people talk and argue, bicker, laugh—their voices rise and fall, and it's like I am witness to some tableau in a dream.

But the lake itself is a thousand shades of molten blue, and there's nothing to do but paint and swim and sneak into his bedroom at the other end of the hallway from mine.

Every morning we tramp together across the road and up the hill, past the old clapboard farmhouse, with its huge veranda. As we walk, he tells me that these upland acres were once a pig farm, but the smell was unbearable, so his father overpaid the farmer and bought the land to get rid of the pigs and their stench.

"Just remember," I say, "it's a farmer's daughter you're talking to."

We follow the path past an abandoned stone foundation, through the woods that open into the upper meadow, and he pulls me down into the tall grass, legs, warm wet skin, kissing me everywhere. In the evenings after supper, he rows me out in a little boat onto the lake as the dusk drains out of the sky. We row out into the middle of the lake, then cut back around the island. By then night has fallen, and when I look back to the dock and the house beyond, I can see the small round figure of his mother, waiting on the porch for our return.

In those first few days, it's easy to forget. Then letters arrive from Kitty, first one then another, imploring her father to come to her camp in New Hampshire—to meet with her and her mother—to try to heal the damage he has wrought.

He will go. I know this even before he tells me. I do not bring it up that evening before supper as we lie upstairs kissing in his bedroom.

He shakes his head. "There's no choice."

"So you will go?"

"I have to. I must make them see. Do you understand? I have to bring peace to it."

"You think you can do that?"

The room is filled with the reflected light of the sun behind the hills, the bed suffused in that yellow-orange glow—we are like two black-limbed creatures in amber.

I run my finger along his mouth. "You think you can fix it all, don't you? Make it right. Make them see?"

"There was never joy."

"Not everyone can feel what you feel, or feel to the end of themselves as you do." I trace my hand along his neck to his shoulder, the strong ropy knob of it. He is propped up on one elbow, looking past me out the window, toward the dusk.

"This morning as I was shaving," he says, "I looked out to the lake and it lay so still it hardly seemed to exist. Only one bright star, its light fading. It was holy—that moment. I've felt it in me since, everything turning into what it is meant to be." Such astonishing conviction. It occurs to me now that art is exactly this: making what's unseen but all around us, visible. Having that sort of faith.

"You're like no one else," I say quietly. "I love that you will try."

His eyes shift to me. "Why only *try?*"

"Because you'll do what you can, and that's as much as you can do. Don't assume you can bend the world to be what you know it should be. You won't win. Just come home."

XIII

THE NEXT DAY, he is gone, and I am alone in that house with his mother and Elizabeth, the brother-in-law Lou sinking into his cups, and Selma with her ankle-nipping terrier "Prince Rico" that she hand-feeds chocolate creams.

I walk through the dank swells of the house without him. The rooms feel like a heavy trapped pool, bleak and still.

I miss him. And I wait. A large star shines through the trees. The star seems even larger, the light blurred, as if it shines through water. Our star, he called it, when we saw it one night from the boat on the lake.

The day he will return, I almost can't sit still. There's a storm. Leaves torn from the trees, the windows shudder in their guides. The car pulls up. I run to the front door, and he's there, rain sliding off his hat. I throw my arms around his neck.

"It happened!" he says, his eyes alight, triumph spilling off him. "After almost six hours of conversation last night, they finally understood. A miracle. But it happened."

I hear the others coming down the stairs behind us. I draw his cloak from his shoulders and hang it to dry.

———

MIDNIGHT. MY DOOR creaks open. I sit up in bed, as he puts his finger to his lips, drawing the door shut behind him. Then he is beside me on the bed, his mouth hard on mine.

"Now," he says, the word mixing with his hot breath.

"I'll bleed."

He pulls me down onto the floor, our hands on each other, feverish, his knee between my legs spreading them apart, and he is inside me, pushing into me. I feel the sharp pain of something torn deep as his hips dig into my thighs, his breath rough in my hair, quickening, then he pulls out, wetness pools on my belly.

He brings me a towel and a bandage from the bathroom, and I lie on the floor, with the bandage between my legs, the vague tint of blood on my hands.

"Come to bed, Georgia," he says softly, helping me up.

"Stay with me tonight," I say.

We slip under the sheets, and hold each other tightly, his legs wrapped through mine.

I WAKE WITH a start, my heart hammering. Old dreams of my mother. How sick she grew—blood in a spray of tiny petals every time that cough shook her small frame. A banging on the door—the landlady had come to collect the rent, but there was no food on the shelves, and my mother staggered toward the door to explain, and her lungs blew apart right there in the hallway, sliding down against the wall, she died. The word aloud in the night, so softly. *Died*. The room is strange. All wrong. For a moment, I don't know where I am. Then I see him, Stieglitz, lying there, his lovely face asleep, so peaceful and so near. The storm has passed. The night is clear. Light falls through the window, laddered shapes across the floor. I spoon myself around him, breasts, hips pressing into him, as if my body could fill every negative space his has made.

XIV

OVER THE NEXT few weeks at the Lake, cousins leave and others arrive—a family chattering, bickering, planning. I quietly nickname Selma's eight-pound terror "Rippy," a moniker that Stieglitz champions. His niece Elizabeth confides in us. She has fallen in love with the gardener, the long-faced Donald Davidson. Erudite, yet without any notable ambition, he is forty and divorced, but they are in love, she insists, and will marry in the spring. She has yet to announce the earth-shattering news to her parents, Stieglitz's staid brother Lee, the doctor, and Lizzie, his docile wife.

"Uncle Al," Elizabeth says firmly, "you must keep my secret since I, after all"—she tilts her head toward me—"kept yours."

"He'll keep your secret, Elizabeth." I look at him sternly. "Won't you?" It's a mock sternness and he knows it, and the three of us dissolve into laughter as Selma comes around the corner of the porch, her seventeen pounds of chiffon dusting the floor as she goes.

"What's all your ruckus about?" she asks haughtily.

"We were just saying your skirt missed a spot." Stieglitz points with his pen toward some cobwebs and two dead moths.

"You're as impossible as ever."

"And you are just as simpering, dear Sel."

Sel can put him in a rotten mood faster than anyone, and I can understand it. Of all his siblings, she's the one I can't bear—just her presence makes me sharply aware of how different his world is from mine.

When she is gone, Stieglitz says, "That sister is a walking, bleating example of why America's in the hopeless mess it's in—unable to embrace anything new, always clinging to some Kingdom of Before."

"Sel has about as much weight as milkweed fluff," Elizabeth retorts. "You give her far too much credit, Uncle Al."

I AM PAINTING well here. I go outside and sit in the grass and make watercolor sketches of the wild roses growing near the trellis. I pare apples and pick grapes. When I have to come in, for the long midday dinner, I skim my spoon over the surface of the soup—too hot for soup, I think. All this food. I am quiet, only half listening—my thoughts drift on the sketches I did that morning.

Toward the end of the third or fourth course, I set my fork down on my plate—a quick ting—it stops Stieglitz in the midst of a heated conversation with his brother Lee. He glances at me. I answer with a faint smile, then look away as they go on talking. Since Lee arrived, the conversation has focused on Oaklawn and the expense to keep it up—taxes, insurance, repairs, all that. The house has been in the family for over forty years, but Lee, who shoulders most of the expense, is commenting that it might be too much house for his wallet to bear. Sel's little dog comes to sniff around my ankles. I give it a brief silent kick. And Lee is asking me now, "How long are you planning to stay in New York, Georgia?"

The table falls still. An awkward silence. Elizabeth clears her throat. I'm careful not to look at Stieglitz. I look at Lee. "I'm due back to teach in Texas in the fall."

I smile and rise from the table. I bend to plant a light kiss on Hedwig's plump cheek, nod to the others, and head for the stairs, walking slowly until I hear Stieglitz's chair push back against the floor, his footsteps behind me. I glance over my shoulder. *Catch me?* I mouth. He reaches out to grasp my sleeve, but I am quicker and start to run, my feet light, almost noiseless, taking the stairs two at a time, then down the hall to his bedroom. He is right behind me. He catches me at the door, pulls me inside. He pushes me up against it, we are shaking with laughter, digging his hands into the waist of my skirt, pulling my shirt loose, he kisses my neck, my breast. I feel his hardness through his pants against my thigh, and the door quivers, thudding lightly in its frame.

"Shhh," I say, "they'll hear us."

"I don't give a damn what they hear."

And in the free brazen sunlight, we make love, his face above me, I draw the pillow to my mouth when I cry out, and we lie there, afterward, skin damp, sunlight blowing in as the curtains stream and fall.

THE DAYS SHORTEN. The sky turns that lean starched blue that comes toward the end of summer. One morning, he wakes me early, and we go out walking. There's a new cooler twist in the air, the light is different—every shape, every tree, roof, hill, farmhouse, the lake, the road—each levered apart into its own, distinct lines—the colors drenched, intense.

As we walk, I tell him how years ago when I was a student, I underpainted a canvas with a thick layer of white, let it dry, then made a picture over it. Days later, when I caught a glimpse of that painting still propped on the easel, I was struck by the brilliance that shone through. The picture itself was unremarkable, but the luminous depth changed everything.

He listens, unusually quiet, thinking. "You're that kind of whiteness," he finally says.

I laugh.

"No, I mean it. It's that purity of vision that gives your art its fierceness. Its indescribable sense of life. You have not been over-taught, and most of what you've been taught, you've rejected, and so the essence of what you are and how you feel comes through in your best work."

A stick cracks under my foot. Those last few words ringing through me, a kind of sinking feeling. *Your best work.* I can feel when it's not there, I can look at a thing I've made and know that I've failed, I can tear it up for being imitative, or imbalanced. But how does one discern what is good and what is best? That's something I want to learn—I want to see it as he does.

Stieglitz seems preoccupied this morning, something weighing on his mind. We walk down to the Lake and lie on the shore, my back propped against a rock.

"Doesn't that hurt?" he asks. I smile. It's one of those odd things about me I can't quite explain—how I like hard surfaces. He looks past me, across the water.

"If you could have a year to do anything, Georgia, what would you choose to do?"

"Paint."

"Are you sure?"

"Yes."

"And you might be willing to put up with some nonsense for that?"

"Nonsense, for example, in a loden cape?" I push my bare foot lightly between his legs. I can feel him there.

"Don't wake that little man. He'll come find you."

"Let him."

"Do you want to stay, Georgia?"

"You mean in New York?"

"Yes, for a year in the studio. Your living expenses would be paid."

"By who? You?"

"No, but I've made an arrangement."

"That sounds mysterious."

"I've secured a patron to pay your room and board. What matters is that you'll be free to paint."

"And us?" I say.

"That is secondary."

I laugh. "Is it really?"

"I've given this a great deal of thought," Stieglitz is saying now. "You need time and space to develop. Your vision is strong, but you need to build your skills in oil. For your work to be taken seriously, you'll have to master oil. You know this."

One year—a stunning gift, that length of time. I feel it ripple through me. So much I could learn in a year. I could make so much.

"That's what I want," I say.

"Are you sure?"

The clouds shift, the sun strikes off the water, grazing my eyes.

"Yes."

XV

TEN DAYS LATER, the rest of them are gone, and we are alone. I am full of paint, but he is restless, throwing himself around like he doesn't quite know where to land now that the house is empty and there is no family around to squabble with. He knows I don't like to be bothered while I am working. I don't like to talk.

One afternoon, late September, I come downstairs from painting and cannot find him anywhere. He is not in the house, or on the porch. I catch sight of him at the end of the dock, throwing stones. His body coils, then his arm snaps out in one quick motion. The skips drive over the surface, denting it. He's told me he will count them. His record is over fourteen. It's a practice left over from boyhood, a way of taming his nerves. Such a curious precision in the motion. A thoughtless, brutal force in how he throws those stones.

The days flow by. I paint the change of seasons, burnished reds and yellows, fleeting shades of green, tones so deep I could fall into them. I am happy. Blue edges of sky on Celetex board, gentle white masses of clouds, maple trees pushing up from the bottom edge of the board, only their upper halves visible. Oil has always struck me as so determined—it lacks the spontaneous free life that watercolor by its own unstable nature evokes. But as I play around with those trees, the yellows and reds, I begin to feel a different kind of immediacy that oil can have—that saturation of color, unapologetic, rapturous, intense. I play with the line where the cloud carves the sky. The curving thrust of a tree—that upward push of it into the blue.

I thin the paint, then thin it further until its texture is smooth on my brush. I work the point along the outer edge—a strong-defined line, all the way around. I feel a quick thrill. How intentional it is! Blending edge into edge, simulating that random bleed of watercolor, but with total control and the sheer force of the colors kicking there on the canvas. Lighter shades now with the flat brush, toward the heart of the oval shape—feathered upward—the wavering curve of that tree flowing toward the sky like flame.

While I work, he writes his letters—letters to his family, his other artists and friends in the city; there is business correspondence to keep up with as well. In the afternoon, he comes to find me. He studies what I've done.

"How fierce those colors are," he says.

"It's starting to work for me."

"So you're glad I pushed you into oil?"

"You can't push me anywhere I don't want to go."

HE BEGINS TO print the images he has made of me. He sets up the potting shed in the old greenhouse up on the hill, black curtains over the windows. He boards and tapes over the hairline cracks, turning the small musty space down to intimate darkness. He pins the prints to clotheslines strung wall-to-wall, crisscrossing back and forth.

"Look at her," he says.

In the developing pan, my face ripples just under the surface. He lifts the image dripping from the tray, and pins it next to the others to dry. I look at them, one to the next. The expression of her hands—my hands—her body, her face, all mine—stern, implacable eyes that belie the soft hint of a smile. I cannot stop looking at them.

"You are in love with yourself," he says, smiling. I study them. Her face does not look like my face.

"You make me different," I say.

"Different from?"

"How I've always seen myself."

"There are many of you," he says, pointing to the prints in turn. "Quizzical, silent, wary, strong."

"Naked."

He ignores that. "This one here I love. How soft your eyes are, looking up at the corner, past it. What were you thinking in that moment?"

"I was probably thinking that my ankle itched and you would throw a shoe at my head if I moved to scratch it."

HE SHOWS ME how to retouch the photographs. Those tiny white flaws made by dust are like stars on her body. I touch the photographs with a point-tipped brush. I dilute dried umber with water to match the exact shade of skin. Very carefully, I paint into the tiny white spot, watching it darken as the dye gathers into the gelatin layer.

"You're good at that," he says, holding up one of the finished prints I've retouched. He peers at it under the magnifying glass. "That is very, very good."

"I'm not bad with a paintbrush."

He is still peering at the print. "I almost can't detect where the spot was."

"Wasn't that the aim?"

"Of course. But even most photographers don't have the eye to do it this well."

He pulls me to him then, and in the close space of the room, only seams of incidental light, he kisses me. It's like darkness melting, how he kisses me. "I love every minute of you," he says, "every expression on that face, every mood, shadow, inch."

"Every half inch?" I tease him.

"And every half of that. I want you here, always."

"That's a bit longer than a year."

"I'm only saying what I feel."

"I'm sure, after a year, you'll be ready to package me up and ship me back to Texas."

"Never," he says.

Never, always. Such big words. It strikes me even then.

"You've given a whole new meaning to my world, Georgia. Everything was ending until you came."

WE TAKE A last swim together naked in the lake. The water is so cold it stings. When my limbs begin to numb, I climb out and wrap a towel around me. He tugs it loose.

"Don't!" I laugh, and tuck the towel back in, and again he pulls it off.

Little Man hangs shrunken with the cold between his legs, the sun is warm on my shoulders, he touches himself, then reaches for my towel. I slap his hand away, laughing. "Someone will see us."

"There's no someone here." He takes my hand and pulls me away from the dock to the edge of the trees. He lays out the towel. The ground is hard, sun splashing through the upper leaves, my hands to the wrist in sunlight, as he pushes into me from behind, harder, deeper. Afterward, we lie there naked at the edge of the shade.

"I want a child," I say to him, running my fingers over his chest. "That child you wrote about in your letters."

"There is much to do before then."

"I know, but soon."

"Yes," he whispers. "Soon."

Flocks of geese flood over us. The slow-moving current of their bodies pass like clicks of time.

XVI

WE RETURN TO New York and the shoe-box room. I'm not going to leave—such a strange delirious feeling—this new life I've slipped into that doesn't yet quite feel like mine.

Twice a week we dine at his mother's apartment on East 60th. She tells me stories of Alfred as a child, how he loved horses and racing; how, at ten, he locked himself into the billiard room on the top floor and practiced billiards hour after hour alone until he could beat his father and his friends. She tells me how when he was very small, not even four, he loved a certain photograph of a favorite cousin, he refused to part with it, so they tied it around his waist with string, and it flew after him as he ran through the house, and bounced along behind him down the stairs.

The dinners at her house are rich and delicious. Candles, a fire, laughter, real joy, an amused glow on the old woman's face, looking on as we tease each other playfully. She beams. It pleases her—to see him happy.

Most nights, we eat out in modest restaurants where we will sit side by side. My favorite is the Automat. I love the beauty and simple anonymity of it—drop a quarter in the slot and pull out a meal.

"This is where our two worlds collide," I say to him one night.

"Here?"

"Yes—the Automat. Your world of fine marble floors," I say, "my twenty-five-cent meal."

He mumbles something, trying to choose between a vanilla crème custard and apple pie. I push the button. The trays revolve around.

"Hey, I was looking at that," he says.

"But if you look from a different angle, it will be easier to choose. See that sag in the custard—I'd get the pie."

Stieglitz scoffs, slips the silver coin into the slot. The latch clicks, and he draws open the door for the pie.

ONCE A WEEK, we walk to Columbus Circle to meet the Round Table for dinner at the Far East China Gardens, where they serve Pineapple Chow Mein for $1.50. The men discuss life and argue over theories of art. They praise those who have come into their circle, and denigrate those who have defected from the fold. I love these conversations, though I am more curious to observe. Stieglitz's vehemence invigorates the rest—he sweeps them all up into intense arguments about art, culture, politics. I pick gems out of the thoughts that fly back and forth across the table—how Matisse, the most brilliant of colorists, calls black "a force." How Cézanne contends there is no stillness in a still life—but a continual play between light and shadow.

"The task of art," Stieglitz says to the critic Paul Rosenfeld, "is not to render things as they visibly are, but to call forth an unseen spirit—to draw what's abstract and timeless out of what is tactile, concrete, personal." Rosenfeld is listening. He is new to the circle—and seems a little stunned by his luck to find himself in Stieglitz's remarkable world. I find him endearing. Short, roly-poly, with sandy hair and kind droopy brown eyes. He's an incisive writer, though—with an acerbic wit.

"The keynote of experience," painter Abraham Walkowitz chimes in. "It is not subjective or objective. Think of Isadora Duncan. No laws, no rules."

"I saw your Duncan drawings when they were shown at 291," Rosenfeld says.

"There have been others he's made since," Stieglitz says. "Stronger and more precise, which capture the exact feeling of *why* her dancing moves us."

Silence then. The table is waiting on that why. Rosenfeld, the unknowing newcomer, asks tentatively, "Why does it move us?"

Stieglitz's voice grows taut as wire. "Because Duncan understands that art *is* the conversion of the body into the luminous fluent spirit, and when she dances, every movement of her body seeks to express that spirit. Therefore, in every movement, she creates, and it is precisely that understanding that Walkowitz is after—not simply the body of the dancer, but its vision and intent."

I listen as the talk ricochets around the table. The passion moves beyond the argument itself. The heat and the words become tiring to me. Sometimes, on these evenings, Stieglitz feels very far away from the man I know. Sometimes, I just want everything to freeze. I want to reach across the table and touch his cheek, to reach beyond that fierce brilliance to what is private and tender and mine.

The conversation shifts—they are talking now about Germany before the war. In 1913, Marsden Hartley was painting with Kandinsky in Berlin, and his art from that time is a keen synthesis of abstraction and German expressionism—bold color, mystical forms, sometimes so raw you can't bear to be too close.

"It was all so romantic then," Hartley says, reaching a long arm to a piece of sauce-soaked chicken with his fork. "Those gorgeous German boys in their smart uniforms, their pageantry."

"Now only hard reality," Rosenfeld remarks.

"It sickens me." Stieglitz shakes his head. "Just when Americans were starting to dip their milky white minds into the avant-garde, along comes this war to blow it all down."

———

WHEN DINNER IS done and paid for, we will stroll together along the edges of the park back to the 59th Street studio. Invariably there will be another artist, or even two, waiting for us on the doorstep, smoking as they wait. Stieglitz will invite them all up the four flights of stairs to an impromptu salon in our two little rooms. He will show them a select few of my pieces—my new oil and some of my earlier things. He will mention the photographs. "I'm working on something new," he tells them. "A portrait." And they are eager to hear more, but that's as much as he'll say.

On those evenings the talk will often continue past midnight. Finally, they will be gone, and the studio will be ours alone again, and we will push the beds together and he will kiss me, move against me, into me, pale skin glanced by streetlight, our bodies like wet fire.

IN NOVEMBER, WORD comes that my father has died. He slipped off the roof of a barracks where he had been carpentering. Fractured skull. Cerebral hemorrhage. There were shards of a bottle on the ground near him.

A scattered flurry of phone calls. My sister Catherine's sweet, calm voice—Claudie's tearful one. Ida has just come to New York to work as a nurse at Mount Sinai. She and I meet with my other sister Anita at her new Fifth Avenue home, but there is little to do, and less to say. The few necessary arrangements are made. It all falls into place, almost too neatly, against the reeling darkness inside me.

The summer I was twenty-three I lived with my father alone in the house in Virginia. When we first drained east from Sun Prairie, he had opened a grocery store, then got into real estate, rented a pier, started a creamery, and failed and failed and failed. By the time I came to live with him that summer, all he owned was a small strip of land with a queer two-story house he'd built out of concrete blocks. He was a ruin of a man, stinking of barrooms. My mother had left him. She'd taken my sisters and younger brother Alexius. She was already very ill by then, her body wasted, dying, blood in her lungs.

That summer, my father and I rarely spoke. I baked biscuits, swept, cleaned, and cooked his meals. We moved around each other through silence full of shame. I had adored him once. When we were children, after supper, he would play the fiddle and dance, heels kicked up, blue eyes sparkling, and when he fell back, laughing, into a chair, I would crawl into his lap. His stubbled cheek bit my skin.

It aches to remember. You will forget, I tell myself, in the long throw of time.

That night in our shoe-box room, I cry. Stieglitz holds me tightly, soft kisses on my damp face. I cling to him. So keenly sharp, so everything—this need of him I feel.

FOUR DAYS BEFORE I turn thirty-one, the Armistice is declared. The war is over. The streets erupt in celebration and chaos.

The last of my things arrive from Texas. I spread the artwork on the floor, sorting what to keep. Stieglitz watches me. "How easy it is for you to be ruthless with your things," he says, "like you feel nothing."

I want to explain that it is not *nothing*—what I feel. There are pieces that speak to what I have come from and where I am going—but everything else needs to be discarded to keep that arc bone-clean.

"Let me keep that one." He reaches for a half-finished watercolor at the top of the pile to be thrown away. I beat him to it, and quickly tear an edge to ruin it.

"I don't want it kept," I say, stuffing it into the wastepaper trash.

That night, when we come home from dinner, we see the paintings blowing all through the street. A huge hollyhock I made over a year ago sticks out of the garbage can in front of our building. Sketches sail around like wild leaves. I feel him flinch, like he'll start toward them. I hold his arm.

"Leave them," I say. "They belong to someone else back there."

I turn him to the steps and we go in.

PART II

I

"PART THE GOWN," he says, "let your hand fall, naturally, across your breast. Higher. There. Tuck your thumb into the fold, near the breast. Yes. Now, don't move that hand, but with the other pull your hair back from your shoulder. Drape it that way." He disappears again under the dark cloth.

"Don't breathe." For the slow glass negatives I have to be unthinkably still—I can't blink or twitch or itch that spot behind my ear. If my hand moves, the image will be ruined.

Still, I think to myself. *Stiilllll,* until my mind drops and my body streams into the word.

When he emerges from behind the camera, I exhale slowly. I arch my spine, stretch my neck, and walk around in the white kimono dressing gown until he is ready. Again he surveys me.

"Hair behind your shoulder. Bring one breast out, touch it, hold it toward me. There." He disappears under the cloth. The room is quiet. I can hear the muted blurred noise of the city through the window. "Both breasts now," he says, speaking from under the black cloth, so it is only the eye of the camera I can see, and the very small, distant white floating creature pinched inside the glass that is me. "Let your arms drop to your side. Chin up, throat back. Look At Me. Georgia."

HIS WORK HAS begun to take over the studio. Boxes of printing paper, bottles, trays and pans. He curtains the windows and fills the bathtub with developing solution. It is only temporary, he explains. The fire is in him now—and I find myself transfixed by his obsession with that woman.

Sometimes he will say only that word, *beautiful,* and then he'll cross the room in a few strides, take my chin in his hand, and shift my face a fraction of an inch in one direction, so the light strikes differently and I become, for that moment, someone else entirely.

ONE AFTERNOON IN February, he comes home early from his office at the Anderson Galleries.

"Leo Ornstein concert tonight!" he says, waving tickets in the air.

"So wonderful!"

"But first I want to use the window." He pulls the camera out into the middle of the room.

"But the radiator is in front of the window."

"You'll stand on it."

"I don't trust that old rickety thing." But he is preparing the plates.

"Come on," he says. He draws a sheet across the window, which is hardly a veil, and I tell him so, but it sheds the light as he wants it to fall. I leave my drawings on the table and climb up. The radiator bars dig into the soles of my feet, warm, but hard to balance on.

"Naked," he says.

I slip off the dressing gown.

"Straighter."

"It's freezing!"

"Lift your arms."

"I'll fall."

"Never," he says. He angles the lens upward. The radiator gives a belch, my arms outstretched, fingertips on the wall, winter cold against my backside. I hold my breath, body taut, an electric rush moving through me from the pain of keeping still.

"Perfect," he says. And it will be. The diffused light sculpts my breasts and hips and thighs, the light ridge of ribs just visible. I am longer, taller in this image, my face cropped. And I realize I prefer it that way—to be curiously absent—the torso of a woman massed out of the air. I've begun to crave the way his eyes rake over me when I am posing for him, so I am only a body. No inhibition, no thought. Pure sensation. There is a strange freedom in that, and it begins to fuel my art.

ORNSTEIN THAT EVENING is entirely abstract music—biting dissonance that achieves an odd cogency as the music evolves. Stieglitz's hand slips over my knee as the young man plays, his dark head bent, listening to the sound within the sound, his fingers violent, moving over the keys. The tall windows of the room hold the winter night— the city outside—a world we've already left without knowing, the rapt, marbleized faces of the women, their heads stabbed on their dark dresses—as the music fills the room.

Afterward we spill into the street, a mill of bodies, muffs, coats, hats.

"You're quiet," he says as we pause at a corner. The moon hangs between buildings ahead. "What are you thinking?"

I take his arm. We cross. The sidewalk underneath us.

"Just feeling that music," I say. "That range he played. It was almost savage. Like he needed to play every note. Like he was playing on the last night of the world."

He wraps his arm around me.

I laugh. "It took me right apart, and now you're walking down the street with little pieces of a person, the skin barely holding her in."

———

THE NEXT MORNING, after zwieback toast and coffee, I brush the crumbs from his mustache and send him out the door. I clean up the breakfast things and make our beds, side by side, last night's music still rilling around inside me as I smooth the sheets. The oddest sort of feeling—I'm moving through an ordinary morning and at the same time standing on some brink of free-falling space. The yellow walls seem to waver, shards of colored light.

A bird sails past the window.

I go into the back room and pull out sketches I made last summer of the natural bridge I visited once in Virginia. I remember passing through it, the smell of the greenery, the cool gray of the rock, and how, when I looked back, the orange dusk struck its edges.

I leave the drawings on the table and begin a new sketch. Lines over the paper, shadow by shadow, details stripped—not the bridge as it was but as I felt it blow through me in that moment I turned and looked back, the moss ripped with light.

Over the next few days, I work my sketch of the stone bridge into color.

I try pastel first. That opaque charge, but there's too much contrast in the tones—the orange and blue don't quite meld. Frustrated, I clean up my things and scrub down the table before Stieglitz comes home and asks what I've been working on.

"Not quite ready," I say.

"Show me what's not ready."

"No." I draw him toward the bed. "Let's do something else."

SEVERAL DAYS LATER, I lay out my oils, brushes, and a blank canvas. One looped stroke to begin, bits of pink and blue rimmed into the ivory tones.

How he made me come last night, in the little bed, night pouring through the skylight, his breath on my skin hot and raw. I shiver, remembering. Crimson mixed into red leaving the tip of my brush, just there—a small, unexpected flash of brightness.

I still don't show him.

THE NEXT DAY when I am alone, I put the two pieces side by side. The first, the pastel, has the opacity I want, but the colors fight—that orange and blue like two separate worlds. In the oil, the emphasis is on the form—almost a drawing—the shape is closer to what I want, but the colors feel weak—almost wan.

I set a clean canvas on the easel, and paint it again. Shapes flare, more vivid tones than I've ever used. My chest tightens as I work—the canvas resists, then bends, as I push on, seams of warmth strung through the cool melodic tones of violet, blue. It's as if it already exists in the canvas and I'm carving it out.

Done. I step back and glance at the clock. Later than I could have imagined. I feel a kind of silver zipping around inside me. My body peeled to the root.

HE COMES HOME just after dark, and this time I have not moved my easel to the corner but left it there in the center of the room with the painting still on it, wet. I sit on his lap, comb my fingertips through the gray brindle of his hair, and we study it, my music, the thrill of it still in me.

"I see now," I say, "what I can do with oil. It *is* stubborn and it *is* heavy, not loose and free, but the intensity of color—*that* can say what I want."

He nods. I wrap my arms around him and draw his face against my breast.

"It's beautiful," he says.

"It's what you make me feel."

II

THE STREAM OF visitors to our makeshift gallery continues, but new names now. Walter Arensberg, Charles Sheeler, Marius de Zayas. Critics, patrons, art dealers. Arthur B. Davies, who organized the Armory Show in 1913, comes, along with Leo Stein, Gertrude's brother. Edward Steichen, also a photographer, brings the art collector Frank Crowninshield, who is the editor of *Vanity Fair*.

Crownie shakes my hand. He is as slick and elegant as the magazine he has transformed. A boutonniere bobs from his lapel. Stieglitz is elated. He shows them several of my new oils and charges in about their "savage force," their "frankness"—the mastery I have already begun to acquire. He tells them the story of how he first discovered my art when my friend Anita Pollitzer brought my charcoal drawings to 291 three years ago on his birthday, New Year's Day, 1916. How the instant he unrolled those drawings, he knew it was a new art. Fearless Self-Expression. An Unaffected Mind. A Woman on Paper.

I will sit at one end of the sofa, sip water, and watch, that black gleam in his eyes as he speaks of me, his hands moving through space.

It is the story of my art that he is making. Only a story—I know this—but as I listen, I find it becomes more difficult to imagine another life, a different life when he was not there. My life before him. It seems almost mythic as he describes it: as if I were born out of the wind and the plains and bone-blue sky, out of the long winters spread across the rolling, frozen land.

Invariably, at some point in the evening, he will draw out a few of his new photographs. The shock hits—like a wave through the room. No one overtly acknowledges them as images of me. These fragments—face, breasts, neck, hands. Nude. Sometimes I feel like I should be ashamed, but I find it almost exhilarating to watch how the photographs unnerve them. How they just can't reconcile my straight black dress, prim collar, with the woman in the photographs, her body, hands, hips, thighs, the taut plane of her belly, the gleam of her fingernails, the triangular thatch of black hair. The prints have grown more explicit and unrestrained.

"Astonishing," someone murmurs, then the invariable stolen glance back toward my end of the sofa as they try to wrap their minds around the austerity of the woman sitting there, and the palladium fragments propped against the wall.

A bold glamour has begun to come into these small rooms. I've been here for less than a year, and already we are seen as an extraordinary couple—the two of us—the old photographer and his daring sibyl, his artist, his young muse. And I begin to see, too—as they can see—how in these deceptively simple images, he comes near to capturing some essence, some manifestation of a universal feminine.

"Revolutionary," Edward Steichen remarks, glancing at me. "They're really like nothing else in our world."

"I've told Stieglitz that," I say. "They're so far beyond just photographs, aren't they?"

Edward smiles. "Done right, a photograph can seize an era in a moment; it can touch, even, what one soul means to another." He turns away then from the photographs, and nods to my painting

Music set against the wall across the room. "But when I used the word *revolutionary*, Georgia, I wasn't just talking about Stieglitz's photographs of you. He says this often, but tonight I've seen it for myself: What *you* are doing there." He points to my oil. "No painter in this country is making abstractions like that."

"CROWNIE WAS FLOORED," Stieglitz exclaims when they are gone. "The photographs just landed him. He loved them."

"Isn't that what you wanted?"

"Of course, but it was effortless. Like a spell. Did you see how easy?"

I nod. I've begun to clear things away. I wash the dirty drinking glasses, slip into my nightclothes, hang up my dress. I dip my toothbrush into the jar of tooth powder, brush my teeth, spit, and rinse.

"It was good to see Edward," I say. Do I know this is cruel when I say it?

Stieglitz looks at me, his eyes flat. "I saw you talking with him. What did he have to say?"

"Just that he loved your photographs—and my art."

"He has more talent in his little finger than I'll have in my lifetime, and it irks me, Georgia, how he's sold out. It's all about money to him now."

"He said tonight that he wants to go back to his family home in Voulangis."

Stieglitz snorts. "That's a whore's fuss and fanfare. He wants to be an advertising star."

I don't agree, but I don't argue. Alfred's fury with Edward Steichen seems to weigh in direct balance with the fiercely close bond they once shared. In the good years of 291, Edward was *the* young protégé—one of the true and adored. When Stieglitz started his magazine *Camera Work*, it was Edward who made the first cover design. They were inseparable. But then Edward grew up: He entered a war Stieglitz did not believe in, directed aerial photography for the Allies, and now there are rumors he's flirting with a position at Condé Nast, which Stieglitz deems rank commercialism. I've always liked Edward—the strength in his face, that slight amused smile. His eyes are penetrating, but kind. He is never thrown by any tirade Stieglitz happens to be on, but is so gentle with him, grateful and indulgent as one might be with an aging father. Edward's own respect for the man who was once his master does not seem to diminish, but he is strong-willed—he does not let anyone pull him off course. Once when I ran into him at a gallery opening, I mentioned it. "Were you always this way, Edward?" I asked. "So sure but so compassionate as well."

"I saw too much in the war," he answered simply. "Too much afterward. Burnt villages. Children. Things like that set your course once you have seen them, and no one—not even the inimitable Stieglitz—can steer you from it." He smiled, his voice sad, but with a clarity I wanted to touch.

That night, as Stieglitz and I lie together on our beds side by side, mine under the skylight, the sound of his breathing deepening toward sleep, I think back over the evening—Edward's remarks about my art, the expression on Crownie's face, how he and the others could not stop staring at the photographs—and lying there, I am aware that we have begun to be swept up in some silent transformation of the world that we belong to.

IV

THE FOLLOWING WINTER, 1920, we learn that our apartment building on 59th Street will be razed. Stieglitz's brother Lee offers us rooms in his house.

"I suppose that's what we'll do," Stieglitz says. "Given how things are with money, there's really no choice."

"There's always a choice," I say. "I've known poor. I've always managed to live on my own."

"But we could never afford as much as Lee and Lizzie are willing to give us."

A twist in my stomach—how strange it will feel not to have our own space, living with his family, first at the Lake, now here.

WE GO TO SEE the rooms. It's a dreary day. The whole building feels like a damp cellar. Lizzie's mother, ninety years old, can't quite grasp the idea of an unmarried couple living together, so Lee has arranged that we'll keep rooms on separate floors. We'll have our own sitting room. We'll use their kitchen to fix our own breakfast, and plan on eating out for dinner. Lizzie shows me a sunny back room where the light is good and I can paint. She's a mousy woman, kind, but she always seems a little downtrodden, like marriage has wrung her right out. She and I climb the stairs together to the top floor where Lee is showing Stieglitz an alcove that he can use as a darkroom.

"I don't like feeling so dependent," I murmur to Stieglitz as we follow them back downstairs.

"Shhh," he says. "It's only for a while."

At the door, he shakes his brother's hand, profuse with thanks.

BY SUMMER, OUR living arrangements at the Lake have changed as well. The family has sold Oaklawn. Too expensive to maintain. Stieglitz alone fought the decision for more than eight months, but as he's the only one among them who can't afford to chip in for its up-keep, at last the decision is made: The mansion and the waterfront property have been put on the market. The family will keep the thirty-six upland acres and the white clapboard farmhouse on the hill that was once a pig farm. By the time we arrive, the renovations to the farmhouse are in the final stages: a few carpenters still bungling about; banging, hammering.

When they are finished, the tennis court is gone. Hedwig's servants, gone. She brings her maid from the city, and there is the local help. Stieglitz's sister Selma arrives, all in a huff because we snubbed her, she claims, through the winter. Despite her numerous invitations, we accepted only one. The walls of the new house feel unusually thin. I can hear her in the room next to mine, roaming around, rattling the drawers. She moves a chair, moves it back. I hear the swish of her skirts, the chatter of Rippy's terrier nails on the floor behind her. Within two days of arriving, she starts harping on about how she wants the desk that's in my room moved into hers.

At first it's a casual remark, made over dinner, but soon it seems all she can talk about is the desk. *Georgia doesn't need a writing desk. She is busy with her painting.* Stieglitz counters, *You only want that desk because you don't have it.* The argument between them ramps up, and finally I tell him to please just let her have it, but he doesn't want to give it to her—it is the principle of it.

"Odious," he says to me. "She is odious."

"And I need peace and quiet."

The following morning the desk is moved into Sel's room, torqued at every which angle to get through the door. It is heavy and dark and swallows the space, but she is satisfied for one entire day, and then in the evening after supper, she mentions that perhaps we should have the desk switched back. Stieglitz will have nothing more to do with her.

BY JULY, THE farmhouse is stuffed with people. I take longer walks, past the driveway oval and the ring of the lawn dotted with fruit trees, past old outbuildings, roofs caving in—barns and a chicken coop, an icehouse, a stable. This was all once farm, I remember, pushing through the rusted fence that separates the fields. I climb up to the woods, past the sand cliffs and the boulders to the upper meadow full of sour grasses and wildflowers. The canna lilies I split and planted last summer have bloomed. Such a plain red flower. Thin stem, the bloom like a splayed hand—aureate, stunningly bright. I clip one and set it in a plain jar on the desk in the bedroom upstairs. I dip my brush into a bowl of water, then swirl it through red paint—that quick thrill of the first mark of color on blank paper, the brush's point to cut that outer edge, the petals opening, their redness thinned in places, pale sunlight shining through. I don't fill in the frame of the paper around them, so it is only the flower without reference—a rupture of color, in disembodied space.

On my way back from a walk one afternoon, I spy a one-room unkempt building. It has sagging doors and a window looking out onto the first meadow.

That evening I tell him I want it.

"For?"

"A space to work."

He walks up the hill with me to see it.

"It needs a new roof."

"Yes."

"And a new window."

"That one there can be repaired."

He looks at me doubtfully.

"You think I don't know a fixable window when I see one?" I say. "Will you get a bid for the roof?"

He nods. "Very well."

But he throws up his hands in disgust when the quote comes in. "Prohibitive!" he exclaims. I don't answer. "So discouraging," he says, "I'm sorry, Love."

When Lee's daughter Elizabeth arrives, I ask her for help, and along with Stieglitz and her new husband, Donald, we spend the next few weeks making repairs. In August, it grows too hot for Stieglitz. He retreats indoors, but Elizabeth and I continue to work, nailing shingles to the roof, frying up there like strips of bacon. I wear my large floppy hat and peel down to chemise and bloomers. One afternoon, Alfred comes out to find us. He's carrying his Graflex and triumphantly brandishing a newspaper.

"Historic day!" he cries with delight. "Ratified! Women have won the right to vote."

"Joy!" Elizabeth says. "I can't wait for the dinner-table scuffle tonight. You will be our champion, Uncle Al. How dull it would be around here if you were as conventional as the other males in this family."

"Alfred isn't one for dull," I say.

"I hear it already," Elizabeth says. "Father's dismay, his very serious concern." She drops her voice to a low somber tone to imitate her father, Lee. "I'm afraid it will skew the upcoming election."

We erupt into giggles. Stieglitz throws us the paper. Reaching to grab it, Elizabeth nearly loses her balance off the roof. I grasp her arm and pull her down. She lies there, laughing, then spreads the newspaper out to read the lead article, her round cheeks flushed.

"Now I can be finished wondering why it took them all so long to see what was always clearly right," Stieglitz says.

"Men can be stubborn," I say.

"Ha! Look at me, Georgia. Look now." He has the camera raised. I smirk and he frowns. "Please," he says sweetly. I shake the hammer at him, then smile, the shutter clicks. I turn away, slip a square ticket of wood against another, set a nail to the shingle, swing the hammer and hit it squarely on the head.

When the shanty is done, Alfred spends the day inside it with me. I retrieve some bits of molding from the trash and make a frame. He builds a stool from a cast-off piece of wood.

"This side of the room will work for me," he says, pacing out one end.

"Oh no." Shaking my head.

"What do you mean, *no?*"

"Just that." I come close to him, touch the V point where his shirt opens, the top button undone, my fingertip light on his chest, tracing the bone. "You have the run of everywhere else," I say. "The shanty is mine."

V

"A WOMAN NEEDS a child, Uncle Al," Elizabeth remarks one afternoon in late August. They are sitting in his corner of the porch. I am on the steps reading.

"Georgia's not just any woman," Stieglitz answers.

"I hear you," I say.

Elizabeth smiles at me, then turns back to Stieglitz. "*Particularly* a woman like Georgia," she answers. "Think of what the experience of a child will do for her art."

"With a baby to nurse, burp, and clean, she'll have no time for art."

"I can help," Elizabeth says.

"And how?"

"I can be not only your favorite niece, but also nanny, caregiver, kindergarten—any and all of what you and Georgia need."

"We don't even have our own home," Stieglitz says. "There's no place for a child."

"There is always a place for a child where there is love."

Stieglitz looks at her over the rim of his glasses, a stern look. "Verbose."

"Romantic," Elizabeth corrects. "And nothing wrong with it. You might have a dash of it in you."

"I am practical."

She bursts into laughter.

"Besides," Stieglitz says. "Georgia is barely more than a child herself."

"Really?" I exclaim. "I am all of thirty-three."

"But young still," he says earnestly, "and developing so beautifully."

The phrase surprises me—something so weirdly awful in it—like Pygmalion and Galatea. I feel a quick wave of anger toward him and toward Elizabeth for stirring this up in the first place.

I look down at the book open on my lap. *Trees and How to Know Them.* My eyes drop to the page. *The bark of all birches is marked with long horizontal* . . .

"And there is the money concern," I hear him say now. "Things can barely continue as they are."

"Things work out," Elizabeth says. "Have some faith in that."

"I don't want to talk about this anymore today," Stieglitz says.

"I'll bring it up again tomorrow, then," she answers.

He ignores her and speaks across the porch to me. "Do you want to go for a row later, Georgia?"

I glance up and hold his eyes coolly for a moment just so he knows I am not pleased. "We can do that."

HE HOLDS MY arm as we walk the path down to the lake.

"Don't ever do that," I say.

"What?"

"Have a conversation about something that matters deeply to me with someone else in that staged way."

"She brought it up."

"Don't do that again."

I feel him shrink, but he nods.

"I want a child, Stieglitz—you've promised me from the start, and if now is not quite the right time, I'm perfectly capable of talking that through. Alone with you. But not like that again."

I HELP HIM flip the dinghy. Together we drag it to the shallows. We row in silence. Halfway around the island, the wind shifts—a sudden squall moving in over the hills.

"Head back," I say.

He turns the boat around, so the wind is with us. A gust flays the surface, driving spray against the hull. Small waves have begun to form. The little boat pitches over them, and he rows with long strong pulls, driving the bow through the chop.

Rain has begun to fall—just a drizzle at first, then drenching. Halfway to shore, a streak of lightning rips the sky across the lake. I see the canoe—just east of the island, two small figures in it. Boys.

"Stieglitz, go back! Go back!" I go to stand. He pulls me down.

"You'll tip us!"

"But look! Out there, those boys!"

As his eyes follow my hand pointing, the canoe rolls, two dark shapes disappear into black water. I see one head surface, his arm pale in another burst of lightning. He clings to the overturned canoe.

"Turn around! Go back!" I shout. "Go back!"

He keeps rowing toward shore.

"You can't leave them!"

"I'll return myself. But four in this boat—we can't do it!"

"There won't be time!"

"I'm bringing you in."

"You can't, not now!"

"You need to go for help. I'll go back for them."

"No! Go back now!"

But he rows on. I grip the gunwale, straining to see the two heads out in the middle of the lake by the canoe, but seeing only one.

"Go back, please. Turn around." The words shred like prayer. "Please."

We strike the dock. I jump out and push him off again. He starts to row into the storm, leaning into the oars, long strong pulls through the rough water.

"Go, Georgia," he shouts back. "Go!" I run up the hill.

My heart is in my throat as I reach the farmhouse, panicked, shouting, my soaked clothes pouring puddles on the floor.

Elizabeth brings me blankets as Agnes phones for help and the men flood down the hill toward shore.

I watch from the porch, gripping the rail. Stieglitz has reached the capsized canoe. He grabs hold of the boy still clinging there—that pale arm I'd seen—the little rowboat tips and sways, but he braces himself and hauls that boy with one pull into the boat.

"They're going to be fine," Elizabeth says, coming to stand beside me. She presses a cup of hot tea into my hands. "Others are headed out now."

"There was another boy," I say.

"They'll find him." Elizabeth brings her arm around me. Stieglitz is rowing again, circling the canoe, looking.

They don't find the boy. A week later, a hunter finds a coat near the shore up the lake tangled in tree roots.

"We need to put this behind us," Stieglitz says to me when we hear the news. "We could not have saved him."

The others have gone to bed. It's a warm night. Stars flood the sky.

"I wish we'd tried," I say.

A deep silence falls.

"He was gone the moment the canoe tipped," he says. "Even rowing back, I knew." He is looking away across the lake, the dark mass of the island floating in the silver water.

"It was probably the right choice," I say.

"There was no choice."

"I'm not blaming you."

He looks at me then, sorrow so blunt it takes my breath.

MID-SEPTEMBER, AFTER MOST of them are gone, I come upon Hedwig in the upstairs hall. She is on her knees. She gapes at me. I try to help her up, an arm thrashes, her voice slurred, she stares through my face as if I am the door she is reaching for. Then her hand drops, and she slumps, the full weight of her pitching to one side.

I cry for help. Stieglitz calls back to me from the other end of the house. A team of doctors swoop to the Hill. She is only just stirring when they bear her away. He weeps when we receive the call from Lee. A stroke. She will recover. To a certain extent.

I hold him, late into the next morning. We take long walks as the leaves burn down into their autumn fire. He photographs lit raindrops on the apple tree. Like tears, he says.

I notice he seems anxious about my work, about what I am doing and not doing, what I have left to learn. Light ripples of tension pass through me when he wanders into the shanty as I am painting. Together, we look over my Apple series. My *Red Maples*. My *Tree with Cut Limb*. Everything I made this summer when the house was bustling seems slightly lackluster, truncated.

"These don't seem to have the life of my earlier work," I say.

"It will come," he says.

But it's hard not to feel the dark current of despair running through his hand into mine as we walk to the post office in town, or sit together in the kitchen in the morning.

"YOU WOULD HAVE to choose," he says to me out of the blue one day. It's late fall. The rest of them are gone. I'm washing dishes in the sink.

"Choose?" I say.

"Between a child and your art. You do realize this, don't you?"

"No," I say, rinsing a plate, watching the clean water drain off its face.

"I shouldn't have brought it up." He takes the plate from my hand and rubs the towel over it, grinding it so it squeaks.

"You are the one with too much on your mind," I say lightly. "I could manage a child quite well."

"Well, it's not the time to make the decision."

"I'm not the one who brought it up."

He takes the two knives I've just handed him. I notice their thin metallic surfaces, light blinks off them.

I drop the bowl I am holding into the dishpan. Water sprays up, soaking us.

"You meant to do that!" he says, stepping back.

"Did I?"

He reaches for my hands to dry them with the dish towel, but I grab the waist of his trousers, push him back against the sink, and press my thigh between his legs.

"You're sopping wet," he says.

"I'm sick of this," I say, "the moroseness, the glumness, it's all such a waste of my time."

"That's not kind."

"No one can undo what's done. Not even you." I unzip his trousers. I touch him, and he smiles.

"Finally," I say. "A smile."

He is hard in my hand.

My blouse is spattered with water. He touches my nipples through the cotton, he twists one as I stroke him back and forth. He touches my breasts, then slides his hand under the waist of my skirt, pushing it down my hips until it slips off, his hand around my backside, his fingers working into me.

"Everything's wet," he says.

His fingers push deeper into me, softly at first, then not.

"I want you," I say.

"Hard over the sink?" His voice low, an edge near my ear. "From behind on the table? Or straddling a chair?" His hand underneath me now, lifting me up, leaning me back onto the table, that sharp quick rush of him sliding inside me.

"I won't choose," I say.

He presses my hands over my head. A candlestick knocks over, rolls to the floor. "You have to choose." His teeth graze my neck.

"I want it all."

VI

October. Paul Rosenfeld comes up to the Lake, bringing the artist Charles Duncan with him. Rosenfeld has just been named the music critic for *The Dial*. He adores us, and is becoming one that Stieglitz can count on. He buys art as Stieglitz tells him to—paintings by Marin, Hartley, Dove—and hangs them in his elegant apartment at Irving Place where we met the poet Marianne Moore last year at a winter soiree. She and I laughed at the fact that we were born on the same day, same year. Rosenfeld has asked Stieglitz if he can buy one of my oils.

"I'm afraid her work is not yet for sale," Stieglitz responds, "but when it is, Pudge, you'll be the first to know."

Soon after they arrive, Rosenfeld exclaims that all he can amount to in the kitchen is scrambled eggs. And so, the next morning for breakfast, scrambled eggs it is. I take over the rest of the cooking and task the men with cleanup. I garden, can vegetables, and press cider from apples. The sweet scent fills the room with a kind of certainty I crave. I've taught Stieglitz how to stoke the furnace, and he shows off his new skill.

"Georgia's so very capable," he says. "I like to think some of it will rub off on me."

"Did you know," I say, "that when Alfred was a child, he spent whole days reenacting the great horse races of the past on a Parcheesi board. Thus, he never learned much in the way of housekeeping. What chores did you do to receive an allowance?"

"There were no chores."

I burst into laughter. "So you were being paid to simply exist?"

"Something like that, I'm afraid," Stieglitz says sheepishly.

ONE AFTERNOON, HE photographs Rosenfeld, Duncan, and me at lunch, sitting around the table set with bouillon, olives, asparagus, bacon, eggs.

"To paradise," Rosenfeld says, raising his glass, then bending back over his food as Stieglitz directs.

Later, I will look at that photograph, and there is something so domestic, so simple—how he caught us, mid-stride—the easy white drape of my shirt, a smile on my face as I spear an olive with my fork, and the fourth place, Stieglitz's, empty at the front of the small table, the loaf of bread on the cutting board beside it, the knife laid perpendicular to a slice just cut. I will look at that photograph—a small print, the size of a playing card—and I will try to remember if it was ever as simple and lovely as he made it appear. This was his gift. This is what we were entranced by. How he could capture the momentary flicker of a soul in the image of raindrops on an apple, or three people gathered around a small table at a meal—such a simple and intimate pleasure—the trees in the background, blurred.

THE FOLLOWING DAY, I overhear Rosenfeld expressing concern that his presence at the Lake might be an intrusion on our work, mine in particular.

"I haven't seen her painting since I arrived."

"No," Stieglitz says firmly. "Nothing but pleasure to have you here. Georgia feels the same way."

"Well I can't tell you how grateful I am," Paul says, his manners as always so beautifully streamlined, "it's such an opportunity to observe the two of you this way at close range."

"You must see her newest things."

"I'd love to."

"It's extraordinary, Pudge—what she's doing right now with color. Her new oils have a daunting power. Almost as bold as those early charcoals."

It's fascinating—to hear him talk this way about my things—when just a few weeks ago he seemed anxious about them.

"I'm thinking," he continues now, "at some point, you should write about her painting for *The Dial*."

"A marvelous idea!"

"Not yet," Stieglitz says quickly. "But at some point soon. Let's bear it in mind."

SEVERAL MORNINGS LATER we are out on the porch, Alfred in his old gray sweater, writing his letters and, beside him on the table, the black portfolio folder that holds a selection of my watercolor paintings and drawings. The men have nicknamed that black folder of my work "Stieglitz's Celestial Solitaire," because he always seems to have it with him, or near him—and he'll take it out and flip through the pictures, and occasionally show them around. They seem to have a particular meaning to him—my early things. As I sit on the steps, I notice Paul observing us, a wistfulness in his drooping eyes. But then he smiles, a warm smile. I smile back.

Stieglitz looks up from his letter. "Let's do a portrait."

"Of?" Rosenfeld says.

"You, Pudge."

"Me?"

Stieglitz stands up. "Yes. You. A portrait of the Writer."

"I'd be honored."

In one of the upstairs bedrooms, Stieglitz has Rosenfeld sit at the small, older desk, his arms crossed, and beside him a typewriter, a stack of books, including Carl Sandburg's recent collection of poems, galley proofs, cigarettes.

Charles Duncan and I watch from the doorway as Stieglitz positions the objects exactly where he wants them to be, and it occurs to me that this is what he does. He moves us through space. I see the glow of warmth on Rosenfeld's face, the joy he feels at being the unexpected center of attention. His bow tie is crooked. It hangs skewed to the right, oddly small under the round portly dish of his face. As I move to straighten it, the shutter clicks, I freeze.

When they leave, the Lake is ours again. Just hours of work and solitude stretching from one day into the next. The air grows cold. I think of the apartment in his brother's brownstone we are moving back to, windows looking out into the dark faces of the buildings behind.

"I don't want to leave," I say. But Stieglitz needs the city—the bustle and comforts that sometimes seem so strange to me.

I dig out a sketch I made earlier in the year, and work it into oil. *Red and Orange Streak*—a dark expanse of sky cut at the horizon line by a chain of red mountains. A wide-grooved orange arc that drives up from the bottom left and off the edge.

"It's a sound," I say when Stieglitz comes in to see it, finished. "That loud raw sound of the cattle in Texas."

It still haunts me—the rhythm of that sound in the desolate emptiness.

He stands before the painting, studying it.

"This is what that country out there means to you," he says.

"Go with me sometime."

The sunlight falls on his shoulders—very soft and tender, tame. The sunlight here.

"You've done it, Georgia," he says. "The union of form and color. This. It's a new American Art."

VII

ONE DECEMBER EVENING, back in New York, Mitchell Kennerley, owner of the Anderson Galleries, comes by and Stieglitz shows him the dozens of prints he made at the Lake this year, many of them of me.

"These don't belong in storage," Kennerley says. "I think it's time for a retrospective of your work."

"No," Stieglitz says quickly, glancing at me.

"When was your last exhibition?"

"Over ten years ago."

Kennerley nods, then looks back at the raindrops on an apple, and a few images of my body and face.

"These are brilliant, Alfred," Kennerley says. "High time for the rest of New York to be introduced to your new work."

AFTER KENNERLEY LEAVES, Stieglitz clears his throat and tells me that he would never do this, never think of exhibiting the photographs of me without my consent.

"But you have my consent. This is your art."

"You don't hear what I'm saying."

"You held showings in the apartment—I was right there."

"This will be different," he says.

"Different people may be looking at the photographs, but other than that, isn't it the same?"

He glances at me, a pause, considering. "It will be an opportunity for your work as well."

I am sitting in the large chair at the end of the table, my legs tucked up underneath me, black shoes set together on the floor.

"Kennerley said nothing about showing my work."

"You will be a sensation," he says.

"My body, you mean. Not my art."

"No. That's not what I mean. This could work as much for your art as for mine," he says. "If we do this, your art will be a sensation even before it's seen."

I stand up and walk over to his prints on the table. Her glistening silver form. They feel very alive to me, the livingness about them— their stunning erotic beauty, their irreverence.

I pull one from the table and look at it more closely. White and black, silver-toned, complete. Her hair pulled back tightly, the cloak around her shoulders, the cords of her neck just visible, a low defiant heat in her eyes that looks directly into the camera, poised, almost insolent. She seems absolute. No past. No future. She belongs strictly to herself, alone.

I remember what Edward Steichen said that night when he came to the shoe-box room and saw the photographs and my oils for the first time: *Nothing like this has come into our world before.*

"Do it," I say now.

"You're like no other woman," he says, his voice quiet. His eyes so strangely earnest search my face.

I say, "We've had our small studio showings. Kennerley is right. New York should see your art. It will bring attention to the gallery. Maybe buyers, too."

He catches my face, his palms warm and firm, and draws me to him.

WHEN HIS FAMILY learns what we're intending, they descend with a slew of objections. "Alfred, you can't do this! What about Georgia?" I remain silent, through these debates, until he summons my opinion.

"We discussed it, and I agreed," I say.

Stieglitz goes to pieces over how to choose which photographs best represent the arc of his work over the last thirty years, and I begin to realize how anxious he is. He's spent most of the last decade building up the careers of other artists, letting his own fall by the wayside, and now he seems to be questioning just how good his new work really is.

There's a tacit agreement between us not to discuss the glaring intimacy of some of the prints of me he wants to include. Some are clothed, many not. The ones of the buttocks are in his "to mount" pile. I remove them and put them with the others bound for storage.

I come across an image of my hands. I do not remember exactly when he took it. I recognize the button on the coat—it was the first year I was here—but there were many days when I wore that coat, and I find a quiet fear kick in me that I can't quite place the day he made that image. There is something unsettling in the disembodied hands—the way the fingers of one seem to claw, almost to tear into the palm of the other. It is one he has chosen. I leave it. She will be called simply *A Woman* in the catalog and will remain unnamed. My face is cropped in the nudes. There will be no image where the naked body and face are shown together.

He obsesses over his words for the catalog. He reads it aloud to me as we fix breakfast in the kitchen, and then again at night before we sleep. *I was born in Hoboken. I am an American. Photography is my passion. The search for Truth my obsession.* At night, I sneak upstairs into his bedroom to keep up propriety's face for Lee, Lizzie, and the mother-in-law.

"So ridiculous!" I whisper, laughing. "They all must know!"

"But they don't want to know they know."

"A façade is so much work, Alfred. You must sell twenty photographs from the show, so we can find a place of our own."

I lie beside him, his hands just touching me, not holding tightly at all. I can feel his anxiety, a tremble in his fingers on my skin. It always surprises me to see him vulnerable this way.

"Why are you so afraid, love?" I say.

He shakes his head. "I just want it to go well."

WARREN HARDING, THE dark-horse Republican, wins the presidential election, soundly defeating newspaper publisher Cox and his running mate, Franklin Roosevelt, who lives directly across the street from us in 47 East 65th. Stieglitz remarks that Harding's victory marks the country's disgust with any policy that smacks of the progressive. "Four steps forward before the war," he says, "now twelve steps back." Instability seems everywhere: large-scale race riots in Chicago, strikes in the meatpacking industry, terrorist attacks on Wall Street. "They don't see how they bring it on themselves," he says bitterly. "Go crazy with fear over anything new, cling to what they think is safe, and cement themselves right into deadness and doom."

My sister Claudia writes. She's leaving Texas and coming to New York—my heart soars when I read the news—my sweet youngest sister. She wants to get her degree from Columbia Teachers College. She'll stay with our sister Ida, or perhaps Anita, who's married a wealthy financier—*imagine all those chandeliers and spare bedrooms,* Claudia writes. So much of home—her familiar handwriting, her self-confident humor that matches mine.

I write back to her—*Such glorious news, the thought of you here! And definitely, you should pursue your degree. You must plan to visit the Lake this summer. If money is any object for your schooling, I can help.*

Who knows where I'll scrape that money from, but I will.

———

I HELP STIEGLITZ hang the exhibition on the red velvet walls of the Anderson Galleries. It is not me, I tell myself, when I look at the woman set among his other things—visions of old New York, ferry boats, carriage horses, aeroplanes, and city streets—iconic images of his earlier career, before he became more well known for dealing in the work of others. Of the 145 prints he hangs to show, 46 are images of me. In the nudes, my face is cropped out.

Three thousand people attend the exhibition. When the reviews begin to appear, his disciples stress exactly what he wants them to stress: the severity, the revolutionary aspect of his vision and of The Portrait in particular.

But other reviewers do not. One critic writes that his photography is "essentially aristocratic and expensive. He spends an immense amount of time making love to the subject before taking it." Some reviewers manage to do both, praising Stieglitz's ability to capture the wholeness of a woman in her fragments and, at the same time, describing my body in rudely intimate terms: "the navel, the mons veneris, the armpits, the bones underneath the skin of the neck . . . the life of the pores, of the hairs along the shin-bone, of the veining of the pulse, and the liquid moisture on the upper lip . . . lucent unfathomable eyes, the gesture of chaste and impassioned surrender."

It's the scandal that drew them. They're not after the art. I am his mistress. It's not a stranger's body they're describing, but mine. My mind tumbles through black space. How could I not have seen this coming? I should have known. What have I done?

I LIE IN bed for most of the day. The little blue scrap of sky outside feels unthinkably bright. I close the curtains. He finds me there that evening.

"Shall we go to dinner?" he says.

"Not tonight."

"You are not feeling well." He stretches out on the bed beside me. "What is it?"

I want to press myself into him, slip under the slight dark curved space his neck makes near the sheet, disappear.

"Have I left you alone too many days?" he says. But he must know. I can't look at his face. I look into that thin dark opening into the pale of the sheet beyond. "I can't bear how they write—it's degrading. This has nothing to do with art," I say to that shallow dark curve of space.

He strokes my hair. "Dearest Love. One must be talked about and written about, for people to buy. They are talking about the woman in the photographs, yes, but now they want to know more about this mysterious young artist whose work they have not yet been introduced to. They are dying to see it. And they will come to see it, when we let them."

"The affair is what they're writing about—not the art."

"You must not care what *anyone* writes," he says firmly.

"But you care—you care more than anyone."

"It's gossip. It means nothing."

I will remember this moment. The space under his neck. I cannot tear my eyes away from it for the whole time we are lying there. Such a narrow space, but wide enough I am sure to flee through.

As the show comes to a close, he announces a sale price of five thousand dollars for one of his prints—a nude.

"A sordid amount," I murmur, drinking tea.

"It's unique," he says. "The plate was destroyed. No other print of that image will ever exist."

I set down the teacup. A bit of brownish-gray liquid has spilled onto the saucer, making a sludgy mark.

"Sometimes it seems like you enjoy this attention," I say quietly.

"Would you prefer I fail?" I glance up. His eyes are cool. It feels strange, that coldness. I turn away.

"No."

"Darling," he whispers, his hand reaching across the table toward me. "Don't you trust me? This will only help you. Even McBride, whom I can never win over, is already aware of your work."

"He's never seen my work."

"That doesn't matter. When it's shown, he'll be looking for it. All of them will."

IN APRIL, STIEGLITZ is invited by the Pennsylvania Academy of Fine Arts to mount an exhibition. He accepts on the condition that they'll include three works of mine. He takes the art by train to Philadelphia. While he is gone, I prep my canvases, canvas after canvas, running white lead over and over and over until the surface is smooth and shines, until it gleams with that thick whiteness—luminous, opalescent. I get out my paints, squeeze color onto the glass palette, perfectly neat, each remote from the others, an impeccable distance. I sit down at the easel, the whiteness of the canvas glares back at me. I put down my brush and go out for a walk.

ROSENFELD INVITES US to a concert of the Detroit Symphony, and after, we go to a restaurant on 59th. As they plow through chocolate éclairs, Rosenfeld is so witty—in his acerbic droll way—poking fun at Paul Strand's new wife, Beck.

"Her father was a vaudeville troubadour," he says with a flair of his fork, drops of vanilla cream clinging to the prongs. "Made his mark as manager of Buffalo Bill's horrifically successful Wild West Show."

I stifle a laugh. "I heard she was a basketball star."

"She's got the legs for it. Apparently, her mother has been trying to matchmake her into a marriage for quite some time."

"Really?"

"Yes, because the tempers between them are so ferocious, she wants her out of the house."

"Strand is swept away," I say.

"She is beautiful," says Rosenfeld. "And in search of something higher and more profound than secretarial work."

"That's what she does?"

"And I am afraid it's a perfectly decent match, perhaps the only match, for her abilities."

Stieglitz shakes his head, cutting off another sizable piece of his pastry. "Strand has introduced her to your work, Georgia."

"Yes, that's right!" Rosenfeld says. "He brought her by, didn't he? And she was so taken by the O'Keeffes she saw, she has decided to roll up her sleeves and plunge into watercolors herself." He shakes his head here and glances at Stieglitz who has an inadvertent smear of chocolate on the side of his face. "A little war paint, right there," Rosenfeld says. "That's the spot. You've caught it. Almost gone."

"So what's her art like, Pudge?" I ask.

"She is quite lovely, though a bit of a moll."

"Her art?" I ask.

"Half a gnat of talent, perhaps less."

I pick triangular pieces out of my grapefruit.

"Strand's been making photographs of her, a serial portrait—sadly imitative of a far greater masterpiece." Rosenfeld looks at me.

"Well for God's sake warn her not to let Strand mount a show that will make her a public spectacle."

Stieglitz glares at me.

"That's not the end of it," Rosenfeld continues, smoothly. "Beck's begun to take after our exquisite Georgia in other ways as well—wearing her hair combed from her face, no makeup."

"I've heard she wears trousers!"

"And the cigarettes," he muses. "Don't forget."

I shake my head. "A woman is never going to gain anything dressing herself up like a man."

VIII

I BEGIN TO resist, quietly, being photographed. I put him off gently. "I have work to do," I say. "You know this." He's restless, though. He has been since his show closed and we were deposited back into the humdrum of everyday life. He's begun to plan for the first major exhibition of my things—more than a year from now. He wants it a secret still. It will be his introduction of my work to New York, and only the closest in the circle know.

By the end of June, the Lake is almost full: his mother, ailing, wrapped in shawls; Selma, along with his other sister, Agnes, her husband, and their sixteen-year-old daughter also named Georgia. We call her Georgia Minor or, more simply, The Kid. Stieglitz photographs her by the back door of the farmhouse, then naked in a window, clutching apples to her bare breasts—like some adolescent Eve—until her mother comes around the corner and ends it, urging her brother to find a more suitable subject.

He fumes over this.

"Convention is inane. I hate being boxed in by it."

I TELL HIM I want to have my sister Claudia visit. She's just arrived in New York.

"I know it might seem difficult with your mother unwell—"

"No, no!" he says, suddenly brightening. "Don't give it a second thought. Invite her up. Ida, too. Have them both come. Yes. A little more O'Keeffe is what we need. I'll write to them myself. Seligmann's coming the week after next—I'll have them come then."

"No," I say. "Not Seligmann."

"He's bringing the Hartley proof."

"The essays?"

"Yes."

"Then invite my sisters for the weekend before."

I'm not keen on Seligmann—a writer for *The New Republic* and *The Nation*. I find him a tiresome sycophant, always trying to shoehorn himself into my good graces. But he's editing Marsden Hartley's new collection of essays, and there's a chapter on women artists I'm featured in. I'm curious to see it.

CLAUDIE AND IDA come up from the city on the train and blow into the Hill—a sudden whirl of fresh air. I throw my arms around my youngest sister, then hold her at arm's length.

"How you've grown up, Claudie! Ida, look at her. Our littlest one. All of twenty-one now."

"And how lucky you are!" Claudia says. "It's so lovely—the lake, this view." She bubbles on. Stieglitz walks out to greet them.

"Hello. Hello," he says smiling. "Welcome! So good of you to come. Wonderful to have you here." He presses Ida's hand, then takes Claudie by the arm, so charming. I watch how my youngest sister looks at him, shyly—he is *that* man after all, the one she did not trust once. She's fallen under his spell.

"What shall we do first?" Claudia says, later at tea. "We have just these few days, and I want to do everything ten times over, at least. A hike tomorrow morning, do you think? We've brought our boots, right, Ida?" Ida nods and Claudia turns to Stieglitz. "Will you go with us and be our guide, Alfred. No bunk excuses please."

"I'll think about it," he says. "There may be things I have to get to tomorrow."

"Perhaps they can wait until the second half of tomorrow," Ida says, wiping crumbs off her blouse.

"That's right," Claudia chimes in. "It's a yes! Alfred will be with us. Now, which mountain—that one there, or that one farther down?" She points. "There must be a lovely sunset from that spot right there."

WE SPEND THE weekend walking, laughing, swimming in the lake.

"He's charming," Ida says. "Every time I see him again, I remember just how charming."

"Much less so before you came."

"Why?"

"All sorts of reasons. His daughter is getting married—there's rumor he won't be invited. And his show is over. Everything got very dull for him after that."

"But you were relieved."

"Relieved to know I'd never let that happen again."

Ida laughs.

"And in the last week or so, he's been moaning on about our 'poverty.'"

"Not everyone would consider it that." I hear the sudden edge in her voice.

"His family may be wealthy, but we're most definitely not."

She doesn't answer, but I know what she is thinking—we could get real jobs, be like normal people. Go out and work.

Claudie is swimming out toward the center of the lake. Her bathing costume is a size too large and drags around her hips. The sun is warm, the air is still.

I ask Ida if she's heard from our younger brother, Alexius, in Chicago, and our sister Catherine who lives in Madison and just got engaged.

"Can't you stay a little longer?" I say.

She doesn't answer. I glance over my shoulder. She's done a good sketch of the bank and the trees, the outline of a great blue heron. She shades in around the shoulder, and the darker shadows marking the feathers.

"Did you hear me?" I say.

"No," she answers absently, without looking up, her round face focused on the paper as the pencil tip scratches back and forth. "I have to be back Monday."

"Such a demanding schedule."

"I love nursing. I can't imagine doing anything else."

"And now it's what Claudie will do as well."

"Seems to be what the O'Keeffe girls are destined for. That is, apart from you."

"I might like that kind of work," I say. "Having a structure and schedule I don't have to make for myself."

Ida's pencil stops then, and she looks at me. Sun on her face, she puts up her hand to shield her eyes. "*That's* not who you are, or have ever been. And you know it."

THE EVENING THEY leave, Herbert Seligmann arrives. The next morning after breakfast, I ask him if I can see that chapter in the proof of Hartley's book that mentions me.

"It's an extraordinary piece."

"Yes, Stieglitz told me Hartley based it on my paintings he saw at the apartment."

"More general really. He recognizes your vision as an abstract artist and he's captured that."

He hands me the pages. I take them down to the dock with a pencil, my feet dangling into the cold lake, and skim through until I find my name. Hartley writes about the life in my work, my place in modern art. He compares my work to that of Mary Cassatt and Berthe Morisot, but there is also this:

> *Georgia O'Keeffe has had her feet scorched in the laval effusiveness of terrible experience; she has walked on fire and listened to the hissing of vapors round her person. The pictures of O'Keeffe, the name by which she is mostly known, are probably as living and shameless private documents as exist. . . . By shamelessness I mean unqualified nakedness of statement.*

I look up. The light rings off the water. A mistake. There's been a mistake.

It occurs to me that this is the only copy. It would be easy enough to lose it.

Stieglitz is on the porch, writing correspondence, a forgotten breakfast napkin still tucked into his shirt collar, the black folder of my work in its usual place beside him.

I hand him the chapter, the section marked off in pencil. "There's been a mistake," I say. "I'd like this to be changed."

"Did you write on this?"

"I'll erase it."

"Give me the eraser."

"I don't have it here."

"Then get it. This does not belong to us. You had no right to mark it up."

"Read it, Alfred." He's trying to distract, to miss the point. He looks at me then, over the steel-rimmed glasses, and it must be something in my face that pulls him from the rut of the debate. His eyes drop to the page, and he reads. His brow furrows.

"I'd like it changed."

"What?"

"These lines—these words, here, do you see? They are about the photographs, but the article itself is about my painting. 'Living shameless private documents'—those words are about the photographs. They don't belong in an article about my painting. You see?"

"I do."

"Then you'll ask him to remove those lines."

"That's the heart of the piece," he says.

"It's not the heart of the piece. When he talks about my work itself—how I use color, what I'm doing with abstraction. That's the heart of the piece."

"It's all excellent exposure," he continues. "It will be good—"

"It's not the kind of exposure I want."

He sighs. "We've discussed this, Georgia."

"We have not. This is *my art* he's written about. We discussed *your* photographs. We never discussed this."

"It's a strong essay."

"It's going to be in a book—'a woman turned inside out and gaping with deep open eyes.' *That* is not my art. *That* is about the photographs."

He studies me as if I am unwell. "It's praise, Georgia," he says. "It may not be the words you want, but it's unmitigated praise. The piece *is* controversial. Just as *your art* is controversial. And this piece is, although you may not see it yet, everything your art is and can be: bold, glorious . . ." His face softens then. He looks at me so intently that the porch is gone, the lake, the house gone, it is only the two of us left in the world.

"Georgia, this is perhaps *the* hardest challenge for every artist. To see their art described in words, because how can words really ever capture the hours and vision that went into the work itself. No words can touch that."

"But," I say. "These words are not about my art. They are about your photographs."

He looks away. He goes on. "Reviews will come. A whole land-scape of them, describing the art of O'Keeffe, and at the end of the day, you will have to realize that all that matters, all that really matters, is that there was a feeling you had once, a feeling that burned in you enough that you took a few days or weeks of your life, and turned that feeling into color and form. What matters is that you keep yourself open to *that*—that raw inspiration, that madness, that passion; you must let yourself be driven by that need. You are a true artist. Your abstractions are ahead of our time. Who else is doing what you're doing? No one. And I'm hell-bent the world will see it. And if some article in some book helps make that happen then I'm going to use it."

I stare at him. There are grains of truth in what he's saying—I know it. But there is something so condescending in how he's telling me who I am, what will unfold, how I must learn. And yet. These things—raw inspiration, the madness, the passion—these things matter to me—he knows this—these are the things I'd trade everything else for.

"And Rosenfeld," he is saying now, "has agreed to write a piece on American painting for *The Dial*. It will feature you."

"When?"

"This fall."

"Who else will it feature?"

"Marin and Dove. I need Dove praised."

"Dove should be praised."

"That's what I said."

"Not exactly. Will there be illustrations?"

"I believe so."

"Then I want one of my paintings printed alongside whatever Rosenfeld has to say. That way he can say what he wants, and my painting will be in there speaking for itself."

He studies me for a long moment.

"I don't know that I can make that happen, Georgia."

I smile at him. "Oh, I'm sure you can."

HARTLEY'S BOOK IS published. I ignore it. But I look for Rosenfeld's piece in *The Dial* that appears that December. There are moments of wonderfulness in what he's written where he claims that in my work, I am building "a new sort of language" through "the unformed electric nature of things." But there are moments of awfulness, too: phrases like "gloriously female," "ecstasy of pain." He describes my colors in terms of flesh and appetite, and I wince, but keep reading. I reach the end of the page, turn it, then see.

A printed image of my abstraction. *The Black Spot.*

One of those pieces I made without knowing where the idea came from or even what it said. But I could feel that thrill in my body as I worked into those shapes, so clear in my mind: dark-blue carving down from one corner, a black edge rising. They burned in me— those contrasting shapes—so much dimension, so many levels of feeling.

I stare at the print for a long time, and a thought strikes me. The thought that I can make my living as a painter.

IX

It's NOT UNTIL the following August that I meet Beck Strand. Stieg-litz invites both Strands to the Lake that fall, but Paul is too busy to make the trip. Beck writes back, asking if perhaps she can come alone.

"Tell her to come now," I say.

"The house is too full."

"She can stay in the inn down the road. Nicer that way." I add, "Then I can see if I like her before she's right underfoot."

The day after she arrives, we invite her to go swimming in the lake, for a row around the island, then up to the house for tea. She is giddy, bouncy, and constantly looking around, saying how lovely every-thing is, sighing—she seems slightly in love with the two of us. She tells me that when she and Paul stayed at Rosenfeld's house earlier this summer I was everywhere with her.

"How so?"

"Your paintings. He told me Alfred finally let him buy a few this spring. Considered him worthy, I guess"—she gives a tentative smile—"and he has one room in his house that's all you—your ap-ples, your blue mountain, your canna lily. We were happy on that

short trip—my Paul and I—he's my only only, you know, and it was
a perfect time for us." She rambles on. I tear off a piece of biscuit and
take a small cut of butter. She is quite beautiful, pale, long-limbed,
kittenish. She calls me her Georginkha. Her O'Keefski. She's been
here for a day and already assumed a certain intimacy between us.
She compliments my espadrilles.

"I bought them shopping with my sister in the city."

"They're very chic."

"Good for walking."

Paul has sent her paper and canvas. "To give the erts a whirl," she
says.

"The arts, you mean?" I ask.

She nods. "Seems I have everything but ideas." Then she bright-
ens. "Say! I need a tie for my middy blouse—do you think Alfred
might have a tie I can borrow?"

THAT NIGHT, IN bed, I tell him we should invite her back for more
swimming. "You should take some pictures of her," I say.

A pause, then, "You don't mind?"

"I have work to do—and she'll be a more compliant model for
you."

So the next afternoon—mid-September already, but the air so
warm—Beck returns, and the two of us go into the lake with nothing on.

"Frigid!" she shrieks plunging in. "Come on, O'Keefski!"

The water is clear, and cold, I feel it flowing into me, around me,
as I float on my back near the end of the dock, my hair trailing on the
surface. She is near me, floating too, her hand brushes mine. My eyes
are closed when the shadow falls across my face, and when I open
them, he is standing on the dock against the sun. He has the camera
out, and I suddenly find I don't want to be there anymore.

She's caught sight of him, and is laughing now. His gaze shifts to
her. I climb out and dry myself off with a towel.

"You're going up?" he says, looking back at me.

"I've got to work." I smile. It's a consent—the smile.

IT GOES ON for days—them gamboling about, him photographing her by the edge of the woods, or in the lake. "All in the nudelet," she laughs delightedly when I meet up with them in the later afternoon. "He must have taken a quintillion pictures of me today."

Thank God he's occupied, I think. I leave them at it, and vanish into my work. I make abstractions of the lake—sensual folds of hills, reflection, sky. I paint the shanty for fun in dark muted colors. To play a little joke on the men, just to prove I'm not all vivid red, pinks, and blues. I can do a drab thing every bit as well as they can.

Once, through the open door of the shanty, I hear her shriek, "Alfred!" Her voice with that coy bubbly giggle, just a short distance away. They must be in the meadow. I know it's what he needs to wrench himself out of his doldrum-ruminations—someone or something to entertain him. Better her than me. I've got work to do.

HE SHOWS ME a few prints of his photographs of Beck.

"They are lovely!" I say, sorting through them, and I mean it—they are lovely.

"Exactly as you said she would be," he says.

"How's that?"

"A very pliant model."

"I said *compliant*."

"I am sure the distinction escapes her."

There is one here—an astonishing image—her head is cropped, just the edge of her throat visible, her breasts fill half of the frame. She is lying in the shallows, just under the water, her wet body shining in the sunlight. She has a hand clutched under one breast, the nipple taut. I feel a quick chill run through me—so exquisite, that image of her body, so frank, his desire. Looking at the photograph, I can almost feel the way it happened. How he waded in, his pants rolled up, standing over her, instructing her to lie down in the shallows, to move her hand under her breast, nudging her gently at first, then more sternly, even as her skin shrank against the icy water, holding her breast toward him, her breast ripe, perfect, the camera and his eyes moving over her.

"You like that," he says, and I feel him behind me then, his hardness pushing into me, he lifts my skirt and I want him to. He slips his hand between my legs. I feel his fingers moving there, peeling into the layers of me. My body opens to him. "You want that," he says, his mouth near my ear, his breath hot, "to be in that water with her, imagine what we could do with her, what would you want to do with her?" The thought makes me shiver, and he can feel it. He laughs softly—a dark laugh that thrills me.

"You are so wet," he says, "I would like to have seen you there, in that cold water with her. You would like that. You would like to put your mouth on that." I push him away, but he draws me back, his voice a dark whisper, disembodied in the black of the potting shed. He unbuttons my shirt and takes my breast out and puts my hand under it, as hers was. I can feel the tug of his teeth, sucking lightly, the nipples sharpen in his mouth, his hand still moving between my legs. I grip the edges of the table behind me.

"Don't tip me into the acid," I say, laughing quietly. A stray light nicks the rim of his glasses as he takes them off.

"Shhhh," he says. Through the door, I hear children's laughter coming nearer, the babble of the baby, and Elizabeth's voice. "Shhh," he says as they pass by. The voices fade, his hand still moving between my legs, moving faster, his fingers creeping into me.

"You're going to make me scream," I say. His hand doesn't stop.

"You'll have to learn to scream without making a sound." He tucks the hem of my skirt into the waist, and then he kneels between my knees, turns me, and pushes me back against the sink. I set one foot on the stool and he buries his face between my legs, and I can feel his mouth on me, harder, sharper, everything in me rising, taut. I grip his hair pushing his face deeper into me, something knocks over behind on the table, I barely notice, don't even care, and in the small cramped blackness of that room I feel his hand grip my buttocks, his mouth moving over me, his fingers moving into me. And the light is a scream—exquisite, cutting—washing through my skull, and I make no sound, and when I open my eyes the room is blacker than darkness, my body limp, spent, I cannot see a thing.

BECK IS AT the house every day, for lunch and dinner, modeling, sewing, reading, lying around, writing letters to her Paul, bang-banging away on the old Corona, typing up articles for Stieglitz. She repairs his undershirt. She knits me a pair of heavy bed slippers.

"They'll keep your feet warm," she says—so obvious it seems almost ludicrous.

"And thick enough to keep my toenails from scratching up Stieglitz's legs in bed at night."

She looks slightly askance at this.

"I'm surprised he hasn't showed you yet," I say lightly, a hint of power in my voice. She's begun to sew a nightdress, a sheer thing.

That afternoon, she gathers a bouquet of dahlias she found on a walk, sets them into a vase, and gives them to me. "For you to paint," she says shyly.

BY THE TIME Paul comes to join us in late September, the family has gone back to the city and we're alone. "There's plenty of spare room now," I say to Stieglitz. "Invite them to move from the Pines and stay with us."

Paul has changed, no longer the soft-faced boy who came to fetch me from Texas. I've seen him since, but it hits me now—how somber he is, oddly anxious in his tweed jacket, knit tie, with a cigarette he's constantly smoking. Paul and Alfred take turns photographing Beck in the bed on the sleeping porch. But then Stieglitz complains to me that Strand is shooting everything that's his—everything in sight, right, left, forward, backward, the lake, the trees, even the old buggy.

"You've had quite a run with his wife," I remark. "Consider it a fair swap."

He shoots me a look, about to respond, then doesn't. But I can feel it smolder, his envy of Strand's youth, energy, his devouring talent. "Strand's gift is pure," he said to me just a few months ago. "He doesn't lose that edge. It's my intellect that gets in the way." I remember this now, feeling the tension in the house rise.

After supper one night, as the four of us sit around the fire, Stieglitz says: "Say, Georgia, why don't you read that piece aloud—the one you wrote for *Manuscripts*."

I glance at him, and know exactly what he's planning.

I shake my head. "It's not quite finished yet."

"Close enough, though!" he says brightly. "Please go get it."

"Yes, do!" Beck says, clapping her hands. So naïve not to smell his design. I glance at Paul. He nods at me, smiling, blind too, so stupidly blind—I would have expected more from him. He knows Stieglitz well. He should be able to read the tone.

"I'd like to hear it, Georgia," Strand says sincerely.

Actually you wouldn't, I think. But then it occurs to me that perhaps it is what they need, to be cut down a bit. She is not me—though she might play at it, modeling for him, and imagining we are all the best of friends. And Paul *is* wildly talented, but his photographs of Beck are derivative at best, queerly resonant of Stieglitz's serial portrait of me.

They are both just sitting here waiting, their eyes blankly full of worship for us. *We* are what they want to believe in. We are the paragon couple they imagine they want to be.

"Very well, then," I say, and leave the room to fetch it. The piece has only a cursory mention of Strand. I know it doesn't do his work justice, barely two sentences sandwiched between my praise of Stieglitz as the singular force driving modern American photography, and the focus of the piece—a tribute to Charles Sheeler, whom Strand actively dislikes.

I can feel the air in the room change as I read, the tension rippling. By the time I'm done, Paul's face is oddly red, flushed with anger and shame.

"Well," says Stieglitz disingenuously. "What do you think?" He is mocking them, and Strand at least has woken up and seen it. Beck still seems a little muddled and looks from one of us to the other, her mind not quite able to compute what it all adds up to.

"That paragraph felt out of style with the rest," Strand says carefully, addressing me.

"Really?" Stieglitz asks. "Tell us then, what would you suggest as an improvement?"

Strand starts to talk, but every argument he raises, Stieglitz refutes. Paul's face burns. Finally Beck grasps what has transpired, and erupts in a burst of childish outrage in defense of her husband's genius—"How could you be so dismissive? So careless? Or was it intentional? How could you?"

Strand turns on her. "Please be quiet," he says, because she is making quite a nut of herself.

She snaps back at him then, "Don't tell me to be quiet!"

Stieglitz has a faint and awful smile on his lips, watching them. I feel strangely heartless. I should feel compassion, remorse, or some trace of disgust for Stieglitz and the games he plays. That's not what I feel. They gave away too much. They gave him too much power and put us both up too high. They have left us no choice really but to stay there.

Later, I will look back on this and it will pick at me. It was wrong—what Stieglitz did that evening, what I did, dismantling Paul, his trust in us, and dismantling something young and tender between Paul and Beck as well. I played along, let it happen, felt nothing. In some clear resolute way, I knew how wrong it was, but it was easier to turn on them than look too closely at what I did not want to see.

X

A FEW WEEKS later, Stieglitz writes a gracious letter to Strand and shows it to me. *I regret that last night you were here. I should have known better,* he's written. It may take a few months, but he will woo them back. This is what he does. A disciple gets a little brash or, in Strand's case, competitive. Stieglitz will set them down a notch, then reel them back in.

He tells me that along with the letter he's going to send as a gift a print he made of Beck on the sleeping porch.

"Is that really the right thing to send?"

He snickers. "It's a fine print."

"You're a rat."

"I prefer rapscallion."

"That too."

"Don't you see," he says, "it will be a nice little weapon for her to have, in case he gets so swept up in his work and forgets his little Beckalina."

"Come with me," I say, pulling at the waist of his trousers.

He sets the print down with the letter, and gives me that look—delirious—it rakes my body. I have less than an instant to run. He takes off after me, sprinting through the house. I start up the stairs, but we don't make it. He pulls me down on the worn scarlet Oriental and makes love to me in the hallway.

Afterward, our bodies are warm and damp, next to each other on the carpet. I touch drops of wetness on my belly where he came— smooth, glimmery.

"Do you think we'll ever tire of this?" I say.

"I don't know why we would."

"Sometimes I feel that every woman should have the chance to have you for a lover."

"Don't say that unless you mean it."

I roll over and prop myself up on one hand. "I have some bold thought like that, then I change my mind." I reach to touch his cheek. How sweet he seems to me even when he's been so bad. He catches my hand. His face sobers.

"Is there another man you want, Georgia?"

"Of course not."

"You know I'd always give you the freedom to have what you need as long as in the end you were still mine."

"I don't want that kind of freedom," I say.

"What do you want, my love?"

"A child."

"Yes." Glancing away. "Soon."

"When is soon?"

"After your show."

"You promise?"

"It's a tremendous decision, Georgia, not as easy as you think."

"Why not easy?"

"When you're painting, Georgia, when you're really in your art, that's where you are. You disappear from the world, from me. And I understand that. I want that for you, because I know that in order to make the art you need to make, you need to give yourself completely to it."

I nod.

"A child would dismantle that."

"I don't believe that."

"Your vision right now is so clear."

"My vision will always be what it is."

IT IS BLISS for a while. I've done so much this year ahead of the January show. I set up all the paintings downstairs in the front room. An avalanche of abstract oils and pastels—my landscapes of the lake, the pond in the woods—they seem to have the same fierce strength as the Evening Star watercolors I did in Texas.

I feel a cogency in these pieces—a common language that binds the body of my work.

There was a teacher I had once, Arthur Wesley Dow, who talked about composition not as an arrangement of pretty things, but as space filled in a meaningful way. I have done this, not only by filling the space of a canvas, but by selection, elimination, emphasis. In the abstractions, the forms are so simplified, they become something greater than themselves—not realistic, but real. Even in my leaves and flowers—the object for its own sake is pushed away. Never rejected altogether, but stripped to its essence, its intrinsic, hidden life.

Stieglitz has been in a frenzy himself, photographing clouds. When the light slants and the breeze is cool, clouds rage over the lake. They seem to rise out of nowhere—so fast, their massive shapes on the tear.

"So difficult to get the rightness of everything," he says. "When the clouds are right, the sky is wrong, and when the leaves are still, the clouds have lost their shape, and there's nothing for it."

But I lose my mind when I see the pictures he's made. A low horizon of tree or hills and then the sky above, clouds rushing, those fugitive evanescent forms he's somehow managed to grasp.

He lifts the hair from my neck. I feel his mouth there, warm, the light graze of his teeth.

"You're not paying attention to me," he says into my neck.

I smile. "It's not always about you."

I cannot stop looking at them—his clouds—his argument against our mundane, ordinary lives. I remember watching him out there, wrestling with his camera up the hill. He has done it—how has he done it? Seized something so ephemeral—an accident of sky and sun and clouds—and fixed it to paper in such a way that all I want to do is fall into the mystical sheen of the world he has rendered.

THE DAY AFTER I turn thirty-five, the news comes about his mother: another stroke. We rush to the city, but she's gone within days.

I have never seen him as silent as he is on the train back up to Lake George, where we will pack up the rest of our things.

"Time's an awful thief," he murmurs, and I remember what she said once just this past summer, looking at him, "If only I was twenty again, my sweet boy, and you were still a baby." For those few last days at the Hill, he does not sleep well. I can see his fitful grief, like a demon clutching tightly, deep inside. I wake to find the bed empty beside me. I go to the window and see him outside, wrapped in blankets, sitting on a chair he has pulled out into the grass, his soft white head, silvery, very gentle in the moonlight. And I know that there is nothing I can give him, nothing I can say, no wise or gentle thing to undo what he feels.

HE TURNS FIFTY-NINE on New Year's Day, 1923. He writes a note to Mitchell Kennerley thanking him for his gift of the space at the Anderson Galleries for my exhibition that will open at the end of the month.

Art is laid out everywhere. There will be one hundred pieces in the show—pastels, charcoals, watercolors, oils—it will be the first time the full range of my work is shown. I have written my short essay for the announcement, to define who I am, how I think, and to debunk what Rosenfeld, Hartley, and the rest have been writing about me. I am not some wickedly female dust storm blown in from the Midwest. I am educated. I am an artist. I paint because color is a significant language for me. I paint to fill space in a meaningful way. My head swirls. I set down the pen and cross out a section. So exasperating, really, that I have to explain myself at all. And knowing at the same time this is my chance to do it.

XI

THE DAY MY show opens, we take the elevator to the top floor of the Anderson Galleries. I pick up a catalog, and leave Stieglitz to settle some business with the dapper-dressed Kennerley. Walking through the rooms, the one hundred pieces of my things lining the red plush walls, I feel something in me settle.

There are the abstract charcoals made before I met him, the watercolor landscapes of the canyon and the sky, my music pieces, my oils from New York. The room is oddly quiet. Stieglitz and Kennerley are at the far end toward the entrance, several of the other Men have come in, their voices muted, and again, I can't escape the sense of how cogent the work feels—the framed pictures not distinct or separate from one another, but living parts of a unique and integrated whole.

The announcement in my hand—"*Not* a catalog" Stieglitz had insisted, the word calling up the stodgy elitism he so detests about museums.

ALFRED STIEGLITZ

PRESENTS

ONE HUNDRED PICTURES

OILS, WATER-COLORS

PASTELS, DRAWINGS

BY

GEORGIA O'KEEFFE,

AMERICAN.

THE PICTURES ARE listed only by number and date. No titles. I begin to feel the weight of their impact like a wave—what I have done, what I have worked for. From the other end of the gallery, Stieglitz's voice rises. I feel a quick shiver of joy. Perhaps this is what he was trying to tell me—that it wouldn't matter what anyone wrote beforehand, because no one could look at my things now and not see them as they are.

I look across the room again and find him. He is not talking anymore, only looking at me steadily, looking nowhere else.

FIVE HUNDRED PEOPLE a day crush into the elevator and pour out into the Anderson Galleries. By the end of the second day, I am nauseous, my head aches, and a chill takes root in my limbs. I beg him not to make me go, to let me stay home, and finally I fall ill enough to warrant it. "The grippe," he says solemnly, "that's what the excitement of a show will do." I stay alone in the apartment, work, read, and try not to think about the reviews that have begun to appear.

He comes home one afternoon with three that have come out in a day. He is ecstatic, I can feel the crackling hum off him the moment he steps through the door, and something in me shrinks away from the paper he holds toward me. It's too penetrating, too intense, his excitement.

"You must read these, Georgia. Don't even stop to breathe!"

"I think it will be better for me not to mix my mind up with reviews."

"You must. I'll read from this one to you." He snaps it out and begins. "'Georgia O'Keeffe is what they probably will be calling—'"

"No," I interrupt. I hold out my hand, and he passes it to me, and then gives me another, a triumphant look in his eyes. His finger lingers on the start of the paragraph, and I follow the tip of his finger into the words. It is praise—yes—stirring praise. But one by one, they echo the Hartley essay.

Little phrases and words: *naked, cleaving, sensuous, the eternal feminine.*

I feel heat rising into my face, burning. They are writing me down, this thrall of bow-tied men, straining me into awful, frivolous terms. Every observation they make about my art is linked back to the body of the woman in the photographs.

I want it not to matter—desperately. I want to let it flow through, sweep over me like dust. Let it be nothing. I push the papers back to him.

He stares, dumbfounded. "How can you not be happy?"

"Can you imagine I would be?"

"These are rave reviews for your art, Georgia," he says. "What more do you want?"

My silence only tips his anger. He slams the jar of paper clips down on the table, gets up and leaves the room, and I sit very still—and I wonder why the jar of paper clips was left on the table. Who would be so forgetful not to put it back on the desk where it belongs? I sit and stare at those thin elegant loops of steel, all jumbled together in that jar. My gut tight.

He comes back into the room. "What would make you happy, Georgia?" he says, more gently.

"Talk to them," I say.

"To who?"

"They'll do anything for you."

"Critics have their own minds."

"Not always."

"And what exactly would you want me to say?"

There's a clip on the table, I notice now. It must have leapt out when he slammed down the jar. I pick it up, take one loop and untwist it so it is straight. "Tell them not to write such stupid things. Everything they say goes back to her—to that creature in your photographs—as if my pictures are hers—you must see this."

"Your nerves are frayed."

"Don't be dismissive of me."

He stares at me.

"I'm an artist, Stieglitz. All this nonsense about the eternal feminine and essential woman and cleaving and unbosoming. This bosh they smear on my work. It rips away the value of what I've tried to do. You tell me not to let talk like this interfere with my work. Well, it does interfere. It will. How could it not? You have to set them straight."

He examines me coolly. So unlike me, to say so much at once, but everything's all tipped over, inside out and upside down between us now—and it is so unlike *him* to be calm and still, not saying anything, his gaze on my face like stone.

"No man has ever been written down the way they think they have license to write me down. You are asking me to submit? To this? And then on top of it, you are trying to say it's *my* fault—that I feel this way?"

"That's not what I am saying."

It is what he is saying. The look on his face rips something in me—as if I am distasteful, someone he does not entirely recognize. I've stretched every twist in the paper clip out. One thin straight piece.

FINALLY THE SHOW is over, considered a success in every respect. Twenty works sold for three thousand dollars, which will see us through the year. Eight weeks later, 116 of his prints go up at the Anderson. His cloud music; apples in the rain, the poplars, and the old barn at the Hill; his portraits of Rosenfeld, Marin, me; six nudes of Beck Strand.

PART III

PART III

I

AT THE END of May, Kitty delivers her first child and falls into a deep depression. She can't leave the hospital. Strange outbursts of rage. Uncontrollable. She sobs for her father, he goes to visit her, but she throws things at him and cries more.

"Everything I touch is wrecked," he says on the train to Lake George. "Kitty is an innocent. I look at her. I look at you, and I feel like a criminal."

"Why me?"

His eyes are flat. "I'm an old man. I'll never be able to be what you want."

I stare at him, and I know what he is saying without saying—the baby—the little one I want that he keeps putting off.

"Don't lump everything together," I say. "Kitty has good care. She'll be all right."

He turns away. The train rocks. We continue silently. Our life on that clockwork tick.

———

HE TEARS OPEN letters from Elizabeth that arrive with updated reports about Kitty.

"Not improving," he says, guilt strung through his face. He seems angry I don't share it.

"There's nothing I can do," I say, which irritates him, that I can be so fatalistic, so heartless, since I was after all—though he won't go so far to say it—the hoo-hah who turned his family inside out.

He tells me he's invited his former secretary Marie Rapp to the Hill. For ten weeks.

"Guests never stay that long," I say.

"They've got no money. Since her husband was gassed in the war, he's had no work."

"They're both coming?"

"Only Marie."

"What about the two-year-old?"

"She's coming as well." He glances at me. "It will be good for you, Georgia, to get a little dose of living with a child." He's trying to get back at me, the thought crossing my mind before I can stop it. I feel a stab of anger.

WITHIN A WEEK, they arrive. Marie was his assistant at 291. Over the years, he's made a dozen portraits of her—none very clerical—and I've never quite trusted the curious intimacy I've observed between them. She will occasionally say something to remind me she was in his life long before I walked into it. I dislike the child the moment I lay eyes on her. A terrible blond little sprite—a first-class whiner with a bone-scratching cry. Stieglitz fusses over her. The second morning they are there, she sits on his lap at breakfast, and he chuckles with delight as she puts her little hands around his toast and squeezes until the butter slips out the cracks between her fingers, then crams it all into her mouth. He wipes her chin, and she rests back in his arms—a kitchen, a little family, sweet breakfast smells still linger-ing over the stove. This was my dream. So wrong of him. So under-handed to play at it this way. As if I am another disciple, another Strand, to be cut down when I want too much.

Stieglitz gives a quick laugh as she reaches up to twist his mus-tache, then her leg strikes out, nearly toppling the orange juice. She wriggles free and runs from the room. A door slams in the hallway, Marie's voice soft, "Yvonne, you must behave." The child answers with a shriek.

"Delightful," Stieglitz says to me, "isn't she? Who would've thought someone so little could make such a racket. Twenty-one cats on a back fence. Just marvelous."

"She's a brat."

He looks at me. "Well that's a child for you."

"No it isn't. A child doesn't have to be that." I stand up and leave the room.

I WILL HAVE little or nothing to do with them. I explain this to him in neat, clear terms. I will set the meals. Marie can be in charge of cleanup. And if she decides to engage *our* housekeeper to oversee *her* child's evening bath (as she's done for the last two nights), then she can wash all the dishes herself. She will not be invited to talk art or politics in the front room after dinner. She is his guest. Strictly. Not mine.

I make this clear and, as I do, I see the funny flinch around his eyes that I have seen when I am too hard for him to counter or manage, when he knows better than to try to say one thing to change my mind.

One evening when he is in the middle of a dinner-table argument with Rosenfeld who has just arrived, contending that the life we live every day is not Life, I wonder what would happen to him if he rose in the morning and met only the unfilled hours, if he did not cram it all up with plans or menus or scheming or busyness, letter writing, conversations, other people's awful children. If he just sat with the silence.

An angry thought—I realize. Directed as much toward the habitual circumstance our summer lives have become—with an open door to whoever wants to breeze in.

He's talking about an idea he's had for a cloud sequence—

"Clouds are, just by their nature, an expression of what is at once transient and incontrovertible. But it's the accidental collision of clouds and light and sky that evokes the *feeling*—there should be a single word for it, don't you think? That certain feeling of what is both temporal and eternal that only Art can express."

Marie listens attentively—quiet sounds of dishes and pots in the kitchen, the housekeeper starting to wash up. Ordinary sounds. Nothing out of place. Quiet.

Too quiet.

I jump up, my chair crashing to the floor behind me, out through the hall and up the stairs. Stieglitz calls after me. I take the steps two at a time, then run down the short hall to the bathroom.

Bursting through the door, I see her there, facedown, her fair hair blousy underwater. I grab her by the arm and pull her up so hard she startles, water spurting from her mouth. She gags and coughs, bathwater sprays into my face, down my shirt, onto the walls, the floor, and her eyes snap open, suddenly wide. She chokes and struggles, gasping for breath, her little fists flailing out, and I hold her arms and strike her lightly on her back, until no more water gushes.

I hear them coming, Marie crying her daughter's name, as she comes up the stairs. The little girl is crying, sobbing, and I hug her to me for a moment, that beautiful child I saved, holding her close, her chubby, waterlogged self—that warm fierce life. "You nearly drowned, you terrible thing," I say tenderly, pushing the hair from her face.

She stares at me—her little eyes tremble, drawing me all the way in. I let her go.

There will be no child. Not because I could not do it, but because he will not. Not next summer. Not ever.

I sop the excess water from the floor, and let the bath drain.

II

I POUR MYSELF into my work.

I keep my things clear, precise, no question, no inch of room open to interpretation. Everything I paint is a nameable form. I paint the lake and call it *The Lake*. I paint alligator pears in napkins, isolated against the white cloth. I paint still lifes. Grapes. Figs. Things that exist. A calla lily turned away. Strict objective forms.

He's been making prints of the images of Beck he took last summer, tickling up her slim buttocks into variegated tones of light and dark under the rippling water. He is delighted with them, and writes her letters to say so. Once when he catches me reading a few sentences he's left to dry, some outpouring of a lustful adolescent fantasy, he snatches the paper away.

"So ridiculous," I say to him. "You're lucky I like her."

"I'm hardly lucky," he says. "This summer has been miserable."

"You have yourself to thank for that."

To prove it makes no difference to me, I tell him to invite Beck for a visit. I am happy to see her—silly Beck—she whirls around the house, a singsongy burst of gorgeous sunshine, and joins me in my hatred toward Marie and the brat. It seems she has forgiven me for that awful evening last fall. We go out for rows on the lake and take turns at the oars.

"I couldn't bear an infant," she tells me flatly one day. She is helping me stake the tomato plants. "I can't stand how they leak from both ends, and smell of shit and sour milk." She tells me she is terrified when her curse doesn't come on time if Paul has been careless.

"It's a terrible thing, isn't it?" she goes on. "Not to want one. I should. I know I should." She sighs. "He is a lot like Stieglitz, you know. Moody and needy and never feeling like what he has done is enough and needing me always to tell him it is, needing and needing. But when he's off on an assignment, I feel so completely shut out."

"Tear me a strip of that pillowcase please." Blackflies buzz around our heads. I swat them away. She rips off a thin strip. I pound in the stake with a croquet mallet and tie up the vine.

"Sometimes it's worse, though, when he's there," she rambles on, "when he's right there, but so absorbed in his work or something very important he's doing, then it's like I take up no more room in his thought than a shower curtain, and that seems almost worse, to be with someone and feel so lonely, that's almost worse than being alone."

She asks if I know what she means.

I tell her then. I can't bear to stay when the house is like this. It all feels like too much—all the rackety commotion, his angst over Kitty, his obsession with that child, his denial of the little one I want, how he likes to think he knows me better than I know myself.

"It wears me to a thread," I say.

Beck slips a hand on my arm. "I'm sorry, Georgia."

I shake my head. It's just too much. Too many in the house. Even her. I do not tell her this.

THAT AFTERNOON, WHEN I hear him and Marie in the next room, I walk in and tell him I need to speak with him alone.

He follows me upstairs and sits on the bed, a dark welling sadness in his eyes as I try to explain in an even voice that if I go to visit our friends the Schaufflers in Maine, it will be more pleasant for everyone. They can get along as they like. He can cavort after the brat, and fawn over his secretary. He can fuss with his prints of Beckalina's breasts and gamy thighs.

"What are you accusing me of?" he interrupts.

"It will be better for everyone if I go. My work this summer has been a failure. You've all but said so yourself."

"I've not said anything of the sort."

"You called that landscape *tragic*."

"That was one picture. Tragic might be right for my clouds, but it's not what your work is intended for."

I bristle as he tells me—again—who I am.

"It will be best for me to leave for a while."

He just sits there on the edge of the bed, looking small, forlorn, the weight of some invisible thing perched between his shoulders, hunching them down.

I FOLD A shirtwaist neatly and set it in the suitcase, then smooth out the places that are wrinkled. They rise up again, the wrinkles, and I press them out flat, until I can feel the ribs of the suitcase beneath. I want to cry.

"All my love goes with you," he says. One of those sweeping, lovely things he retreats to when we come to a moment like this.

III

MAINE. THE SEA is vast. The cold sting of salt air strikes my face, and I feel my heart rise. The cottage is small, spare, and plain. After supper that evening with the Schaufflers, Florence and I walk the beach down to a schooner-wreck. I return to my room. The birch logs snap and crack in the fireplace, and I sit in the window and look out into the dark. It reminds me of the sky in Texas—the beautiful forever of that night.

The next morning, I run across the boardwalk in my nightdress over the cranberry bog to the beach. I walk the water's edge, the cold shallows rinse in around my feet. I scavenge odd bits, seaweed, rocks, and shells; a large branch worn and tumbled by the sea into an antler shape, cool and smooth like bone. I bring it back to the cottage and arrange the seaweed and shells into still lifes on the table. That afternoon, I sketch their simple forms. I make quick studies on paper. I stretch canvas I bought in a shop in Ogunquit.

His first letter arrives on the second day.

I know you need this time away, he writes. *But I love you. It is so clear and deep—the way I love you* . . . I feel my heart kick over. He writes about how queer he's felt since I've been gone. No interest in photographing. He's just messing around with prints. *I want to Palladio, but the sunlight's not steady enough, clouds keep mucking through, and the air is damp. I suppose I'll Artura instead.*

He writes about odds and ends—Dempsey's heavyweight championship victory over Firpo; an evening walk he took along the Bolton Road. *The house has that heartbroken lonely feeling it gets when you're away, when that something that you are is missing from it. No matter who else is here.*

They've always been so beautiful—his letters.

I asked him once: "Do you love me, Stieglitz? Or is it an idea of me you love?"

I read his letters in the kitchen, sitting on the little rocking chair with the red cushion, my feet up. There are white oilcloths spread on the table, onions boiling on the stove, the room filled with the heady scent. The ceiling is high and dark, the floor unpainted, the walls unplastered. It's a room made to use, the kind of room I love, and his letter has that beautiful ache his letters have always had. And, for the first time in what seems like months or even longer, I *feel* him, in my body, moving through me, that sense of missing him, wanting him. Sometimes, I think I'd trade every other thing just to have this clear deep sense of him inside me.

A knock on the door. Florence comes into the cottage. She smiles when she sees the letter. "Another arrived in the mail today," she says, handing it to me.

I WAKE UP when I please, go to bed when I please. I meet the Schaufflers for supper, and occasionally lunch. I spend most of my time alone. No one to fuss over or wait on. No one to tell me to shut the window if the night air is too raw. The quiet here is almost complete apart from the rustling of the grasses and the low hollow pound of the waves against the shore. There are live lobsters wandering around in the pantry. I hear them sometimes at night, the scratching scraping sound their claws make as they scramble around.

I tell myself it doesn't matter. What he does with Beck. Flirts or sports with her. She's just a model, posing for the kind of photographs I refuse to pose for anymore. I've encouraged it, haven't I? To keep him busy, out of my hair. I put the thoughts in neat order and make a study of seaweed. One of a shell. Only studies, though. Nothing worth keeping. My work feels strangely uninspired, but the days are beautiful, the sun rising and the green willows through the window, moving sweetly, everything so soft. Funny, how keenly I feel him here, more keenly here than when we are together.

He writes that Strand came for a short visit, then left, and Beck is messy, nothing creative about her. She's always in a rush to speed up, trying to grasp what she can't—her pictures are as scattered as she is. Good with a typewriter, though. Rosenfeld has discovered she's quite useful on that front. He's been writing chapters for his new book. He slips pages under the door, and she Smith-Coronas them for him.

I tell myself it's good for us—this separation. Eighteen days now.

IV

I FEEL IT the instant I return to the Lake—the shift, the awkwardness between them, some sexual static gone awry. A line crossed. He is anxious and furtive. Everything about him, his eyes, mouth, hands, lie. He doesn't look at Beck, and when I do her eyes shift away. Her laughter is forced, and I know. Even Rosenfeld's smile is desolate. He's seen the gleam of our ideal union stripped.

Stieglitz takes my arm. "There's something we need to discuss."

He sits on his bed, and I listen, while he tells me that it was all a mistake, and he is done with these carousel infatuations, this foolishness.

"*What* foolishness?"

"That's how Elizabeth describes it."

"Elizabeth?"

He hangs his head, and says he needs me to hear him out. It was all a mistake, the flirtation, but how lonely he was without me. He suffered, couldn't sleep, Beck came to him one night and held him, and it became a something it never was. There was no Actual Sex, he says quickly, but she and everyone else have read everything the wrong way. And perhaps it was good for him, he continues, a good lesson, my going away like that. Since now he's realized how much he needs my severity with him all the time, my sense of order.

"Tell me the truth," I say.

"The truth is you're the only woman in the world who should be close to me," he says. "My love, my dearest, sweetest love. Poor Pudge," he adds. "I'm afraid he saw me at my worst."

I listen and let him go on.

Only after supper that night, in the living room, sorting through the records to choose one for the gramophone, I get into it with Beck and remark how inane it is for a woman to wear trousers. Really.

She tries to buck me off. Stieglitz just sits there, his eyes flick from one of us to the other, as if he had no hand in this.

"What are you trying to be?" I say to her. "Why does a woman get herself up like a man anyway? What is that? Explain it."

Stieglitz lifts his glasses and brushes something invisible out from the lens.

SHE LEAVES WITHOUT a word to me, the pages she was typing up still set in a neat stack beside the Corona. It is only later that night that I let him near me, back into my bed.

"I want only the truth from you, Alfred. Do you understand? From this point on."

"There's no other woman on earth who can touch what you are to me. That is the truth."

We lie in silence for a while.

"I needed that time away," I say. "The sea, that space. I needed it so much I was almost afraid I wouldn't come back."

"You're home now."

"Everything was so beautiful there—even us. I wish I could explain."

"You don't have to."

"I want you to go with me," I say. "Stay in a little cottage. Just be alone together."

He nods, a soft smile. "There's work to be done here. It's our season now."

"I was afraid—" I say.

"Shhh."

"I must never leave you—"

"Don't talk now, Sweet." His voice quiet, gentle, but the more gentle he is, the more the anxiety snaps back inside me, rising.

"I needed it so much, that time away—"

"Shhh—Georgia, dearest. You're home now. It's just us."

V

IT SHOULD FEEL like any other fall, but it doesn't quite. I do what I've always done. Paint in the shanty until November, then move my work into the house. He shovels coal into the furnace and keeps the fire going. That's his chore, to keep things warm and lit to tend the aloneness I love that so unnerves him.

He turns into his work. Stalking around, vest inside out, shoelaces undone, the cape thrown casually on when he goes out to traffic with the Infinite, just a lone slight figure, wind whipping his cloak around, the handheld Graflex angled straight up. He shoots the clouds until his neck kinks, a crick so severe he can barely move it. I put Sloan's Liniment on it for him, order him to bed, only to find that a few hours later he is gone again, slipped out to his darkroom in the potting shed. I come on him there, the photographs he has made surfacing toward us out of the developing trays, rippling through the water, those long brushed strokes of clouds.

The irony is not lost on me. I remark on it—how I'm choosing things on the ground for my work while he's usurped my sky.

They feel stark to me. My still lifes. The colors intense, even vibrant, yes, simplified forms—my leaves and birch trees, my seaweed studies from York Beach, my picture of two avocados on green drapery. That bit of reflected light on their skins feels almost too meticulous, even forced—unnatural. That's how it seems to me. Unnatural.

The intention of my work has changed. With the exception of the pink moon over the sea I made in Maine, there's no sky in the paintings I made this summer.

As we're packing to leave the Hill, the sky begins to gather, darkening—then a blizzard of whiteness.

"Snow on the lake!" he says, staring from the window as it falls. "I've always wanted to see this."

I hold his arm and we walk out into it, laughing together, falling into each other like children. We roll down the hill, snow in our faces, in our mouths.

By the time we take our boots off inside, my clothes are soaked, my hands red and numb. He builds up the fire. I notice he is silent. I look up. Without a word, he takes my hand and draws me to the mirror in the hall. Reflected in the glass is the window behind us, and through it, the exquisite frozen world. The face is not my face, it's a younger face, smiling, unlined, the cheeks flushed, eyes so bright—

"Look at you," he says.

We eat in silence. Almost happy. Almost ourselves again. He ministers to the fire, and the night comes down, and we sit in the window together looking out at barns swathed in whiteness, the moonlight brutal, carving channels through the snow.

"Maddeningly beautiful," he murmurs.

VI

HE DECIDES THAT my 1924 exhibition in March will be staged as a joint show, his work and mine. My paintings will be in the larger room, and his tiny cloud prints will be in the two smaller rooms of the Anderson Galleries. He is thrilled. I find it hard to feel the same level of excitement after the fiasco of last year's show of my work and the tone of the reviews.

Carefully, I pick the paintings to be shown. Conservative pieces— no more than three abstractions—the rest as objective as I can make them. I want them seen as I intend them to be seen.

In the *Brooklyn Eagle,* a woman I knew at the Art Students League writes of the girl she knew there. How they called me Patsy. How I modeled for other artists. And while she praises the precision of my brushstrokes, she focuses more on the girl who is now a woman, "no longer curly-haired and boyish, but an ascetic, almost saintly appearing, woman with a dead-white skin . . . capable of great and violent emotions." She contends that "psychoanalysts tell us that fruits and flowers when painted by women are an unconscious expression of their desire for children."

In almost every other review about my art that spring, there's a reference to Stieglitz's discovery of me. The comparison is glaring, our work described in such different terms: His cloud photographs are "a revelation." My paintings are "the work of a woman who after repressions and suppressions is having an orgy of self-discovery." I hate it every which way. The words. This leaden weight in my chest. Learn not to care, I tell myself. Let them say what they say or figure out how to change it.

But my work sells. We clear several thousand dollars. Coomaraswamy, a curator at the Boston Museum of Fine Arts, requests a donation of Stieglitz's photographs. He is irked that they don't offer to purchase them. But he gives them twenty-seven of his best prints. He mats them himself, not trusting even Coomaraswamy to do it as he wants it done.

I keep thinking about the money my paintings brought in. Enough for a space of our own. Before we leave for the Lake, I drag Stieglitz to look at apartments. There's one on East 58th I particularly like, the top floor of a four-story brownstone. I would have a studio to work in. I leave our number with the landlord. He can't promise it will still be vacant by the time we return in November, but I tell him that if it is, we'll take it.

Stieglitz grumbles about the rent after we leave. I point out that he's not used to paying much, if anything at all, for rent.

"I'll have a show once a year," I say slowly. "You can sell my paintings. That will cover our rent."

"With art, you can never know what will sell," he said. It strikes me as peevish—the way he says it.

"I'll figure out that part," I answer. "You can do the rest."

My sister Catherine writes from Portage. She has given birth to a daughter—a baby girl. I write to tell her how it must be nice to have her way of living, a nice banker husband, a normal everyday sort of life. Halfway down the page, I stop. I ball the letter up tight in my fist, tighter, then take a fresh sheet and start again.

———

WE ARRIVE AT Lake George that April in a downpour. But I am happy—for the first time in months it seems—happy to be here again in this soaking-wet nature away from the city. I have the boats fixed. I plow the garden and plant it with vegetables. I get everything in but the potatoes. And I feel a thrill of joy, dirt under my fingernails, my body wrung to physical exhaustion. No room to think, I sleep soundly.

One morning, walking past the old garden, the explosion of color stops me. Delphinium and freesia in bloom, their petals deeply hued, the sunlight washes them to fire. I remember a small still life by Fantin-Latour I saw once. A quiet vase of flowers on the table. The mind and scale of it suggested a quiet domesticity. But what if I took that simple delicacy of a flower and kicked the shape open? What if I made it not life at arm's length, not constrained, but altogether different?

I make a small sketch there in the garden, and back in the shanty, I go through my canvases until I find a large one—vertical—thirty-five by eighteen. One strong driving line up the center, abstract forms curving off it, the background erased so it is only the warm curves of those flowers and their leaves—yellows startlingly bright, pale crimson, violet, green. Pendant heads of lily of the valley. Forget-me-nots. Blue spills in around—no stems, no roots—as if the forms bloom out of the sky.

For the next few weeks, I paint flowers. On canvas-covered board, I paint petunias—such a simple household flower, arranged as one would expect a still life to be, but cropped, without a vase or background—just blooms. Then I take those same flowers and translate them onto a thirty-six-by-thirty canvas. Massive. Inflated. Their edges soft, like they're just coming into form. Teal lines for shadows, a layer of white for the luminosity in the petals. One bloom is central. Then another below, extending past the bottom edge. It's fun—this play with flowers—like nothing I've done. Smudge in pinks and blues—edges blended where the colors meet. The flower no longer in its proper role. It's not living in the world as we know it. It grows out of a celestial hill, the light deepening toward dusk, toward the darker curve of the horizon. Past it, the sky rises—surreal, abstract— another flower massing inside it, on the verge of rushing over the hill.

I'm nearly finished when Stieglitz comes in. He stops when he sees the canvas.

"What exactly do you think you're going to do with that?"

I smile at him. "I'm just painting it."

"I don't see where it will take you."

"You mean if it will sell?"

"I just don't see the point."

"I want to paint a flower. That is the point. I want to paint it so big that people will have no choice but to stop and look and really see it—as it is. The way I want it to be seen."

He pauses, my words registering in him. "And I love that about you."

"What?"

"That you know what you want. How you are so magnificently lovely when you're clear. And that is lovely." He points to the flower. "I may think it's silliness to paint a flower that way, but it is also lovely, as you are."

"Well, I'll be in soon," I say.

He hesitates. It takes him a moment to realize I am asking him to leave.

I DO NOT stop painting the flowers. He asks me to explain my reasoning. But I don't want to explain, and I tell him I'd rather just do it.

I want to show them—my giant flowers—in the group exhibition we're planning for next winter. *Seven Americans,* he's already titled it, the show will feature all of his artists plus himself: Demuth, Strand, Marin, Hartley, Dove, and me. He's made arrangements with Kennerley. The Strands, his niece Elizabeth, and Rosenfeld have created a collective rent fund that will keep our rooms at the Anderson Galleries open through the year.

BY THE FIRST of July the heat is stifling—the air filled with a yellow dust that coats the house. When I come out of the shanty one afternoon, I find him on the porch in his wicker chair writing a letter to Strand. His black folder of my work is on the table across from him. I pick it up. He glances at me, wary.

"Don't you think I'll be careful?"

He gives a little harrumph, then he bends back to the letter he is writing, he dips his pen, his script flows in fluent lines. I turn the pages of the folder slowly, through my watercolors, colors bright and sharp, mounted on black paper, then the charcoals. I keep turning, until I come to his favorite. *Special No. 13.* A drawing of the Palo Duro Canyon. His pen has stopped, his eyes are on my hands at the corners of the folder.

"You love this piece," I say.

"Yes."

"Why?"

He does not answer right away. In the distance from the dock, I hear voices, the joyful shrieks of Elizabeth's daughters, then Elizabeth's calm voice—the voices changed, caged by water.

"Because it is you," he says.

"Isn't everything I do, me?"

"This is how I met you first."

"But it wasn't the first one you saw."

"Maybe not. That doesn't matter."

I was teaching in South Carolina when I made that drawing of the canyon. I'd already been out to visit Texas several times by then, seen the country and the vastness of the sky out there, and I missed it. I remember how sharp the feeling was—the ache of wanting to go back.

He draws the folder away from me now, not harshly, but as if he cannot keep himself from doing it. He runs his fingers just above the paper, not touching.

"Who else would see a canyon like this? *Who else* would see a stream like this, or the backs of cattle?" he says, a flinch of sadness in his voice.

"Why is my early work more real to you than what I am making now?" I ask.

"I'm not saying it is."

"You are."

"No," he says. "But when I look at these drawings, I see that entirely free creature you were before you came to me."

I look down at the picture. I remember the night I made it—this *Special No. 13*. The stub of charcoal and cheap paper laid out on the floor, my knees digging into the wood as I leaned over it, my body tense, elbow held in place until the joint ached, I drove my hand across in long unhindered strokes. There were moments that fall of 1915 when it possessed me so fully I was sure I'd lost my mind, my mind swirling with those shapes—my heart broke for weeks as the charcoal swept across the page, broke through everything I had read or learned in class, everything I had been told that art should be.

WHEN ELIZABETH COMES up from the dock, she asks me to go for a walk. The grass feels overwhelming—the noon sun beating down.

"You don't seem yourself," she says gently as we head up the hill.

"Life isn't quite my strong point these days."

She glances at me. She has a light-blue dress on, with a sailor collar. She always wears simple clothes, more practical than any other Stieglitz.

"Your work is going well, though."

I nod. We've reached the upper meadow.

"Hasn't it been so unthinkably hot this summer?" she says.

"Yes."

"Everyone gets so crabby when it's this hot."

I laugh.

"He loves you, Georgia."

"I know."

"He's desperate to marry you."

"Did he send you to work on me?"

"No," she says. "You know I'm neutral. As close to you as I am to him. I know he can be difficult."

She watches the ground pass under our feet.

"He wants to marry as soon as his divorce goes through this fall," I say.

"And will you?"

"I don't know. I've stopped thinking about it, really. The divorce has just dragged on so long."

"Well, that was Emmy's doing."

"I know."

We step into the shade. The long shadows of the trees fall across us as we walk.

"Let's look at it from a different angle then," Elizabeth says. "Why wouldn't you marry?"

"I just don't see the reason to."

"I told Donald the other day that I feel like you're unsure because of that funny business with Beck. You know that meant nothing."

I look up.

"I just don't see the point, Elizabeth. We're fine as we are."

"He loves you, Georgia. Everything became alive for him when you came."

"It just seems easier to keep things as they are," I say.

A bird calls in the trees. I stop, she stops, and we listen. It does not call again.

HIS DIVORCE GOES through. Again he brings up the marriage question. He cites all sorts of reasons—little reasons, bigger reasons, legal, financial, tax penalties, estate planning, the challenge of something as simple as signing a lease. And then there's poor Kitty. Her doctors have told him that if we marry, it might banish her delusions that her father will return. He is sixty this year. I am thirty-seven.

"I couldn't change my name," I remark to him one morning when he raises it again.

"What does that mean?"

I shrug. "After all we've done to fashion 'Georgia O'Keeffe,' it would lose its value to change it."

He looks at me, uncertain. "I never said anything about changing your name."

"And love?"

"What about love?"

"Is that a reason as well?"

"You never seem to quite understand what you mean to me," he says slowly. "Even when you think the worst of me, Georgia, to me, you'll never be anything less than Absolute."

"Are you trying to win me back?" I say.

"Sometimes I feel like I'll spend my entire life trying to win you once, all of you, just for an instant."

"That's ridiculous." I say, and laugh.

"No. It's true. And I just wish you knew it. I've never been more committed to any person or thing as I am to you. I sometimes wonder how you don't seem to know."

MY FLOWERS HAVE gone by. I paint a landscape abstraction instead. Dark red, just a sliver of blue.

When he comes into the bedroom and sees the abstraction, he is elated. "Extraordinary!" he exclaims. "On the old order. Do you feel that?"

I shake my head. "I don't think it will find a buyer, nor am I sure I want to show it."

"It's good enough to keep," he says. I look at the painting. It could be the hills across the lake, which is how he sees it. It could be the walls of the Palo Duro canyon.

"Will the old order always be the point of reference for what's new?" I ask without thinking. "I'm sorry. I sometimes just want you to love what I'm doing now as much."

"I just said I did."

A piece of my hair has fallen loose from the knot I brushed it into. He reaches out and tucks it back behind my ear. His fingers linger. "I love everything you do, Georgia."

"That's not true, and you know it."

He pulls me down onto the bed, and kisses me. "It is," he insists. "Everything."

He makes love to me. And it is slow and beautiful, the lovemaking—I don't want it to end. We fall asleep there on the bed. I wake after dark, my canvas gleaming, still wet on the easel. I've left the window open, and the room is growing cold, but I don't want to wake him—he looks so sweet and pale and soft. I lie there with my arms around his body while he sleeps, and I listen as the cool night sweeps through the room, touching chairs, desks, surfaces, looking for something it no longer recognizes.

VII

IDA COMES FOR a visit. Stieglitz gallivants around, flirting with her, and it is fun and light, the flirting. He photographs her with a rifle and a squirrel she took down with one shot.

Rosenfeld arrives several days later and, over the next week, I notice something slight and lovely developing between them. I mention it to Stieglitz. He grumbles something about how Paul should be focused on his writing.

"You aren't jealous?" I tease him.

"Of course not."

"Look how happy they are. Can't you feel it? How it's all so new and sweet between them."

I can see the spark in Rosenfeld's long eyes when he talks to my sister, and I notice a certain self-conscious grace in how she makes the beds, each fold of the sheet so even.

ONE NIGHT, IDA reads our palms. We're stuffed with dinner, an over-rich meal, and we roll into chairs in the living room. Ida takes Stieglitz's hand, her finger tracing out the lines.

"You lack talent, but you have a great will."

We all laugh, Rosenfeld harder than the rest of us. Ida glances at him, then back at Stieglitz. She pulls her face into a mock seriousness.

"You see this break in this line here. That says you're an incurable flirt—"

More laughter.

My sister glances at me. "Do you confirm that, Georgia?"

"I can answer that!" Rosenfeld launches in. I feel a quick wave of gratitude. Dear Pudge. Always there to save us.

ONE NIGHT AFTER they're gone, I hear him bungling around in the hall, a crash, then a tumbling cry. I leap from the bed, rush out, and find him in a bruised heap at the foot of the stairs. I kneel beside him and take his head in my lap.

"Are you all right? What have you done to yourself?"

"First time in forty-seven years I've fallen down those stairs," he says wanly. He smiles to see me cry. "You do love me then," he says. His eyes seem small without the lenses of his glasses magnifying them. "Marry me, Georgia." My lips graze his forehead. I can smell his age.

"Did you fall down the stairs just to get me to say yes?"

"No, but I would."

"Come. Let me get you to bed."

I help him to his feet. He gives a cry when he bears weight on his ankle. "I'm a rickety old carcass," he says with disgust.

"No, no," I say softly. I put my arm around him and together we walk up the stairs.

"Marry me," he says again, when we have almost reached the landing.

"And we'll have our own apartment," I say.

"That one on Fifty-eighth."

"Yes, that's the one. Or, if paintings continue to sell, maybe rooms at the new Shelton."

"Anything you want."

"Ah, you say that," I add, not harshly. "But there was something I wanted very much that you refused." I feel him sink a little into me.

ON DECEMBER 8 we take the Weehawken Ferry across the Hudson to New Jersey; I've finally agreed, but we can't get a license in the state of New York, because Stieglitz is a divorcé.

"New Jersey's a better state for major life events," he says.

"Because you were born in Hoboken."

"If I had to crawl to Canada to marry you, I would."

I laugh. "Oh stop!"

"You know I mean it."

It is raining, the sky sliding into the sea, foggy drizzle, an untethered gray.

Marin picks us up at the ferry slip. My hands are soaked. I can feel the cold water leaking into my sleeves. The road is slippery. Marin turns to joke with me, to ask if I am ready to be Mrs. Alfred Stieglitz, and perhaps it's the look on my face that causes his gaze to linger. The car skids into a puddle, veers sideways before he can stop it, toward a grocery wagon. He jerks around and tries to pull the front end back to the road, but turns the wheel too hard, too fast, and it twists in his grasp. He hits the brake, too late, and I can only grip Stieglitz's arm as we spin across the street and sail into a lamppost.

And we are all safe—luckily—essentially uninjured. As we crawl from the wrecked car, I laugh and say that of course this would happen to us. Here we are, trying to do something upright and conventional, and even the heavens toss us an elbow.

After the hubbub of police and witnesses we pick our way across the shattered windshield glass and walk in the rain to the hardware store, where the owner who deals in screwdrivers, sandpaper, and nails is also a justice of the peace.

Three days later, December 11, we return to Cliffside Park. Marin is our witness. There is a bruise on his temple from where he hit the car door, the skin pearly blue, taut. No ritual, we've decided. No reception. No rings.

On our way out on the ferry, I told Stieglitz that I would not say the words *Love, honor, and obey*. He argued with me on that point.

"There's no reason to," I said simply.

"It's a marriage," he insisted.

The wind lifted sheaves of spray off the waves, and cut the surface easily.

"You know I can't promise to obey, Alfred. That's what you loved about me to begin with." I pressed my fingers gently to his lips until he smiled.

VIII

MARRIAGE CHANGES LITTLE. Everything continues on course, exactly as I told him it would, except for the fact that I feel a bit boxed up in a formality that has nothing to do with what I am. I am annoyed with him that he pushed me into it, annoyed more with myself that I let him, and maybe it's the tiniest rebellion when I go off and paint a city night scene of 47th Street near the Chatham Hotel. It's large—as large as my flowers—the staircased lines of the buildings angled and clean, a streetlamp with a reddish orbed glow, the moon half hidden in the night clouds.

It rings with life, and I know it. I tell him I'm going to hang it in the *Seven Americans* show.

"That's a bad idea," he says. "Even the men don't do the city well yet. It will be enough to introduce your flowers."

We argue over it fiercely—an argument that lingers, flares up over dinner at Joe's Restaurant or on our way home from the new Metropolitan Opera House. It makes him insane that I won't agree. He likes things settled, and I won't let this go—it's my picture, I want to hang it in my part of the show. He reminds me it's not my choice—I am only one of seven artists in this exhibition—we have to do what's best for the whole.

"And who decides that? You, I assume?"

And so it goes on, never quite resolved, the issue still a sticking point when he tells me that Seligmann is bringing Jean Toomer, the celebrated black writer, to the gallery. The plan is to meet them there, then go to dinner, but I've had enough Round Table small talk, and I decide I'll come up with some good excuse—a headache perhaps—to sidestep the rest of the evening. But when I meet Toomer, I change my mind.

He looks like no one else I've ever seen. Fine looking, exceptionally so—his face just irregular enough to be interesting. There's quiet eloquence in how he speaks. His eyes are striking, a unique iridescent tone to his skin. Rumors have been dashing around him all year. He went to visit Waldo Frank, seduced his wife, Margaret, and now she has left Frank and moved with Toomer to New York.

At one point at dinner while the men are talking, I feel a pressure on my face, and it is Jean—looking at me across the table. For a moment I meet his gaze, and he does not look away. He comes back with us to our apartment and stays until after two. I stay up, talking with him. When he finally leaves, my body is tired, but my mind still hums from the conversation.

I go into the bedroom and start to undress. Stieglitz sits on the edge of the bed, taking off his shoes. "A handsome man," he says, "wouldn't you say?" I don't answer.

He looks at me then, the air momentarily bent.

I'M FURIOUS WITH Stieglitz on the opening night of the show, when I walk into the Anderson Galleries and see that the men have, down to the last, sided with him and refused to hang my *New York Street with Moon*. I know it's too late now, but this is the last time, I think to myself, when I'll let him determine what will or won't be hung of mine.

Flanking the entrance hall are Demuth's portraits of us. Marin's skyscrapers and flinty seascapes follow, then my magnified petunias, Strand's close-ups of machine parts, and Dove's collaged assemblages of mirrors, clock springs, sand, and wool, which are baffling, to put it gently.

Within days, the self-indulgent puff of the catalog has ticked off the critics. They go after us. They ransack the work of all the men apart from Stieglitz, whose cloud prints they continue to praise. And they love my flowers—the galvanizing charge of color. I'm particularly pleased to see how Edmund Wilson in *The New Republic* lauds the "razor-like scroll edges" of my leaves.

Stieglitz is out-of-his-mind enraged at how the others are trashed.

"Those critics are one and the same," he says. "Ignorant traitors."

I notice that the only writer who remarks that my things this year feel "clinical" is a woman. I feel something tick inside me when I read that. I agree. There's a restraint to my things now—even in the magnified flowers, a certain pulling back. It would take a woman to see through a woman, wouldn't it? I shove the thought down.

LESS THAN A week after the show opens, Stieglitz falls ill with a violent attack of kidney stones. Too ill to go to the gallery, he fumes.

"I need to be there."

"You need to get well."

"I've never missed one day of a show."

"Get yourself well and you won't miss more."

He drags himself around the house. He pens a scathing response to McBride whose review in *The New York Sun* poked fun at the "super-publicity" the Stieglitz group uses to attract attention to itself. By the time I come home from the gallery that night, he's doubled over in pain. He refuses to go to the doctor. He refuses morphine. I call Ida, who prescribes two quarts of buttermilk.

"I detest milk," he says when I tell him.

"It's buttermilk."

"Any kind of milk."

I pour half a glass, and he reaches for the bottle and downs it.

"I've got too much to do," he mutters, "to be taken down by a pebble."

Within a day, he grits through the pain and passes the stone, fishes the odd knuckled thing from the toilet, and hurls it out the window.

IX

AT THE LAKE that summer, I begin to take my meals alone. I pick watercress and lettuce from my garden, tear the washed greens into a bowl with chopped garlic and onions, then walk outside and eat on the porch looking out at the water.

I wake before dawn, when the moon is still up, its light so smooth and still. I row the little boat to the island. There's an old birch tree I go to visit, several lean trunks twisted together at the base. I paint half a dozen large canvases of that tree, its harmony, the balance of trunk to leaf. I have no intention of showing them—my trees—at my exhibition next winter. I've begun to understand that there is work I will do that I will put out to the world and there is work I will keep as my own. That feels important to me. Like it needs to be that way. That slight, but very clear delineation.

JUST STIEGLITZ, ROSENFELD, and I are at the house that fall when Jean Toomer arrives with Margaret Naumburg. I am walking up from the shore when I see them above on the hill, Toomer, and Margaret with Stieglitz. They are engaged in a conversation on the lawn, Stieglitz pointing to something farther down the lake, then up the hill—making one broad sweeping gesture with his arm—telling some primeval story of how the lake was formed or how his family discovered it on a chance trip from Saratoga, bought some land, and then more, sold some, endured, and so on. As I come up to them, Jean sees me first, raises a hand, and smiles—a kind of free and happy smile—the others break off. We exchange a few nothings. Then Margaret and Stieglitz take up their conversation again.

I stand near Jean, close enough to imply that that's what I want, his skin a kind of glow you could put your hand to. I find myself wanting to. His eyes shift and linger for a moment on my face.

Like Rosenfeld, he's come for a working holiday, to write, but over the next few days Stieglitz takes a dozen photographs of him—sitting on a rock by the white rosebushes, his elbows resting on his knees, his top coat and open-neck shirt. In the evenings, we talk about his writing, about *Cane* and the new work he is struggling to complete. We talk about the Walden School that Margaret started in 1914. She does not believe in the simple acquisition of knowledge. Too restrictive, she says. Education should be about cultivating a child's ability to think openly, in creative ways. When "The Marriage" with Frank ended (she calls it that: The Marriage), she resigned from her position as director at the school—one finger twirls through her brown hair as she explains how she suddenly found she needed to cut free of all structure just to keep her mind straight on who she was and what she wanted on any given day. She glances at me as she says this as if I, a woman, might understand. I stare back at her blankly.

When a record comes to an end, I swap it for another on the gramophone, and notice that her head has fallen to rest against his shoulder. She has her hand on his lap, their fingers interwoven. Stieglitz is talking, Rosenfeld and Jean nodding gravely as acolytes do. With the thin hardness of the record in my hand, I stare at her pale fingers. For a moment I can see their bodies together, the first time he kissed her, undressed her in her husband's house, her whiteness and that luster of his skin. The record ends. He draws her to her feet, his arm circling her waist, and leads her, sleepy, into the hall and toward the stairs. Their tenderness pierces me. The private laughter, the looks exchanged. I find it irresistible. One afternoon, I see them in the hallway when they think they are alone, he runs his finger lightly down her breast, tugging at the fabric of her dress. She catches his hand and knocks it away.

I lead them on a hike up Prospect Mountain. Stieglitz stays behind at the house, concerned that the dry cough in his chest might with exertion turn to something worse. We picnic in a meadow on the ridge, and I send them over to the rim to watch the clouds roll in over the lake while I pack away the plates and forks and napkins. A shadow falls across me. "Almost done?" he says. He holds out his hand to help me up. I feel him pull me through the air to standing. Rosenfeld and Margaret are wading through the wildflowers toward us, talking, laughing. His finger trails down the center of my palm.

"Be careful," I murmur with a smile, and slip my hand from his.

"Of what?" he says casually. I study his mouth. I want to kiss it. Unforgivable.

I shake my head, and laugh. "You might not want to know."

That night, I see them from an upstairs window, their shadows are long and rippling on the grass, they are arguing, their voices, low, strained, but the breeze sweeps off the words. At one point, she turns, abruptly, and starts back toward the house, he reaches out to grasp her arm, she wrenches loose and continues walking, I can see her face broken up, unkempt and wet with tears. A door closes below. And he stays there, for a good half hour longer, outside in the dark. He sits in the grass, and looks straight ahead, and the stars rain down—a thousand stars. He does not seem to notice.

When I come back from my walk the next morning, they're all on the porch, except for Jean. Margaret is there, she looks tired, her eyes puffed. I sit on the steps, and Rosenfeld cheerily asks after my tree.

"I like trees very much because they don't move or talk back."

"Or ask questions?" he says.

"Exactly."

He laughs. "Oh, you are perfect," he says delightedly.

Jean comes out, and Rosenfeld, in his gentlemanly way, offers his chair.

"No," says Jean, "the steps are good enough for me." He sits down on the other end of the step where I am. I look at the grass just past the shade thrown by the roof, the darker line of green dividing the reach of the house from the open sunlight. Something has changed between Jean and Margaret—I notice this—he did not bend to kiss her when he came out as he usually does. He is silent, watching some local children below on the hill. Stieglitz says something that makes Margaret laugh, a kind of tinny laughter.

"I want to see the new croquet court in the greenhouse," she says.

"A marvelous idea," Stieglitz answers, and they go off, Rosenfeld after them.

Jean's leg is stretched out, a quiet smile on his face that has nothing to do with anything—no place or reason at all. I feel my heart skip. I fiddle with a thread at the seam of my shoe, and we sit there, in a sudden awkwardness.

I say something about the fair weather, and he answers some sort of nothing back. I remember when I saw him with Margaret—when he touched her breast, I can almost see it as if it is happening still, his finger moving slowly down, then tugging the neckline as if he would strip her right there.

"You'll go back tomorrow," I ask lightly, though it doesn't come out exactly as I intend. He glances at me, and I see it then, that uncomplicated fire. I feel a stark jolt through my hands. He doesn't realize this could be a mistake—this thing between us that is nothing but has the weight of something, this wordless, drifting intimacy someone might see.

The clock chimes.

"Shall we go and find the others?" I say.

He does not answer. The wind has faded, the air tenuous and sheer.

STRIPPING THEIR ROOM, I find the pen, his, rolled under the bed where they slept. The gold is cool, and I feel my heart rise. I think of him, his face—what it would be like, feel like, to have his face above me, his skin on mine, swirling wild pieces in my body. Later, I take that feeling of him and transpose it into a tree on canvas—that sense of desire in every color, leaf, trunk, limb, fused by an invisible force.

It's just lines, I tell myself as I squeeze paint onto the palette— clean piles of color, the light slips off the glass. It is only lines—this house of angles where the spirit resides.

When the painting is done, I scrape the color from my palette until the glass is spotless, clean again, and I can cancel the thought of him.

Stieglitz works alone in the Little House through October. He makes 350 prints of the cloud series that he titles Equivalents. "I tore up another three hundred," he says. "I kept only the ones that expressed that true feeling. The others were beautiful, but that's all they were."

He prints several photographs of me. Her face has begun to change. There's a line between her brows, her lips have tightened, a slight downturn has appeared at the corners of her mouth. She is not the same. Her gaze is fixed, Spartan, that quiet exultant glimmer in her eyes gone, replaced by a stern hardness that could be misread as cruelty.

EVEN AT THE time I noticed it. Just a blink, that noticing, then gone. I realize now I should have let it sink in. Let myself really feel what that hardness meant, the story it told.

There are those moments, always, looking back on a life when you can see the points—fully lit in hindsight, real or imagined—where the path split, where you could have made a different choice and the cost of the choice you made.

PART IV

I

THAT FALL, 1925, when we return to New York, we move into the new Shelton Hotel. There's a life-sized wooden Indian in the lobby opposite the registration desk. The hotel has a library, a solarium, and even an Olympic-size swimming pool; it has a cafeteria where we will take our meals, fireplaces in every room, a roof terrace in the spring.

The sales of my paintings have paid for this.

My arm hooked through his, we walk through a suite of rooms on one of the higher floors. Vaulted ceilings, the windows are huge, looking out across the landscape of buildings and streets, the spires of St. Patrick's Cathedral. From this height, I can feel the gentle sway of the steel in the wind.

"Perfect all around!" I say.

We will only rent for the months we are in the city. The hotel staff will do the housekeeping, leaving me free to paint.

The bedroom is tiny. We squeeze in the bed, a bureau, his favorite deep armchair. The sitting room is my studio by day. I have the walls painted gray, the furniture slipcovered in white. No decorative chintz, no distraction—only a few shells and rocks scattered in little piles on the mantel and the windowsills. Stieglitz asks for curtains. I refuse.

"I love it here," I say to him early one morning after we've made love. We lie wrapped together under the coverlet, the wind beats against the windows and the panes sway, all tumult and windshift, distance pouring out in every direction. "It's almost like not being in the city, but we are. You can have your city and I can live here in the sky."

I help him transform the new space he's rented in the Anderson Galleries. We will call it simply The Room. I tack unbleached muslin over the black velour walls—the natural sunlight reflects off the muslin and the room feels airy, free. Once it is ready, he's there all day, fussing over Marin's installation, which will open the season.

There is a clean lovely peace between us. We take breakfast and supper together in the Shelton cafeteria. I work alone in the apartment. I make pencil sketches of the skyline, then a series of oils of the city. I paint until dusk and, when the phone rings, I pick it up and ask whoever is calling if they could please call back when the light is gone.

II

BLANCHE MATTHIAS HAS offered to write a feature on me for *The Chicago Evening Post*. She comes to our apartment for an interview. Stieglitz has told me the article won't make much difference, since it won't print until early March when my show is on the verge of closing. But I like Blanche. She's sophisticated—wealthy but straight up. She's traveled through the Orient, the Middle East, and Europe, and I've always liked her, not just her person, but her poetry and essays on art, and I see this as an opportunity. When we are alone in the sitting room, her notebook and pen ready on her lap, she asks what I think about women and art.

"There just hasn't been much," I tell her. "We do things differently from how men do them, and men can't really see or feel what it is we do, because it is so different." And I explain to her that perhaps that is why I've been written about as I have by men—when all I am really trying to do is say something that I feel in color and form, something that matters, something that has life.

"It's really just that simple, and there's no reason to argue or stew, because the time it takes to complain is time away from work."

She asks me how I work, and I tell her how I make notes on every color I choose. Each has a certain relationship to life. I paint that.

"That sounds like Kandinsky."

"He's so theoretical. He links hue with pitch and claims different tones of color cause a particular vibration in the spirit. But art is more about sensation. When someone looks at a painting I've done, I want them to feel what drove me to paint it in the first place. When I make a picture of a flower, I don't paint it as I see it, but as its essence moves me. I eliminate every detail that's extraneous. I paint it as I want it to be *felt*."

She scribbles a few things on her paper, then turns the page and asks if I am an exponent of expressionism.

I laugh. "I have no use for that term or any other." I tell her how this all began for me when I was teaching art at a small school down in the Carolinas. "And one October, I took out all the decent pieces I'd ever done. I placed them all around my room, and studied them, and in each picture I could see the influence of some teacher I'd had, or another artist I'd known—and I began to realize that I'd never done anything original. So I packed it all up and put away my color box, and got down on my knees on the floor with some paper and charcoal. For weeks that fall I was dizzy, my head spinning with shapes that meant something to me. When I was finished, I looked at them and I could see that they said something new."

"A rebellion."

"It wasn't that grand. And in a sense that was the most wonderful thing about that time in my life. I wasn't doing it for anyone, or in reaction to anyone. I was alone in that room. I was no one. I was those shapes, that paper, that charcoal. And then I rolled the drawings up and sent them to a friend in New York."

She writes on her pad of paper, her pen flying over it, then she stops, and glances up, waiting. Through the window behind her, dusk has fallen and the sky is that steep violet that I love. The room is spare. We have been here for three months and only a painting of

Dove's hangs on the walls. A red flower in a vase, the only spark of color. On cold days he still mutters about the lack of curtains—how those windows let everything in. Should I say that I am a landscape artist who has become famous for someone else's portraits of me? That as my art has hit the world it's been instantaneously recast by those who see what they want, not what is there? The words are on the tip of my tongue. My hands rest on the arm of the sofa. I press my palms down, the muscles tense, gripping slightly, unnoticed.

I explain instead that what has been written about my things says more about those doing the writing than it says about my art.

"You alluded to that earlier," she says. "Shall I include it?"

"Yes, please."

She does not write it down. She is still looking at me, a curious look, as if she has unwrapped something and is not at all sure what to make of it.

"What?"

She shakes her head.

"Tell me," I say.

"You are fearless," she says.

"Not really."

"You dare to paint what you feel." She drops her pen to the page and writes for a moment, then continues. "You know there was one photograph of you—it was an early one, taken up at Lake George, you are standing and the sky is behind you."

I nod. There were many that were taken that day. Out of so many, though, I already know exactly the one she is referring to.

"There's something remarkable about it," she says. "A simple ferocity in your expression that reminds me of your art." I hold up my hand to stop her.

"I have nothing to say about the photographs, Blanche."

"Excuse me?"

"They're not mine."

She looks off balance. The sudden hardness in my voice has thrown her.

"One last question then," she says.

"Yes?"

"Stieglitz?" she says tentatively, unsure perhaps if she should take this route. "I've heard him described in so many ways: philosopher, wizard, master, discoverer of Marin, friend of Einstein."

I smile at her.

"What would you say about Alfred Stieglitz, Miss O'Keeffe?"

The dusk outside has fallen a step farther, toward near-black indigo. I consider this woman almost a friend, an ally. And in the last hour we have spent together, I can feel the bones of the piece she will write. The things she will say about my work will be things I want people to know. This will be a piece I'll want cited, and so I answer her question this way:

"I would say that Stieglitz is, first and above all, a brilliant artist whose photographs have transformed America's understanding of modern art." I do not look at her. I want her to absorb only the words and not whatever my eyes might betray. "But Stieglitz has never allowed himself the time to achieve his own greatness. Rather he has dedicated his life to others. He fights for his artists tirelessly, fights so that we might have the time and space to work, and he fights for the integrity and future of art itself against all of the forces and politics that seek to diminish it."

I look at her then. "Write that," I say. "Please."

MY EXHIBIT IS scheduled for the second week in February 1926. Once again, he doesn't want to include my city paintings. He likes them much less than the flowers, he says. At least the flowers have color, but they can be too pretty, too frivolous, and he doesn't like the way people remark on that prettiness when my art is so much more.

"Do you see what I mean about the prettiness?" he says, as if he's entirely forgotten that the argument started on my cityscapes. I tell him I don't care if the flowers are pretty or not. They mean what they mean to me. I make them because that is what I am led to do. And I don't care what anyone else thinks about my city paintings or that the men say I am mad to attempt something so ambitious.

"I don't care, because when I look out from this window all the way across city to the river and past it, right now—exactly now—this is what I want to paint."

"Which is precisely the point," he says. "You should care."

He is hearing only what he wants to hear and stripping out what's useful to his argument: that he should decide what goes in, not me.

"The city paintings are going to be in my show this year," I say. I remind him then that he was wrong about the flowers when I first started making them. He called them "silliness," he said no one would buy them, and what a surprise it's been—to both of us—that the flowers are the reason we were able to move into the Shelton.

THE WALLS OF The Room blaze with my things. *New York Street with Moon* sells the first night of the show for twelve hundred dollars. The flower paintings are snatched up as well. Within the first several weeks, sales total nine thousand dollars. Stieglitz is ecstatic and extends the show through March.

I take the train alone to Washington where I am to speak at the National Woman's Party dinner. My friend Anita Pollitzer who arranged it was surprised and thrilled when I agreed to come. There are five hundred women in the audience, a sea of faces, and I tell them that it matters—to earn one's own living, to work hard, and to consider oneself an individual, with rights and privileges and responsibilities—the most vital of which is self-realization.

When I return to New York, he clings to me. He makes love to me in our room, the free night pouring through the windows. He runs his mouth along the inside of my thigh and kisses that spot between my legs until I cry out and stuff my face into the pillow, my mind rinsed, breathless. He lowers his weight onto me. I grip his back and pull him deeper in. Afterward, we lie together, he holds my face in his hands and pushes my hair back with his thumbs from where it has stuck, wet, against my cheeks.

"I walked the streets for hours while you were gone," he says. "I don't know why it is, but I can't bear it somehow, when you're away. Like everything is missing."

ON MARCH 2, Blanche's interview appears in *The Chicago Evening Post*. It is the best thing that's ever been done on me.

"I'm not sure I'd go that far," Stieglitz says.

"And look what she wrote about you!" I point out the paragraph where she quoted me word for word about his indefatigable work for others, how he once set aside his own career for the sake of his artists, how his new series of photographs—his clouds—secures his place as one of the great visionaries of our time.

"I want to make copies for The Room," I say, squeezing his hand as he reads the paragraph through again.

"That was generous of you, Georgia, to say those things about me." There's a tremble in his voice. He is moved.

"So we'll make copies then."

He looks at me for a moment. His eyes search my face trying to gauge the slight steely brightness behind my smile.

"Do it," I say.

"All right. We will."

III

I PAINT THE black iris over and over, falling more deeply, more irrevocably, into the secret dark of it. At the Lake, I paint cannas but differently, giant canvases. They aren't still lifes. Some are abstracted to the point of being unrecognizable. Their edges explode off the canvas, but they are always nameable. Pansy. Calla. Tulip. Rose.

Stieglitz is not himself. He reads a little, pokes about in the kitchen. One night cleaning up after supper, he washes the dishes, wipes them dry, then sets them back into the rack as if they are still wet. He inadvertently throws leftover scraps of food into the bread box. Finally, he mopes off to bed with an undetermined illness and a smuggled copy of Joyce's banned latest, *Ulysses.*

He is bored, and I am busy, and perhaps to get back at me, he invites Eva Herrmann and Ethel Terryll, the daughters of his old friends. He rallies, as he often will for guests. He finds himself exactly where he likes, in a knot of young women, who giggle and adore being photographed. He begins to make nudes of them, the first nudes he's made since Beck. He flirts with the cook that Lee and Lizzie have brought. Her name is Ilse, a young blond thing with a round face, rounder breasts, and a small waist cinched in her red apron. One day I hear him telling her that the rolls she bakes are delicious, the most buttery, sweet biscuits he's ever bitten into. "I could eat the whole tray and still be hungry," he says. Her girlish laughter drifts through the house. With my city paintings, the money from my sales, and perhaps most essentially Blanche's interview, some balance between us has changed. He'll claim it's innocent—what he's doing—these girls are entertainment for him while I work, but we've been here before, and there is something loud and blatant about the way he is doing it that feels like a punishment.

It's a Thursday, midafternoon, when Eva Herrmann comes to the shanty and knocks politely on the door. I slip back into my shirt. It was hot. I'd taken it off. I go to the door and let her in. Her face is grave as she pulls a stool over and reaches for my hand and tells me that when she walked into the kitchen just now, he was kissing the cook.

I slip my hand from hers—deft and quick—and ask her to leave. I begin to work again, my mind trembling, all seized up like a record caught on a scratch. I lean back against my stool. The door ajar, the sky is starkly blue, the slant of light on the hill so perfect I just want to tear it to pieces.

I leave my things where they are—paint on the palette, the brush on the table. I don't clean up, just that tight stretched feeling in my chest like a drum. I walk toward the house. There's a commotion on the porch—new voices, children, and I suddenly remember that today is the day the little Davidson girls arrive. Elizabeth has stayed at home and sent them on alone.

I cut around toward the back of the house.

"Georgia, there you are!" Lee calls. "Come over here, please, and see the girls. They've prepared something for you." I turn and walk stiffly over to where the little girls wait just inside the front hall—their matching dresses, sandals, and bonnets.

Little Sue steps toward me and curtsies, holds out her hand, and says shyly, "How do you do, *Aunt* Georgia?"

I slap her light and fast across the face. "Don't ever call me Aunt."

Like a falling house of cards, the sounds behind me as I move toward the stairs—the child whimpering, a woman's murmur to soothe her, the shocked silence of the rest, and the echo of crisp, determined footsteps, mine.

I spend the rest of that day in my bedroom. Stieglitz comes to find me, and I tell him to leave. It's just too much—the taut weight of anger and shame. The question searing: "Who is this person I've become?"

The sunlight is pale on the walls.

Not one for children. I remember those words—words from the summer Marie came with her two-year-old Yvonne. We were alone in the kitchen when he said it. *You are not one for children.* A vague, knowing smile on his face. So awful, that smile, it made my throat constrict, like he was seeing into a future I'd not yet arrived at. The future we seem to find ourselves in now.

THAT EVENING, I tell him I am going to Maine. He denies the business with the cook.

"You think every awful thing you hear about me is true."

"Why would Eva invent that?"

"You imagine a simple flirtation means something it doesn't."

I feel a sharp flash of rage. I know what he thinks he's saying. In his mind, the two are separate—love and sex—how he feels about me and what he does with someone else. I think of Beck, how I saw it coming and did nothing to stop it. But this. Somehow it feels worse. A kiss. The word itself is a word I love, and I can't escape the leveling feeling inside that I've brought this on. I've done something to make this happen.

My mind is not working right, torn in too many directions at once. I brush my hand across my face. Tears glisten.

———

ON OUR WAY to the train station: "I didn't make the bed," I say.

"What?"

"The bed. I didn't make it."

"That's all right."

"No, you see, it isn't really." My voice sounds small, far away, a voice falling through an hourglass, because I thought to myself: I should fix the bed before I go. But as I stepped into the room, I suddenly realized that we would not be in that bed together and he might not be alone.

"I started to make it," I say, "and then did not."

"She meant nothing, Georgia. There was nothing."

"It means something, though, to me."

WHEN I RETURN from Maine, they're gone—the nobody cook and the rest. We are careful, he and I. We move around each other gingerly. Not one harsh word exchanged.

I unpack the shells I brought back, and paint them. My palette has shifted—austere, almost alabaster tones—the shells' edges clean, severe. I tell myself it does not matter. What he did or did not do. It should not, cannot matter. Whether it's something or nothing. I should not care. A body, a kiss, or those fugitive clouds he tries to seize rushing over the hill. It does not matter that once I threw myself into him like water into water.

CROSSING THE YARD, I find an old weathered gray shingle on the ground near the barn. It reminds me of a shingle I fashioned with a white sail as a child and set to float in the rain barrel.

I bring that piece of shingle upstairs to the sunny bedroom, and set it with a shell on my table. They seem to say something to each other—the bleached whiteness of the shell and the gray of the shingle—and I paint those shapes and repaint them until the shingle becomes just a darkness, its curved shape like the petal of a very dark flower, the shell a loose dab of whiteness beneath. I look so closely and for so long, my mind begins to soften, my seeing separates. They become fluent, flow together, those non-living things, they shift and continue to shift, losing their hard edges, gradually abstracting from their own forms.

IV

"I want to evoke something different in The Room this season," he remarks one evening. We're back at the Shelton, and I'm sorting through things for my upcoming show.

"Different how?" I say.

He sits on the sofa near me. "I want people to understand that when they enter The Room, this is True Art, what they're seeing." He glances at me then, a playful smile on his lips. "I want solemn reverence."

"And you think you can institute that?"

"I don't see why not."

"Oh, you make me laugh, Stieglitz."

"Hours of silence. That's what I'm thinking. Mondays, Wednesdays, and Fridays."

"All day? No one will come!"

"No. Only certain hours. In the morning. Ten to noon."

"Does that mean *you* will have to keep silent as well?" It gives me a kind of pleasure, this sweet, gentle teasing, it's like the way things used to be.

"And a crystal ball," he says.

"No!" I laugh.

"I'm serious," he says. "I want people to understand that The Room holds the spirit of 291. It's not like any other gallery in the city, and it's not some stuffy museum. I want people to walk in and feel something different, something in the space itself. That will help them *feel* the impact of the art."

"I don't know that you can make people feel that way."

"Of course you can," he says.

THE TONE IN the reviews of my work has begun to change. I don't remark on it to Stieglitz—it's all still praise and, for him, that's enough—but it pleases me to see that the emotional faucet has been cinched. I'm convinced it's because of the Blanche Matthias piece and the copies I made that we still keep to hand out at the gallery. The critics have begun to incorporate some of the terms and perspective I used in my interview with her to describe my intent and vision. McBride praises the intellectual palette of my paintings. Helen Read lauds my giant close-ups of flowers, fruits, and shells. Mumford compares my work to Matisse, although he still, aggravatingly, continues to spell my name with only one *f*.

Six paintings sell for a total of seventeen thousand dollars. I collect these details in my mind—noting that things are finally becoming what I want them to be: The critics are taking my work on its own terms; money is coming in; everything is as it should be.

So why can't I feel the fineness? It all feels a little mechanical, some tiny something in me broken, or between us, removed.

Perhaps it's the work itself that feels wan to me. When I look at my things, I don't entirely like what I see. The shells, white flowers, even the cityscapes, they are almost too controlled. I ask him if he sees it. He disagrees. He loves the elegance of the neutrals. Though color is my strength, he's never quite trusted my passion for it, and seems a bit relieved that it has fallen from me.

———

ONE MORNING, THAT fall, lying alone in bed, I find a small round thing in my nightgown like a marble for a doll's game. A balled-up thread. Then I realize it's not in the cotton but under the skin of my breast, a small hard sphere rolling around under my fingers. It doesn't hurt.

I show Stieglitz, his face is stricken when he feels it, and I have to pack away every ounce of my own fear just to calm him.

"It's not a lump," I say.

"That's exactly what it is."

"It's too small. Just some funny blister under the skin."

He doesn't let his fingers off it.

HE SITS WITH me in the doctor's waiting room, completely undone. He picks at his fingernails. I've never seen him do this.

"Don't be so anxious," I say. "How sweet you are. You love me."

His eyes shift to my face, strangely dark. "Love you?" he says. "You're my *life*."

"Alfred. I'll be fine."

But the words glance off him, and his fear starts to kick up a wild flailing in me. I look away. "Stop this," I say. "Please. I need to know I'll be fine."

We're called in. During the exam, he sits in the visitor's chair, his shoe tapping the floor, as the doctor's cool, expert fingers probe. I feel like a yard of cloth stretched out on the table—inanimate, taut.

"It just seems to be that one," the doctor finally says. He has stern blue eyes. My palms sweat, a jittery feeling that must be my heart as he tells us they'll have to cut in and take that thing out.

STIEGLITZ SETS A light kiss on my eyelids before I'm wheeled through the sterile scrubbed hallway of Mount Sinai—the antiseptic reek, brutally polished linoleum floors, nurses in their hospital whites moving crisply about.

I close my eyes to feel it again, that dry brush of his lips grazing my eyelids as the ether pulls me down, the room funneling to a tiny circle of light, my mind unpeels.

THE CYST IS benign. But it takes time to recover; the pain in my side so intense, I can't raise my arm. I can barely sit up.

"They went deep with the knife," I joke when he comes to see me in the hospital. "Did you tell them to go after a good chunk of my stony heart?"

He doesn't like that kind of black humor.

The pain is searing, even after I'm moved back home. The shape of my breast is altered, puckered skin around the stitches, the cut long and bruised.

He does not leave my side. He insists on changing my bandages.

"You don't know how to do that," I tease him and twist to peel the gauze away myself. The pain rips through me. So sharp—that pain—like a nail through my ribs. I gasp.

"Darling," he says, easing me back onto the pillow. He gently removes the bandage, adds fresh ointment to the wound, and covers it again. He taps a small white pill out of the bottle on the night table and gets me a glass of water.

"What do you need? Books? Paper? Do you want to sketch? How is the pain? You need to tell me *before* it becomes too much."

I laugh. "For which one of us?"

"It's true," he says. "I hate seeing you in pain."

He spends one entire afternoon sitting in the chair by the bed, reading aloud to me from Sherwood Anderson's *Tar*. He flows in and out, bearing plates of orange slices, crackers, hot soup, and tea. It feels lovely—the intimacy between us, like soft fire moving again sweetly, quietly, as it was once.

Even after he returns to the gallery, he calls once an hour to check on me.

I MISS MY opening that January. There's still too much pain, I can barely stand. He sends Rosenfeld to the apartment with flowers.

Rosenfeld has just returned from the Southwest, and as we sit together in the living room he waxes on about the untamed beauty of Taos.

"So many artists out there now, writers as well. It's becoming a cultural mecca."

"I've heard Mabel Dodge orchestrates all that."

"You've met her?"

"Once."

I don't add that she struck me at the time as a larger, female counterpoint to Stieglitz—moving people around through space, importing the important ones, all that.

"I'd love to see what art you would make out there," Rosenfeld says. "The colors and the light are so intense."

"As magnificent as Marin claims?"

"Every bit. You'd love it, Georgia. Of anyone, you."

"Sadly right now, I can barely visit the kitchen."

He looks at me, with those wise drooping eyes. "That place reminded me of you, that something about you no one can touch."

I brush some bits of nothing off my skirt and tell him that's very nice of him to say, and perhaps I'll go sometime when I'm well enough to travel. I do love to travel, and only wish I could get Alfred out of the Manhattan, Lake George rut.

He smiles at this. A good friend, Pudge. He loves us both and knows Stieglitz well—flaws and all—better than anyone apart from me.

I THINK ABOUT it more after he leaves. I used to tell Stieglitz I missed that sort of country—wide-open plains, real spaces—but his face would cave in the strangest way and so I stopped telling him.

John Marin has been going to Taos for years, and the Strands were lured out last summer by the plump and lavish force of nature, Mabel Dodge Luhan, an heiress once married to a Bolshevik who's spent most of her life trying to outrun her bourgeois childhood. Beck, whom I've slowly begun to forgive, has told me it's like no other place, and while she was there, she felt so serene, cut loose from everything.

I know that western sky. Sometimes when I'm alone painting, a blind lifts and I let my mind drift back. I remember walking out into the red sun in Canyon until the night fell. I'd lie down on the scorched hardness of the desert floor, looking up at the stars raining down like small silver bullets into me.

It was all I wanted then—to feel that roar of the infinite that exists within our finite selves. At times it seemed unbearable—that hunger I felt once—like the edges of my skin could not contain it.

I miss that.

V

HE'S DISTRACTED, I notice, which I chalk up to the fact that I am ill in bed until he remarks, in passing, that Dorothy Norman—the young wife of that Sears, Roebuck heir—has returned to The Room.

"You might remember," he says, "she was the one banished so summarily, I'd say rudely, by that disparaging remark Louis Kalonyme made when she came by one day."

"No, I don't remember your telling me that."

"She delivered her baby in November," he continues, "and she dropped in last week on her way to a luncheon. She wants to be engaged in the work. She said she'd be happy to do anything for us that we need: manage the goings-on, open the mail, answer the phone, and so forth."

"For *us*?" I say.

"You must meet her. You'll see what I mean. Her innocence is unusual. She's not at all jaded as the rich can sometimes be. She's having dinner with the Strands next week."

"What about the baby?"

"What about it?"

"She'll just leave the baby at home all day?"

He shrugs. "That's hardly my affair."

EARLY FEBRUARY, SIX weeks after my surgery, I'm well enough to slip into a plain black coat. On his arm I walk in to see my show. I meet Dorothy Norman then for the first time. She is younger than his daughter but reminds me of his wife, Emmy, whom I may always perhaps think of as his wife. That same coy gentility. She has girlish cheeks and a doe-eyed look. Stieglitz, in his favorite tweed suit, makes the introduction and, among other things he's already told me, explains that Mrs. Norman is involved in the Civil Liberties Union.

"Why not quit that nonsense and just support the Woman's Party?" I say.

"Other causes interest me more." A sweet smile as she answers, but her lips are tense, a coldness in that lipstick line I was not expecting. A funny shiver in my chest, a quick pain in my wound when the muscle tightens.

THAT SPRING, WHENEVER I come by The Room, it seems she's there, answering the phone, reading old issues of *Camera Work*, or taking notes as Stieglitz answers questions, her head bowed, on the verge of kneeling at his feet. She wants to write a book on him, he says. She's begged to be allowed to be there, and he's told her she is welcome as often as she likes.

She begins to root herself into the circle—Dove, Hartley, the Strands. Only Rosenfeld apparently will have little to do with her. But I see the looks exchanged when her name comes up, how they all avoid my eyes. Trouble stirring. When I mention it, Stieglitz reminds me that the week after she met me, she graciously made a one-hundred-dollar donation to the rent fund, and even went as far as to ask if she could borrow his camera to do the installation photos of my show.

"Under your guidance."

"What are you implying? She's married, with an infant."

"That she leaves at home with a nurse."

"You treat her coldly," he says, almost accusingly.

"No differently than any other bootlicker."

He glares at me.

We're at breakfast in the Shelton cafeteria. A boiled egg and toast on the plate before me, an orange.

"The Room gives her a sense of purpose."

"That's of no consequence to me."

"She is nervous around you. She told me you look at her queerly."

I don't answer.

"You could be kinder. She's just young and old-fashioned. She wishes you would call yourself Mrs. Stieglitz."

"Since she is Mrs. Norman, it would seem that's not her decision to make."

We don't talk as he spreads a thin sleeve of butter across his toast. I slice my egg into halves, then quarters, then I slice those quarters once more. I eat them slowly, watching my fingers on the fork and knife. I could ask him if it's her money he is after, but in my heart I know him well enough to know that's not it.

It's true I dislike her. That flushed juvenile brightness. There were girls I knew at boarding school in Virginia who had that same quality—cinched waists, wide shining eyes, flounced and ruffled dresses—they huddled in cliques and giggled. One night after curfew, I stole onions from the kitchen, then caught and killed a chicken from the coop, and cooked it up in the wood-burning stove in the dormitory. They were in awe of me from then on. I was the one they could never quite make sense of, but I taught them all poker and my daring enthralled them. Toward graduation, as I illustrated the yearbook with ink drawings and irreverent cartoons, all they talked about were the boys they would marry.

"What about you, O?" my friend Susan asked.

I laughed. "I won't have the kind of life you're signing up for. I'm going to give up everything for my art."

I EAT THE last piece of my egg.

"Listen to this, Georgia," Stieglitz says now. He reads aloud an announcement in the *Times* that the painter John Sloan sold thirty-two pictures to an unnamed collector for forty-one thousand dollars. "Unnamed collector," he says. "Unnamed. If that's not a bucket of nonsense—who would *pay* for thirty-two Sloans?"

I push my plate of egg and toast away, and begin to cut an orange. It's her softness he's so taken with, that breathy, ingenuous tone in her voice. I don't realize I've cut my hand until the blood comes in a veiny trickle. A small cut, but deep. I drop the knife and feel the acid sting of the juice.

Stieglitz looks up. "Heavens!" he says rushing to my side. "What have you done to yourself?"

A FEW WEEKS later, he announces to the press that six of my calla lily panels have been acquired by an anonymous collector from France for twenty-five thousand dollars. *The New York Times* prints a story on the sale. The news sparks a frenzy when it hits the other papers: "Prim ex-country schoolmistress who actually does her hair up in a knot is the art sensation of 1928!" Stieglitz feigns a stunned disbelief when we are asked about the sale.

"It is extraordinary," he says over the phone to a reporter calling to request an interview. "Yes, of course, I am thrilled, of course, but at the same time, not entirely surprised. That amount is after all what her art is worth. Europe knows that. O'Keeffe *is* modern American art. This only proves what many of us have always known."

He is in his element. He is also, I know, constructing a truth out of smoke. I watch him as he nods, listening, the phone tucked against his ear, not a touch of uncertainty in his face—he knows exactly what he's done.

"Yes, absolutely," he says. "Four-thirty, Wednesday. Miss O'Keeffe would be happy to meet with you. Here, at our rooms at the Shelton. I'll leave your name with reception."

I ALMOST CAN'T bear the landslide of publicity. But the announcement of the sale has done just what he planned: catapulted me to new heights and confirmed him as a visionary. He knew what I was worth before the world did.

As he arranges interviews, I make a list of errands that need to be done. Such a charade, this scheme he's concocted. I drop our shoes off at Slater and his cape at Barrett & Nephews to be cleaned; I look for the blue cups I like at Macy's, but it seems they are sold out; I order frames at Of's.

When the reporter from the *Sunday Magazine* arrives at the Shelton, I find that my face has stiffened to a mask. I can barely smile. I sit and answer questions and try to play down the exorbitant price.

"But is it true?" the man says, snakelike, leaning forward. "Twenty-five thousand dollars!"

"Yes it's true," I say brusquely. "But the idea that you can make an artist overnight is not. There have been many paintings, many years of hard work and hard experience."

I am in my bedroom, writing to my sister Catherine, when he comes home that night. I start to get up to go and meet him, but I hesitate.

"Hello," I hear him call. He appears in the doorway. "How was the interview?"

I set down the pen. "Someone will find out," I say.

"Find out what?" he says.

"That it's a hoax."

"It's a perfectly legitimate sale."

I think of Mitchell Kennerley with his pipe, his Englishman accent, his thinning hair, swimming in debt. He was forced to sell the Anderson Galleries back in January, and the only plan he has is to buy it all back after his marriage to his wealthy European lover.

"Kennerley does not have twenty-five thousand dollars," I say.

"His fiancée wants them."

"She's never seen them."

"He signed the contract. You signed the contract. Quarterly installments."

He has not yet taken off his cloak. One of the buttons, I notice, is loose, a big round shiny button, hanging by a thread. And I think about how I had to walk twenty blocks the other day to find the shirt and tie he wanted. Exactly the same as the old shirt and tie. When I pointed out the fray at the collar, the stain on the tie, and suggested new ones, he was nearly sick. He can't bear to let go of old things. It would have been funny if I hadn't had to go in such a mad search to replace them.

There was a painting I did once when I was very young. A picture of a man, but my hand was a child's hand, and I could not get him right, he seemed to bend where I wanted him straight, and was straight where I wanted him bent. What he became on paper was not at all what I intended, and finally there was nothing to do but turn the page a different way.

ONE EVENING IN June, he slips and falls, spraining his back. He can barely walk from the cab to the doctor's office. That night, as he fumbles to pull off his underclothes, he tears a tendon in his hand. He is a mass of bandages, tape, and splints. I tell him we should stay in the city until he's better, but he insists he wants to be at the Lake and limps to the train, his weight resting heavily on me.

The space between us is tensile, wrought. Tiny arguments, no more than usual, but harder for me to set aside. Bickerings over the bathroom door, the rain, the pain from the wrench in his back and what he should do for it.

Nothing new is stirring in me. No shapes. I paint what I know—what is safe. Some calla lilies. Roses. A peach on a glass. But the colors feel flat, bodiless. Midway through a second picture of the peach I find myself in a muddled place, oddly dislocated, clinging to the edges, the geometric order of the shape feeling space.

My hand trembles. I close my eyes. That sudden hard fear and nowhere to put it.

You're the strong one, Georgia, my parents used to say. The survivor.
Tears sting now, squeezing out against my will.

EARLY ONE MORNING at five, what we've always called "our hour," I
crawl from my bed into his, my body pressed against him.

"I miss you," I whisper.

"I'm right here."

"But I miss you."

He sighs. "Oh, Georgia. Why are you unhappy?"

I swallow and avoid his eyes, the sorrow going down somewhere
deep. He draws me closer and strokes my back like I am a kitten or a
child. Pat, pat. I pull slightly away, he sighs again, and we lie there,
separately, as the sun rises through the window. Ten years ago, this
month, I came to the Lake for the first time.

At breakfast, he mentions that I've used the wrong cup for his
cocoa, so I pull out another, only to have that one rejected as well.

"Please pick out your own," I say lightly.

I empty the drying rack, put the silverware away, setting forks
with forks, knives with knives. I can feel his eyes on my back. Then
he gets up and starts rummaging around the shelves for a cup that will
satisfy. I go on doing what I am doing.

As I pour his cocoa, he remarks that before we left the city, he was
looking for some mounting paper, because he'd given Mrs. Norman
one of his cloud pictures, and how aggravating it was not to be able to
find the mounting paper he wanted, it didn't seem to be in stock anywhere, and where did I think he should look?

"You gave her an Equivalent?"

He stares at me. I stare back.

"You're missing the point," he says. "No mounting paper of the
old sort. Not in stock, anywhere. We're all at the mercy of commercial manufacturers."

Something deep in me turns over. He is so protective of those clouds—they are not pictures of the sky, he will say, but of life. And it levels me—not just the gift, but the offhand way he relayed this bit of information, as if not delivered as an attack, but as a minor detail.

I stir the cocoa. As I hand it back to him, my grip on the handle slips and it falls, nubs of cocoa, ceramic. Pieces everywhere.

VII

I WANT TO go away. I plan a trip to Wisconsin in July to visit my sister Catherine and her family. I will stop to visit with my brother Alexius and his wife and the new baby in Chicago.

"Come with me, Stieglitz." It's the first warm day at the Lake and the lilacs are in bloom. Their dusky scent fills the air. We are out on the porch. He is scrapbooking the clippings from the show, as he does for every show.

"Come with me," I say again.

He shakes his head. "I'm too old to make that kind of trip."

"Sixty-four is not old."

He looks at me then, something hard to interpret, then goes back to cutting, pressing, turning the page.

I arrange for a housekeeper, Margaret Prosser from the village, to look after him. He brings me to the station. Bags packed, cash tucked into a money belt around my waist. He kisses me, and I board the train. I find my seat. Through the window, I can see him standing between the station pillars. The black triangle of his cape between the white triangle of the pillars. His eyes find me, that piercing glimmer, and the train gives a shudder and heave as we begin to move. He grows smaller, his eyes fade into his face, and then he is only a speck, vanishing into the black shape of the station door behind him, his hand waving.

Halfway across the country, I cry. My face turned away toward the window until the handkerchief is soaked through.

MY BROTHER ALEXIUS meets me in Chicago at Union Station—the war has aged him. He drives me to the Art Institute because I want to see the Bartlett Collection—Monets and a few van Goghs. His swirls of color stun me—how he used such quick strokes of paint, jab after jab to build those larger arcs of moving light and wind and space. At noon, Alexius comes back for me, and we go to the hospital to see the baby, just born, with his wife, Betty. The sweet constellation of the three of them fills my heart with warmth. The baby is in my brother's arms. The small skull rests in the palm of his hand. Alexius's face is worn, his figure sadly drained of its own life, but his eyes shine every time they fall on his child's face.

"She's lovely," I say. "Such a simple thing—isn't it?—all those toes! You're lucky." He glances at me. Perhaps he hears the wistful sadness in my voice.

"You always looked after us when we were young," he says.

I laugh. "I know, imagine that."

"You were good to us, Georgia." He drives me back to the station to catch my train, heading west, toward dark country. I order poached eggs in the dining car. Everyone on the train is playing cards.

STIEGLITZ'S LETTERS ARE waiting for me when I reach Catherine's home in Portage. It feels queer to see them there. Catherine and I walk down to the river with her daughter, Little Catherine. We cross over a bridge, and Little Catherine, who's five years old and not shy, weaves her little fingers through mine as we walk the woods on the opposite shore. In the afternoon, I lie down on the daybed on the porch, and when I wake, I find her little body lying near me, asleep, the little features, so like my sister Catherine's, and that echo of our mother's features as well, like this raw bit of creature is the spit of what we were once, and I am the air around her, flowing in and out. I watch the rise of her little chest, slow and even, as she breathes.

He is a thousand miles away. Does the wind stir through the summer green of the lawn on the hill? Does it sweep up to the porch and touch his face, and will he pause and feel my presence in that soft bolt of wind?

My heart feels like stone. Catherine, who has always been sensitive, notices.

"What's troubling you, Georgia?" she asks when we are up late, talking together in the kitchen.

"Things have just been difficult."

"With Stieglitz?"

"Yes. And *he* can be very difficult!" I laugh.

She looks at me—not laughing—her eyes, dark and gentle, probe. "That's not quite it, though, is it?" she says. "Is it another woman?"

I feel something in me catch. I shake my head. "Sometimes I wish it were that simple."

"You don't wish that," she says.

Growing up, I was the one the others looked up to. The one who knew who she was and what she was about. It comes back to me here, as I watch my sister with Little Catherine—that luxuriant joy in her eyes every time they fall on her daughter's pert face. When I think of the five of us, my sisters and me, I can see how our lives have begun to find their track, to become the lives that will be ours. Anita— social, elegant, rich. Her husband, Robert the financier. Just this spring, Anita bought one of my flower paintings, a white lily framed against red that she shows off to her guests when she entertains. Claudia and Ida, both full-time nurses now, have dedicated themselves to that exquisite pleasure that comes with caring for others. And Catherine. Lovely gentle Catherine was always the one with that goodness about her—a woman in the truest, most noble sense of that word. She is the only one of my sisters I occasionally envy. Catherine's life is closest to the life I sometimes feel I could have had. The life I have missed my chance for.

In his letters, he calls me his Dear Runaway, his Faraway One. His Sweetestheart, as always. And as always when I read his letters, I feel something warm rinse through me. He writes of the news at the Lake—new pipes are going in, trenches dug. He has rewaxed some of his prints and respotted them, though I am much better at spotting than he is, he writes. He has been trying to read a bit of Shaw, but it doesn't suit his mood, so he has picked up Lao-tzu's Tao instead. *I am happy for you that you have made the trip out there, to your America, the place of your beginnings, but it makes me sad too. Sometimes I think— a killing thought—that you were lighter when you came to me, that being here has never been quite enough for what you need. I have never been quite enough.*

I look up. I'm sitting on the sofa by the window. Catherine is cooking dinner. I can smell roasting potatoes and the lighter scent of cooked ham. The dark is falling outside, and my face has begun to surface in the long window—an older face, only traces of the girl who came to him, dark hair pulled sharply back, as I wore it then.

He used to pull it loose. I remember this. In those first few years when we were together, he loved how it fell when I was above him in the night bed of that small studio with the orange floor, my hair falling like a thin black shelter around us.

I read the letter again like if I keep reading, I will find my way back. Then I fold it and put it away.

I TELL CATHERINE I want to drive out to see the farm where we grew up, and I want to paint a barn. We load her car up with canvases and paints, and the three of us set off—my sister, Little Catherine, and I. Things look different, a few landmarks gone, the roads wider than when I was a child. Halfway there, I know where we are. We pass the stretch of marsh with tremendous willow trees on either side. Little Catherine is delighted and claps her hands as she presses her face against the window. The trees are thick and tall and green.

Catherine keeps her eyes level on the road.

"What are you thinking?" I ask.

"Does he make you happy?"

I hesitate before I answer. "Happiness has never been exactly what I'm after."

"Marriages move through ups and downs. They change. It is hard sometimes, that changing. You will be happy again."

"It's more than happiness, Catherine. Happiness is only a piece of it."

We drive past large fields of ripening yellow grain and windrows of cut hay. We pass sunburned men working. We drive until I find the barn that I like. Deep red—that redness like life—with a high-pitched roof and a stone foundation. Bars of white fencing wrap the barnyard. Little Catherine has fallen asleep, curled up with her pink blanket and doll. Catherine goes to speak with the farmer. I get out my oils. When my sister gets back to the car, she takes out her book to read.

"No," I say. I pass her a board, a brush. "Paint yours."

She looks at me, surprised. "I don't paint. You and Ida. Not me."

I don't answer. Finally, she reaches for the board.

At one point as we are working, she says to me, "It's not coming out as I see it."

"That doesn't matter so much," I say. "Paint what you feel about the barn."

Little Catherine wakes up and wanders into the field. She watches a dragonfly.

When we are done, I set our paintings together, hers and mine. It takes my breath—my sister's painting—the small and awkward purity of it, devoid of self-consciousness, like a raw dream.

"That's beautiful," I say.

"Oh stop, Georgia."

"No, I mean it. I like yours much more."

"My first time with a paintbrush in my hand since I was nine. Don't be so kind."

"Have I ever said a thing just to be kind?"

She looks at me, then back at the paintings. Mine is cleaner, stronger, but there's an untouched life in her small work I recognize, something pulsating I knew once.

"Give me some advice," she says. "I'll give it another try when you are gone. What would you do to improve it, or if I tried to paint it again?"

"I'll leave you paints and brushes. You can find out for yourself."

VIII

THAT WINTER, WE do not go out nights. We do not have guests. It's just the two of us in our rooms at the Shelton. We've moved to a larger suite on the thirtieth floor. Every day, he goes to The Room to prepare for Marin's show, the first of the season. Mine will open in February 1929. Looking through my paintings, I feel a sense of dread. There's just not much there.

I wear a flaming-red cape to my opening. My lilies, cityscapes, my leaves with torn edges, and an abstraction of Alexius with its wild, cloud-tousled sky, which I made in celebration for my brother when the baby was born.

Dorothy Norman is there. In a slim black dress, she glows, something deep and supple in her young face. I see how her eyes raise to him when he asks her to do something for him, how quickly she responds. I hate the thought. I hate him for having her here, for not knowing, or not caring, what it does to me.

That night, when we are undressing for bed, I confront him. He denies they are lovers. That it's anything other than innocent.

"Are you in love with her?"

"Of course not," he snaps. I meet his eyes with a calmness that would have been impossible before. "Don't start this up again, Georgia," he says, angry now.

"Don't turn this onto me."

"There's no one else. There's never been anyone else."

I look at him. That's not true. Beck. The cook. Perhaps there were more. Such a manipulation to use those words *never, no one else,* and yet I know, at some level, he's convinced he has not wronged me. I know how he sees it: these other women, these dalliances, he believes they're inconsequential against what I am to him. And sometimes I just want to stand in that clarity, that conviction that allows this to be so clean and upright in his mind.

FEW PAINTINGS SELL but, for the most part, the critics continue to rave. They don't seem to have a sense of what I've turned my back on. I'm not happy with the art I am doing. My forms feel too safe. They lack the bold force and freedom of my earlier things, and it strikes me that ever since his photographs of me were shown, my work has a different quality. As if I've been trying to undo the words he and the men trussed me up with. I remember how decisive it was—when I realized the danger of sending a free, abstract shape out into the world. If it had any mystery at all, they would only misinterpret it, sexualize, sensationalize it, reduce it to gendered terms.

And so I made things on the ground. Nameable forms. Leaves. Trees. Flowers. Strident colors yes, but hard-edged lines, a certain polish and restraint. No longer from a fierce driving need but only as an answer to them.

They don't seem to notice, and I find it curious—not heartbreaking as it should be—but like it's happened to someone else.

HE COMES HOME late one evening, and I lean in to kiss him good night and smell her. Perfume. The distant, sweet, glassy scent of sex.

I step back.

"What now?" he says.

"Don't lie to me."

He meets my eyes. "There's nothing to lie about."

"Don't, Stieglitz. I know what you are doing with her."

"Stop."

"This is all wrong. Don't pretend it isn't."

"I'm tired, Georgia," he says with a sigh.

"Is it always about you?"

He turns away from me, and sits down to remove his shoes.

WE ARGUE MORE and more frequently. A small thing will set it off. He accuses me of never going to The Room.

"Your sitting room?"

It enrages him that I call it that. I tell him I don't want an exhibit for a very long time. He tells me that that's ridiculous, but there is fear in his eyes. "Unthinkable," he says.

"Because my shows are the mainstay of the season? Is that what concerns you?"

He looks at me for a long moment. "Art is what you're meant to do, Georgia. And your art is meant to be shown because it says something. *That* is what concerns me."

True and not true—twisting words around again, there's no way to get a foothold.

IX

LADY DOROTHY EUGENIE BRETT has moved into the Shelton. Quite a grand Englishwoman, she has a tremendous silver ear trumpet nicknamed Toby, and I can't help but like her. She drags Stieglitz and me down to her room to see her pictures—her Ceremonials. She tries to talk Stieglitz into a showing. "We'll have to see," he demurs.

When I mention I'm thinking of taking a trip to Europe this summer, she immediately jumps in with that haughty Englishwoman clip that instead of Europe, I *must* go to Taos, to visit Mabel Dodge Luhan at her fiefdom.

"Everyone seems to say so," I answer. "Mabel used to invite Alfred once a year."

Lady Brett turns Toby in Alfred's direction, asking, "And how did you find it?"

"I didn't go."

"Why on earth not?"

He mumbles something about his heart and the altitude. She asks him to please speak up, and that's the end of it. But later that month, when I see Strand's new photographs of Taos on exhibit at The Room, I decide.

I TELL BECK I want to go.

"You should," she says. "You'd love it there." We're out for lunch together. She's got her white shirt casually unbuttoned at the throat, a cigarette hanging from her mouth, that gangster air to her she sometimes adopts. "I'll have Paul talk to him."

"I'll talk to him myself."

"It would be good for you, particularly now—" Her voice breaks off.

I frown. Mrs. Norman. They all know.

"I'm sorry," she says.

"Stupid nonsense," I say. And it is. This obsession he has with pretty young things. But it's also distracting, aggravating, humiliating—and I keep thinking to myself I'd rather leave for a while and let it run its course.

"Men are awful," Beck says.

"I just want to get out from under it. I want to do something new for my art."

"Let Paul talk to him." Her cigarette glows as she inhales.

No, IS WHAT he says, which shocks me. Absolutely not. Georgia's too fragile right now to make that sort of trip.

"That's what he told Paul," Beck reports back.

"FRAGILE?" I SAY when he comes home.

"This business you keep on about not wanting another show."

"Oh, is *that* the business that's wrecking things?"

I'm not proud to admit the deep satisfaction I feel when I see the look on his face.

"You need to focus on your work," he says, with less conviction, though.

"That trip will be good for my work."

"I don't think it's the right time."

"And I don't think that's for you to decide—what's right for me."

Silence then. Bleak and steep and strange.

THEY ALL FALL in to convince him. Dear Pudge, Lady Brett, Paul and Beck, even Hartley.

Think about Georgia's art, they say. There's no place like it in terms of light and views. Think of her early work—what she did with the sky in Texas, those Celestial Solitaire watercolors you're still always dragging around. There's so much out there to inspire.

Slowly, they wear him down. But it is Beck's offer to accompany me that finally shifts his mind.

"I told him I'd look after you," she says to me, a triumphant gleam in her gray eyes—"be a sort of nanny."

"The nurse sort, I hope, not the nanny-house sort," I say.

"Just a little spy."

I scoff. "Wouldn't that be fantastic if I were up to something worth spying on?"

She laughs.

"He knows you'll keep a tight rein on me," I say.

"That's right. I'll have you with a cig in your mouth before a week's out."

I TELL HIM we will still have our summer.

"When?" he says snippily.

"I'll be back in July."

"July first?"

"Yes."

It's startling—after all these months of feeling so far away from him—to feel his need of me.

"Do you know I want you to do this if it will make you happy?" he says.

"I do know that."

"Do you know I love you?"

I'm silent.

He sighs. "You're always going away."

"I'll be back soon."

He paces the bedroom, picks up his tie clip, sets it down, moves to something else.

"Lie down with me," I say. He looks up, his face sad. And it's that pause that shreds my heart. For a second, I almost believe that if I stay, I can hold him close enough and fix it, change it—there would be a place, a way that we could rinse it all from us, and find ourselves again in that small studio on 59th with the cot and the skylight and the orange floor and sunlight streaming through into that time when it was just the two of us, and we were lovely together, bodies of light, that pure uncomplicated desire when I was his only world and he was mine.

"Lie down with me," I say again and he does, without a word, and I hold him. I kiss his eyelids, smooth under my lips like shells.

BECK AND I board the *20th Century Limited* on April 27th. I don't stand up to watch him go.

The river flows into hills, and the hills fold down into the flatness of nothing. As the train rushes on, Beck falls asleep beside me, her silvering hair, her face with the short deeper lines that have begun to form between her brows.

Before we left, she and Paul stood a distance apart from us, far enough that we couldn't hear their voices. They were arguing, some kind of awful row. He was telling her something, and I saw her face wither, and knew, watching them, that their marriage would fail.

Stieglitz knew as well. "It won't last, will it?" he said to me.

"No."

"It was never quite right, was it?"

"I don't know if you can ever really call that until after."

He shook his head. "If you look at them clearly, you know. Her lack of direction—his lack of conviction and faith. That's always been Paul's failing. For all his talent, and I'd give my teeth for it, he's never quite had the drive to see his gift through."

"Could be," I murmured.

"I so love you, Georgia," he said to me as we stood there on the platform, his arm around my waist, watching them, as if they were strangers, as if they were not us.

I BREATHE AGAINST the train window now. My face softens under the fog of my breath on the glass. I wipe it away with my hand as we pass peach and plum trees in bloom, and bare trees with nothing on them yet, new green shining everywhere, and mountains in the distance, very gray. The train rocks, and I ache for him. It was vast once, the passion we felt that still hits me at times like a smell, so sharp I feel I'd throw myself down into hurtling darkness if I believed that would keep me with him, would keep us bound together in the way we used to be.

It comes to me now, our life before, in disparate pieces, like the memory of a country we once sped through.

PART V

PART V

I

I FEEL IT the instant the door of the train opens in Santa Fe. The sharp sting of the air on my skin, scents of piñon, sage. The dazzling emptiness seems to extend in every direction.

We never told Mabel we were coming for sure, and Beck hesitates when I suggest it now.

"No," she says, that little-girl pout she gets. "I want you to myself."

But for such a vast country, news travels astonishingly fast. Several days later, we take a bus to the corn dance at the San Felipe pueblo. Mabel finds us there. Once the host of infamous soirees in Greenwich Village and a champion of the avant-garde, Mabel threw herself at Taos and fell in love with what she will call her strange and sweet country. On her fourth husband now, an Indian named Tony, Mabel lives in an adobe mansion she built on a vast sprawl of land. In the summers, she imports philosophers, artists, and writers, to spice up the tedium.

She is stocky—slightly bull-like, but irresistible, with her intense eyes and cropped black hair. She is shocked we came to Taos without telling her, and overturned when she realizes we are not intending to stay with her. Because she's the kind of woman who loves the challenge of going after what's out of reach, she sets out to convince us that her home, Los Gallos—as we must have heard—is like no other place. A compound on twelve acres, it overlooks the mesa. A stunning view. She looks meaningfully at me when she says this. There's a studio where you could paint that looks all the way to the mountains.

She is formidable, and to Beck's chagrin and my delight, it seems we have no choice but to follow her.

HER HUSBAND, TONY, comes for us the next morning, with another Indian, to drive us the seventy-five miles from Santa Fe to Taos. I sit in the passenger seat beside him. He barely speaks. He is a landscape-made human, a barrel-chested man with a long nose. Mabel told us he prefers buckskins to what he's wearing now: a blue sweater, tan-colored breeches, and black boots. He doesn't read or write and refuses to learn. When they married, Mabel changed his name from Lujan to Luhan in some vague attempt to tame him. "They fight like cats," Lady Brett had told me once. "They'll have a wild brawl and he'll up and leave Los Gallos and go to the pueblo, and Mabel will lose her mind with jealousy and a fear that he won't return."

The car slides around the narrow turns along the riverbank. In the woods off the road, patches of snow are slung through the trees. We emerge onto the high mesa, the roar of mountains all around, bruised purple shapes under the heady blue of the sky.

"My watch has slowed," Beck says from the backseat.

"Those don't work good here." Tony's voice is low, sharpened to a point from being seldom used.

"You're wearing one." I point to his watch.

His dark eyes are solemn. "I set it to the sun," he says. His finger taps the wheel. "You drive next time?"

"I will!" Beck pipes up from the backseat. "Georgia doesn't drive."

"Why not drive?" Tony asks me.

I shake my head. "I never learned."

A smile touches his mouth, his eyes fixed back on the road. "Then we'll teach you."

LOS GALLOS IS astonishing. We pass under a bell, through carved wooden entrance gates that swing into a flagstone courtyard. A sprawling masterpiece all built by this inimitable woman. She left a big life in the East, snipped it with one cut and tossed the whole of the page behind her. The Big House is a three-story adobe, ladders leading from one level up to the next. It's a flamboyant mix of New York artwork and Navajo hangings, ornamental tiles, caged parrots, and antique French chairs. We will stay in Casa Rosita, the trim little guest cottage at the edge of the desert, where Beck stayed before when she came out with Paul.

As promised, Mabel gives me a studio to work in. She leads me into a round high-ceilinged room with a kiva fireplace, white walls, and windows looking out across the plains toward the mountains.

Walking back to the main house, she warns us to mind the sun. "Don't let it do its work on your face," she says. "It's deceptive. The air is so dry, you don't feel the heat as you do back east. The sun is much stronger than you realize. Have you brought dark glasses?"

"No," I say.

"You will have to buy some." She draws out her own pair and hands them to me.

I put them on and look out across the sage to the horizon. The dark lenses mute everything—color, scale, even shape. I take them off and hand them back to her. She looks at me, a superior glint in those eyes.

"You'll regret it," she says.

I nod. "Yes, I understand what you're saying."

THE NEXT MORNING I walk out alone into the cold dawn. I feel a quiet exhilaration rill through my body watching the sky go to flames. Piercingly beautiful—this country—so much space between the ground and sky. I walk over to the Big House and go into the large sitting room where there's a grand piano, a daybed, and a Max Weber painting. Tony comes in and sits on a chair near me. Without speaking, he and I become friends.

He takes us to the footraces at the pueblo, where the boys strip to nothing but a loincloth and race in pairs of two. They wear moccasins, feathers, beads, bells, paint. The old ones, wrapped in their black shawls and blankets, call from the edges, urging them on, and the sky rings with the sound of shouts and the beating flush of feet against the earth. I look out past the pueblo toward the desert. Curious, how something as inarguable and simple as wide-open space can rearrange me back into myself.

I think of Stieglitz and feel a sudden stab of fear, like if I really let myself fall into it, I'd keep falling. Leave my life behind and never go back.

AS PROMISED, BECK and Tony teach me to drive. "I'm no good at it," I say when I inadvertently hit the shift and we jerk into reverse. Beck has told him that Stieglitz is nicknamed Old Crow Feather, and now Tony calls me Mrs. Crowfeather. He tries to be patient. His low voice rises only when I bear down too fast and hard on the gas so we lurch forward. He shows me how to work the clutch and use the brake but, on our fourth run when I hit a gatepost, he shakes his head and directs us back to where Beck is waiting. He gets out there, and says he won't drive with me again.

So it falls to Beck, and we go out together hurtling into the roadless distance. The cool rushing air makes my head light. I catch a glimpse of a dead tree far off.

"Let's go there!" I say, and swing the wheel hard in my hand. The car whips around, the front end aimed toward that withered tree. I press the gas to the floor without restraint and speed across the plain.

"Slow down, Georgia!" Beck cries, but I laugh at her fear and drive faster—it's impossible how at home I feel right now. The world is flooding through me, the wild gorgeous recklessness of it, the sky rushing by. I am flying, free.

I notice Beck's hand white-knuckling the door handle.

We stop.

"Get out of the car," I say. She looks at me, confused. "I need to drive the way I want to."

"You don't know how to drive."

She doesn't understand I know exactly where I am and what I'm doing and there's no way I'm going to give this up.

"Get out, Beck," I say again, and it might be the way I say her name, that lingering kick on the *k*. I see her face fall as she reluctantly climbs out of the car, closing the door behind her. I don't look back to see her standing, watching as I go. I drive faster, the speed catching up to the wind, becoming wind, faster, and everywhere around me, the sky.

I BUY A car. A black Ford sedan with steel-blue interior for $678. Beck is all in at first, until the very last minute when she falters.

"You'll go out and kill yourself and I'll be the one who has to tell him."

"If I'm dead, it'll hardly matter," I say.

"What will you do with it after the summer?"

"Bring it back across the country with me. What else? We need a car out here, Beck. We can't always be asking Tony or someone else to take us out looking for good things to paint." I see her waver. She pays for half the license and the insurance. We name the car Hello.

EVERY MORNING, I scramble onto the roof of the cottage to watch the sun rise.

My mind begins to loosen. There's a sharpness to the colors here, and the world back there, his world, seems so far away, like a page I've turned.

Beck and I go out on long walks, looking for things to paint. Or we take Hello and drive out into the desert until we find a place where we feel like stopping. We bathe in the irrigation ditches and lie naked in the sun, the desert ground hard and dry underneath us. My hands darken. My nose peels with sunburn.

In the evenings after supper in the Big House, we play cards, drink liquor, then Beck and I walk across the field to our little cottage. Sometimes when she has drunk too much, she talks about her troubles with Paul, how she doesn't think they'll be able to make it work. She talks until she has talked herself into tears, and I sit down with her on the floor, my arm around her shoulder.

Over time, I tell her, the weight of what you're feeling now will seem so slight. Like a flower that opened once, long ago, so long ago you won't recall the scent.

I hold her tightly until her breathing grows quiet and her head falls against me, her face lovely and tentative, like a child's.

I lie awake as she sleeps. The cottage feels empty, and the emptiness rings. Like a tingle under the skin. And for the first time in a dozen years, it occurs to me that perhaps Stieglitz is not my life, but a detour from it.

II

As the days pass, the angst in his letters seems to grow. The more joy I pour into mine, the bleaker his become. The building that housed The Room has sold. He'll have to find a new space. He's moved all the art into Lincoln Warehouse for storage. My absence has begun to take root. He's packing for the Lake but afraid to go without me. Restless, too restless. He tries to sleep, but can't. He worries. He can't help it, he writes, he worries about the state of my nerves when I left, the state of things between us. He worries that I don't seem to know— that I've never seemed to truly understand—what I mean to him.

No letter came yesterday. Are you all right, my Sweet Wild Girl? When no letter comes from you, my mind crumbles—a fear that something terrible has happened.

I fold the letters into a neat pile and I write back to him on Mabel's letterhead. There are stacks of it set on every table through the house. A design of Los Gallos takes up nearly half of the page, so you only have half left to fill. I make sure I write him once a day.

"You are an awfully dutiful wife," Beck says wryly.

"The more he worries, the more work it will be for me," I say with a smile.

"He'll be fine," Beck says. "They always are. No matter how much of a fuss they make."

"When I owe him a letter, the easiest thing is just to write it. Otherwise, it drags on me."

"Well you shouldn't let it," she says, apparently more adept with my life than her own. I don't point this out. "I'll write him, Georgia. I'll tell him you've never been better."

"No, don't say that. That will only make him worry in a different way."

"I'll tell him you're the picture of serenity, not an ache or pain since we've arrived."

"Don't tell him about the driving," I say.

"No. That I'll leave to you."

WE TAKE HELLO out into the desert, then find a spot I like. We walk around, picking up things off the desert floor, bones, rocks, and bits of shell. We are far off, miles from the house, the day I find the first cow skull. The whiteness gleams. I run my hands over it to feel the shape, my fingers through the sockets of the eyes. Beck kneels beside me.

"Touch it," I say to her. She presses her fingers to it, uncertain. Her hand drops and I laugh.

"Do you ever think our lives stand for nothing?" she says as we walk back to the car. I carry the skull against my chest.

"You mean because of this?"

"Everything seems so old out here, ancient. Like it's always been here. It makes everything I do feel pointless."

The sage stretches away on either side of us, the silver glint of it like the sea.

"I love that feeling," I say.

She glances at me, then gives a little sigh and does not speak again until we reach the car. I sort what we've found into piles: the throw-away pile, and what I'll take back to Los Gallos. Then we set up our things and begin to sketch. Beck will last for an hour, sometimes a bit more, but her impulses are unpredictable. She draws in fits and starts, then begins to doubt. She sets down her pencil and lies on the ground near me as I continue to work, her arm over her face to shield the light from her eyes. She is lovely, lying there, with her gray-blond hair sprawled out. I can see the light tug of her blouse where her breasts rise, and the shadow of her nipple through the cotton. I continue working.

"It's hot," she says. "Don't you want to lie in the sun?"

"I'm not done yet," I answer.

She makes a little noise, irritated, a few minutes later, then takes off her clothes and lies back down again. After a while, I finish my sketch, order my things, and lie down beside her.

"It's so nice here," she says, that kittenish smile on her face. She's happier now that I'm not working, either. Her body is beautiful. I remember the photographs he took of her, just under the surface of the lake. Sometimes I think those photographs he made of her body were as beautiful as any he has made. When I see her lying here, next to me in the sun, her scent, her warmth, her long-limbed magic, I see her as he must have. Her body like art.

I WORK THE sketches into paint. I am playing with watercolor again and I love it—how the water is free—the color always to an extent at the mercy of what the water is doing. I love its suggestion of that random life present in nature.

My pictures begin to fill the studio. In the corner, a rising pile of bleached bones. From time to time, I'll pick one up. The whiteness gleams, fluent and cool in my hand.

BECK AND I go out walking behind the *morada* toward the *penitente* cross in the hills. The evening air is so clear it seems to ring. The cross looms large and black ahead of us, implacable against the unruly luminous sky. Once, as a child, at Catholic mass with my father, I saw God in the patterns of stained light on the floor, and while the priest up there droned on and my sisters sat with their backs straight, their prim hands folded in their lap, I shut my ears and dipped my foot into the overlapping pools of that sudden, holy light.

Back in the studio, I paint the cross, the juxtaposition of its black strength against the moving sky. I paint it again and again, its strict form always quartering each canvas in different ways. I paint it as I saw it that first night against the red sunset. Then I paint it again, as I never saw it, with the mass of Taos Mountain right behind it. The arms of the cross cut the sky like the mullion of a windowpane I'm looking through, slim rectangles of dark blue in the two upper quadrants, then lighter below. I don't want it to be quite straightforward, heroic or iconic. I don't want it to be just a cross in a landscape. I want to show how it lives, how the road and the mountain and the backlit evening sky curve around it. I want that frisson, that uncanny, ethereal life this country seems to hold.

I put the stars in last—eight dots of white. The sky is alive with stars, and was, long before the cross was set into this landscape, and will be, long after.

OTHERS ARRIVE. THE notorious dinners in the Big House grow to be extravagant affairs. Spud Johnson brings a young photographer, Ansel Adams, and his wife. Adams is from California but came to the Southwest to cure a sinus problem. He is in awe when he realizes I am the wife of Stieglitz, whom he calls the greatest photographer of our time. There are local artists: Cady Wells and Russell Vernon Hunter. Charles Collier comes, and Marin arrives in June.

Mabel and Tony fight often—it starts as a squabble, then the argument rises to a high pitch, shooing the rest of us out. "Mabel is so possessive," I remark to Beck one day as we cross the field back to our cottage, their voices filtering out the windows of the Big House behind us. "If she's not careful, she'll squeeze the life out of him and she won't like what's left."

The days here pass so fast, and I am full of paint, in love with this country, the vast desolate yawn of flat land moving away.

Dear Hello is covered with dust. There's been no rain and the car has a thin layer of red earth caked to it. She needs a good wash, I say to Beck, so we slip into our bathing suits and use the hose, but the gush of water is not enough to get it clean, and there are no sponges we can find. Mabel is gone and there's no one to ask where a sponge would happen to be, so we use sanitary napkins to scrub it instead, Beck laughing, giggling, as we go through half a box, stuffing them into a bag that we'll shove to the bottom of the trash. Then we strip down to our skins and turn the hose on each other.

Tony takes us on a trip to Canyon de Chelly to see the ancient cliff dwellings. We get lost in the woods, every road seems to lead nowhere. We have nothing for supper but oranges and whiskey. We go into Santa Fe for the rodeo. Beck picks out matching black sateen shirts for us. I wear a strand of white beads and a silver ring with a large blue stone. I look quite unlike myself. And Beck and I stand together in front of the mirror, studying ourselves and each other, before she slips a cigarette into the side of my mouth and shows me how to get it to dangle just there, without falling.

His letters have brightened. He has come through something, he writes. And now he has embarked on an adventure of his own. He didn't want to tell me at first, afraid I'd be too concerned, but he went for a fly in an airplane with Donald. Flew higher and higher, then upside down. He has started taking lessons. *I want to take you up, my Love, spin you around up there in the Blue and watch the lake running downhill* . . . It makes me happy to feel the joy in his letters, like it might be possible: for him to live in his free state, for me to live in mine. I am halfway through the last page: *My Sweetestheart, my only heart, our togetherness can't be touched. I've known that since I met you, from the moment I unrolled those drawings. If there's anything I have faith in, Georgia, it's what you are to me. Not just lips and legs and shoulders and the flare of cheekbone I adore, but the free and nameless part of you—the far side of my soul—that's what you are. We should have had a child. That was a mistake. I see it now.*

A thousand kisses, dearest. I send every one to you—

I look up.

Sometimes it seems I know everything about her, that child we might have had. When the thought of her takes me off guard— I sense, I know, it would have been *her*—it hits me: the smell of her skin. Sweet soft soapy, burnt sugar baby smell skin. I know just how the light would strike her hair, how it would fall in a long black wave down her small back. She would have blue eyes and her nose would wrinkle when she didn't get her way. She would be willful. Turning cartwheels on the grass, her legs flashing out from under her skirt, as she turned head over heels, again and again, down the hill.

Once I thought I could be an artist and have a real life, like the life my sister Catherine has. I once thought I could disappear into the world of color and shapes and, when I surfaced from it, satisfied, my family would be there. A child, a husband, their shining faces and open arms. I saw it once so clearly—art and life—and my vision of how those two halves could fit was clear. Perhaps it could have been if I had been willing to put my art second. It would be easy, I realize, to blame Stieglitz and say he took this from me. But that is not entirely true. I've never been willing to put my art second. And the best things I've made—my charcoals, my abstractions, a few of the flowers and trees—have that quality of life ringing through them; they were done out of a kind of ruthless ecstasy when my mind was singularly focused and free, in uninterrupted solitude. I could not live an everyday life of skinned knees, meals to cook, beds to make and also have that kind of solitude, which does not make my longing for the life I did not choose, less.

I get up from the table and walk away from the house, away from the letter and the thought of the child, away from the sharpness of the memory of what I will not have. I walk into the distance and the brightness and the wind-torn skinflint earth that gives nothing back.

THAT AFTERNOON I find Beck reading on the bed. She sits up when she sees me.

"What is it?" she asks.

I shake my head. "Will you do something for me?" I ask.

"Anything."

I take out the letter, and she sits on the floor beside me as I read it aloud. I have never done this. Our letters have always been only for us. And it's the oddest feeling hearing his words in my voice fill the room.

I look up when I finish. Her eyes are lowered, she looks down at the Navajo rug underneath us, the shadow of her lashes on her cheek.

"Are they all like that?"

"Each one is different."

"But he always crams in so much of himself like that?"

"Yes."

She is silent, then she says, "I don't know what I'd do if someone wrote to me like that. I don't think I'd be able to do much besides wait and tear them open the minute they came."

I fold the page back together, slip it into its envelope, and put it with the rest. It feels better to me somehow. Like I can leave the thought of that child behind.

"He writes such big sweeping things." She is looking at me now, her eyes intense on my face. "But they *are* entirely real. More real than ordinary life. And that's Stieglitz, isn't it?"

I nod.

"You know," she continues, "I remember the first time I met him, the first time he really talked to me. It was like standing in sunlight. I'd never felt anything like that before."

I could tell her that he is the kind of man who is drawn to things that are free. It's not their beauty he sees, but that other thing, that vital thing past beauty. Life, we could call it, for lack of a better term. He is also the kind of man who can never quite let things exist in the state in which he finds them.

I could tell her, too, that when you are an artist, when you are the kind of person who can vanish for days inside yourself, and you are given this kind of promise:

I will sweep up the details so you can paint.

I will find the words to make you a star. I will make you great. I will frame you, hang you, explain your greatness. I will tell others what to think, what to adore.

As I adore you.

It can be so seductive, the glint of this kind of promise, this kind of man. Particularly when you know it is true when he writes, "I will love you completely, to the end of forever, as no other woman has ever been loved." No matter how untrue it might sometimes seem, this is what he believes, and it is irrefutable for that reason. Truth more than true.

Beck leaves early. Her mother is ill, and she needs to return to New York to care for her. I hug her before I put her on the train, then let her go.

I TAKE A horseback trip to Kiowa to visit Lady Brett, with Tony and some of the others. The horses need shoes so we get a late start and wind up passing through a thunderstorm. We ride in single file, in our yellow slickers, the rain coming and going until we arrive and drag our sleeping bags and tents up the hill to a dry place under the pine trees where we will camp. Brett's house is a crazy house—chipmunks eating up the bed, and toilet paper hanging by a wire in the outhouse. Everything is so haphazard, and it seems to fit Brett so neatly. Seeing a woman fit so well into her own crazy-unkempt life fills me with pleasure. We travel on to Alcalde—to poet Marie Garland's ranch. The silence is more complete than at Mabel's. I can wander and meet no one for hours. And the hills are different. They are like sand and change under the touch of the wind. Nothing still.

We drive northwest to the Grand Canyon. There are five of us, and we take two cars, Garland's Rolls-Royce and the Packard. We keep the convertible tops down, and the wind washes through us as we drive. Starting at 8 A.M., we drive all day, from Bright Angel Trail where the sun rises alone into the canyon, along the soft gray hills that give way to red cliffs. The rain has cut the roads to pieces. I love it, the steepness and the danger of it. For days, we are lost in this country. No mail to send, no mail to receive. I write a telegram to him: *Heading into Navajo territory tomorrow. Will wire when I can. It could be several days.*

I send it and feel a sharp pang of sadness, something cut, then sweet and deliriously light.

WHEN WE RETURN, the household of Los Gallos is on its ear. A gruesome story. All over the paper and for days, the talk has been of nothing else. A man Mabel knew quite well was found with his head severed, chewed on by his two fierce dogs.

There are letters waiting from Lake George. It's been days since he has had word from me, and he has fallen into despair. He says he prowls the house like a ghost, staying up all night, pacing the floor. He's afraid I will not come back. *The Lake is desolate without you. Meaningless.*

He's begun to destroy his work: negatives, papers, images of Kitty, images of Venice, of 291. He says it is a good thing. A growing into clarity. A purging. *I have come to understand that there are things worth saving. Those things are few. The rest must go.* He builds bonfires—letters, prints, magazines, all sorts of truck. He throws it on and watches the past burn; the coarse smell of the palladium fills the night sky, leaving his eyes red with smoke, so even the following morning there's a horrible redness that can't be rubbed out.

He sends small clippings folded into the letters. In the last, he tucks a photograph of the two of us kissing under the tree out in front of the house at the Lake. Below the photograph, he has written: *I have destroyed 300 prints today. I haven't the heart to destroy this . . .*

It is the ellipsis that undoes me, those three tiny dots that say nothing in themselves. I remember that kiss. I was on tiptoe, he was just above me on the hill, and his cloak enveloped me, and he drew me in against him, and held me, so tightly and so close, as if to say, There is this and only this and I will never let you go.

It's the strongest pull I know—the pull back. Over every other thing, it seems, still.

I look up from the letter. The room is plain, the adobe smooth, bare. After Beck left, I stripped the decorative ornaments from the walls. It was the emptiness I wanted—only the heat through the window, the scent of flowers, and the sound of the little stream flowing by outside. The peace in that emptiness.

I send off a wire.

I leave for you on Friday, if not sooner.

THAT NIGHT, I go to meet the others in the Big House, but they seem shadowy, like paper cutouts. I leave them after coffee and take the horse for a ride along the ridge. It's dark by the time I come back. I put the horse in the corral and cross the field, alfalfa grass crackling under my boots. I see the others through the window of the Big House, their lit forms moving through the orange light. I look back toward the mountains I just rode from, and I let the wind breathe into me, and out of me.

III

HE MEETS ME at the train in Albany, and it is the sweetest homecoming. I almost cannot believe how happy I am to see him again, how restored things feel between us. He looks, strangely enough, more sound than he has looked in years. Perhaps it was the bonfires, I whisper, giggling, as we lie together in the bedroom in the early morning. He moves his hands over me, my neck, my breasts, he touches me at that spot in the center, and makes love to me until my thighs ache.

"I'd forgotten how perfect it can feel here," I murmur.

He pulls me in tight against him and kisses me hard on the mouth. "Do not forget," he says. "Don't ever. Promise me."

We spend the day outside. The lake shimmers, the grass bright and lush, the air strung through with the scent of wild grape—and Stieglitz at the center of it all, stubborn, aging, glorious. The bliss between us is as it was once and, at the same time, new all over again.

Later, I spread out all the work I did on the floor. It's good. Really just so good. I call him in to have a look, and he comes and sits in the chair, his body folded over the arm, his vest with one button off, his face with a halo of white hair, dark eyes piercing, looking over my things.

"So fine, aren't they, Stieglitz?"

He nods, smiling. He is happy.

"Do you see," I say gently, "how good it was for me to go there?"

CHARLES COLLIER DRIVES my Ford cross-country and delivers it to us at the Lake.

"Hello," I say formally, addressing the car, "I would like you to meet Alfred. Alfred, may I present Hello."

He takes photographs of me with the car, playful images of my hands, the wheel, my dark weathered face, a coy look back at the camera. *Like it used to be,* he says afterward, holding me to him. *How I love photographing you, no one like you.*

THAT FALL OF 1929, news comes of the stock market. Stieglitz stews over it. Will it affect art sales? Of course, it will affect everything. But we'll still go ahead and open the new gallery in December. It will be called An American Place. The young ones—Strand, Beck, and a few others—have been working away at it down in the city. So dedicated, they've raised over ten thousand dollars in pledges to fund the new space.

We make plans to return to the Shelton. We will attend the opening of the new Museum of Modern Art. He is not keen on it. He looks down at those matrons, Mrs. Rockefeller, Mrs. Bliss, who snubbed his opinion as they were building their new museum, but the second exhibition will include Demuth, Marin, and me, so he has grudgingly agreed to be decent.

IN NEW YORK, breadlines wrap the corners by the soup kitchens. Walking the streets, I pass humped shapes under blankets, men with their hats pulled down over their reddened ears, mothers clutching children with torn coats.

I have lunch with my sister Anita at her Fifth Avenue apartment. Her daughter Cookie comes in—almost twelve years old now and with her mother's slim grace. She has lunch with us, before stuffing grapes in her pocket and running off to play. Anita confides in me that she would like to buy a few more of my paintings. Her husband, Robert Young, whom they are now calling the "daring young man of Wall Street," netted a small fortune during the crash selling stocks short.

AT AN AMERICAN PLACE, along with the main rooms, there's an office Stieglitz nicknames the Vault and a storage cubicle he converts to a darkroom. I choose white for the ceiling, high-gloss gray for the walls. It's an austere space, spare and modern. Frosted-glass doors. He draws up an engraved ivory card, with simple black script listing everything that the Place is not:

No formal press reviews
No cocktail parties
No special invitations
No advertising
No institution
No isms
No theories
No game being played
Nothing being asked of anyone who comes
No anything on the walls except what you see there
The doors of An American Place are ever open to all.

"Very Stieglitz," I say with a smile when he shows me the final version—his sly poke in the eye to the Modern and the ballyhoo of their recent exhibition that included my oils and six of Marin's. Despite his vindicated pride that they chose to feature two of his six artists, it infuriates him that they did not include the rest. He has always condemned what he sees as the shortsighted politics of institutions, the decisions made by faceless, rich trustees.

Just after the New Year, I learn that my brother Alexius has died. His lungs and heart had been a shambles since the war, and he caught the flu and could not survive it. He has left his wife, Betty, pregnant and with their young child. In my February exhibition at the Place, I include the abstract portrait I made of him three years ago. Beside it, the other paintings float on the walls—pictures of the Ranchos de Taos church, wooden crosses, *New York Night,* and *The Lawrence Tree,* that pine tree at Kiowa Ranch I lay under at night, staring up into the giddy swirl of branches and the blue-black falling sky. The only Lake George image is a portrait of the farmhouse I made last fall. A closed flat white door. The sea-green space of the window. It looks strangely two-dimensional against the rest. I debate leaving it in, then decide to anyway.

Stieglitz is concerned about sales. He says my new work is too daring and the world, since the market crash, is too anxious. "*You* are anxious, sweet," I say.

When I look at the work, I don't see daring. I see only the smooth forbidding beauty of a land I can't wait to pour myself back to.

DOROTHY NORMAN IS still at the gallery, managing things, keeping track of the bills. He remarks on how good she is at fundraising, skilled at plucking money out of air, but he does not seem preoccupied with her anymore. He rarely mentions her at home. Whatever was between them seems to be over. Her presence in our life has cooled, faded to the edges of things. And my work feels alive.

The Cleveland Museum of Art buys my painting of a white New Mexican flower for four thousand dollars. Can you imagine! I say when he tells me. So much money for nothing more than a flower. The money almost seems unfair when others are in such bad straits. Dove can't scrape together the twenty-two dollars he owes Stieglitz. He's lost his single source of income—magazine illustration—and doesn't have money for food, let alone paint. He and his wife are desperate. Once, at the Place, I watch as he tips black ink from the pot on Stieglitz's desk to cover a frayed spot on his overcoat. He rubs cigarette ashes into it. "Fixative?" I ask. "You fix what you can," he answers, with a grim smile.

In March, I agree to a public debate at the Breevort Bar in the Village with *New Masses* editor Michael Gold. He's an opinioned, talky man, and he starts in by chastising me for not taking a more political stance in my art. For not reflecting, as others have begun to do more frequently, the working classes who are downtrodden and oppressed. Isn't that the task of art?

He blusters on, and I study him calmly even as I feel the flush rise in my face, praying only to the low light of the bar that it will not betray me. I think about a woman I saw in the street several weeks ago. A thin, tattered boy clung to her, and she held out his hand. It filled me with rage to see her use him this way, to do her begging for her, but I pressed three coins into his hand, and his fingers grabbed them like a trap. I remember this and sit, listening to Gold, until it is my turn to speak.

And then I remark coolly that art is, fundamentally, a personal struggle, and that women as a class are, fundamentally, oppressed. My work is to free myself of male influence and say something that is inimitably mine. My *success* as an artist, to use a word that has been flung about quite liberally, is a victory for every woman. I see that woman in my mind when I say this. *Would she agree?* But I realize, too, it's not an option for me to meet this man halfway. It's not an option to offer a concession.

He is on the attack—and already has left me only a corner of ground to stand on. He sneers back that my argument is a convenient way of sidestepping economic inequity. The expression on his face makes my throat tighten—such certainty, cartoonish, the scorn in it. I find it almost shocking that I maintain an even tone in my voice when I answer him that to limit the conversation to economic oppression denies the very human issue that is at the root of this debate. And that human issue involves every woman. That is the real content, just as the form and color of a painting are its true content—deeper and more relevant than the image a picture conveys.

MABEL WRITES AND invites me back to Taos. I want to go, but can't decide. Everything feels so sweet and peaceful here with Stieglitz. I leave the letter with her invitation lying open on the table next to me as I work, but when he comes home that evening, I tell him I will go. He says he understands, as clearly as I do, that this is what I need.

"I may have to go every year," I remark, "to fill myself up again."

And so the decision is made—I'll leave in June.

I go up to the Lake alone to plant the garden and open the house. I sweep the winter from it, cobwebs from the corners, the gathering of must and stillness.

One afternoon, walking by the springhouses, I come upon a patch of jack-in-the-pulpits, just off the path.

I make six paintings of their dark-veined forms. The hooded bloom curling over the straight phallic stamen, and that curious vivid inner life, like an altar in the center, hidden in the leaves. I work through the series, canvas after canvas, the edges change, green corners become blue, leaves become sky, until all that is left is the pistil.

"These are for you," I tell him when he comes from the city and sees the Jacks for the first time.

He is busy at the Place, overseeing every detail to ensure the end of the season goes well. Every weekend, he comes to see me at the Lake. He walks into the house looking for some new thing I have done.

"I wish I could stay," he says wistfully. "By the time I take down the last show and wrap things up, you'll just be setting out to leave."

One clear night, we go for a walk. He holds my hand. "There it is," he says. Our star. The bright, strong one out over the road leading to the pasture, just glowing away up there like some young white bloom, burning.

That night we lie in bed together, my fingers braided through his. As he sleeps I remember how he would hold me above him, his hands on my ribs, when we were first together in the shoe-box room. It was something I loved, something I will always love, how he held my face, that touch that said you are like nothing that has come into the world before, and you are mine.

I fill the walls with my new pictures. So they will be here, after I am gone, reminding him.

IV

AFTER THREE MONTHS away, I return in September with over thirty paintings—landscapes, crosses, flowers.

"Every day was full of color," I say to him as we look at my work one evening, his arm around my shoulders. We sit together on the couch, turning the pages of my sketchbook filled with drawings of iris and freesia, a tree near Bear Lake, and sketch after sketch of the hills.

I tell him how once when I was driving across the sage, I watched the sky change, the low line of storm clouds gathered and began to race.

"And I raced that storm all the way back to the house," I say.

"Did you win?"

"Almost."

He laughs.

"After rain out there, Alfred, the trees are huge and black and soft. You must come with me the next time I go."

"Isn't that always how trees look after rain?"

I shake my head. "Out there it's different. Everything there is different." I show him the paintings I made at Bear Lake. I loved how the long pure line of the light reflecting off the lake made it feel solid. The mountains rose and fell like waves around it. There was snow along the ridge.

"I found an enormous dead silver tree there," I tell Stieglitz, "that had fallen across another. I climbed up onto it, and found a seat, and I rested my feet in a crook of a branch. It was a queer place to sit"— I laugh—"but exactly right for a queer sort of woman like me." And even as I say it, I realize that for every wrong thing that has passed between us these last years, he is the one person I could explain this to.

He photographs me wrapped in the black-and-white-striped Navajo blanket, and then framed by the shanty window, holding a cow skull I shipped back, my fingers splayed along the jaw.

He's been practicing his flying, and he takes me up in a little rental plane. We soar over the lake, the pressure of the wind shudders against the plane's body, and through the window I pick out the tiny curving shape of the road, houses so small against the varying tones of color that mark the hills and woods and fields. Sunlight scatters on the lake below, the shadow of our plane plows across the surface, and we are happy. He is loving, sweet and calm, listening to my stories and telling me how he's been reading Santayana and how, a week before he came back, he beat his own record at mini golf by three points.

It is like every other fall at the Lake. I paint. He proofs his photographs. We pack our things to go back to the city.

The day before we leave, I find the letter. From his niece Elizabeth—always the confidante, the one who can be trusted—to her beloved uncle Alfred. *Don't forget to register Mrs. N's letters to us, when you feel the time has come—We will keep them for you carefully— till you have worked your way through this tangle.*

I feel a faint dark crush.

Elizabeth told me what a wreck he was last summer when I was gone—how terrified he was that he would lose me from his life forever; how he tried to assuage the desperation by telling that old story of how we met—our predestined passion. She told me how he confided in her that when I was absent from the Lake, he could not get past the sense that everything familiar was turned inside out, into a kind of hell.

And all along, Elizabeth has been keeping his secret, safeguarding his letters to Mrs. Norman, so I would not discover them. All along, this other thing—this dalliance, their affair—has continued.

Such an arrogant trait—how he insists on holding on to certain pieces of correspondence for posterity, some library or museum, even while he burned so much last summer when I was gone. How much better off we'd be if he could learn to burn a thing like this.

I consider walking upstairs to our bedroom where he's resting to ask what exactly was in those letters that they're worth this kind of lie. He'll only deny it, or turn it back around on me. If this is the muck he wants to play in, I'm not going to fight him.

I fold the letter and put it back with the others where I found it. Close the drawer.

V

I STILL PLAY hostess when we have parties at the Shelton, but I've begun to move in a circle of new friends, including artists I met in Taos. I have dinner with Claudie and Ida when they have evenings off from work. I go to concerts and salons with the troika of Stettheimer sisters: Ettie the novelist in her red wigs and brocades, Florine the painter, and Carrie the elegant dollhouse designer who plans extravagant meals that last long past midnight. Her infamous "feather soup" is all the rage.

I only go to An American Place to hang the shows. Apart from that, I am rarely there. For my January show, I mix the Jacks among my abstractions, my adobe churches and gray sandhills, the red landscapes beyond Abiquiu.

I'M GOING BACK to New Mexico two months early this year, I tell him. I'll leave in April.

"There's too much here to do," he complains.

"I'll do it before I go."

He does not answer. He wants me to sort through all the works by his artists that he has in storage, to determine what will stay in storage, what will go to the Place, and what will be returned to the artists. I work five long days at the warehouse, and then it is done.

THAT SPRING, I rent a cottage on Marie Garland's ranch in Alcalde, looking out across the plains toward the dusty blue shapes of the Jemez Mountains, the starkly brilliant sky. Within a week, I've met myself again.

Day after day, it is the desolation of this country that enthralls me. How the wind sweeps the light and throws it into vibrant shifting patterns of color and shadow against the cliffs. I breathe. My mind loosens like a fist and empties. I do not think of him. I drive, I walk, I paint, and I am not the woman that he made.

I MAKE THE Model A into a studio to take out on the land. I loosen the bolts, swivel the front seat around, and prop my canvas on the reversed front seat. I sit in the back and paint. Even the thirty-by-forty canvases fit. Light pours through the window.

One morning, I drive out from Alcalde toward Abiuqiu, then farther north, a stretch I drove last year that says something to me: pale sandstone spires and black mesas. The road twists, rising higher, then widens onto a high plateau.

I paint the distance. Not a shape inside it, not a mountain or church or cross. Just distance. Line after line of horizon. Raw sienna, burnt umber, ocher, gold—the colors leave my brush, becoming light-struck dirt.

There's a timelessness to how the light here washes over the land. As I work, the air begins to beat, years condensed to an instant, tones of sky and earth blend. How easy it becomes then to strip the details from what I see—trees and rocks and brush and sage—so all that exists are long unified forms of sky and land, and the sense of my mind rushing in. Hours pass, lips dry, a fine dust on my cheeks, shoes soaked in it, as my brush sweeps over the canvas. A thin white line far

off, just glimpsed, that might be a reflection on water or an answer—
rarefied light outside of time.

After dinner that night, I sort through my finds: flowers, rocks,
bones, clumps of fossilized mussel shells, hundreds of thousands of
years old, still with a dark blue trace of the sea. With a rag I clean a
massive ram's skull, wiping grit from the eye sockets. I run my fingers over the dry flat planes of the surface, rough and gray around
the corners. His pile of letters at the other end of the table seems
weightless against the skull.

I go outside to lie on the bench and look up through the maze of
branches to the stars. There's a kind of ecstasy in the night here. You
cannot escape it, the sense of some hidden thing folded into the sheets
of space, some identity, ancient and raw, moving under what appears
to be dead.

I WRAP UP my paintings in early July. I pack the bones into a barrel
and send them off, addressed to myself in Lake George. I send a separate letter to Stieglitz, *Please do Not open my packages when they come.*

Several weeks from now, I'll pry off the barrel lid, and he will
watch, askance, still fuming from the sixteen-dollar freight charge, as
bits of the desert and dirt crumble onto the floor.

VI

LESS THAN A week at the Lake. I shouldn't have come back.

Heat. Low sky. The green close, smothering. Everything feels foreign and, at the same time, nothing has changed. Stieglitzian bickering, clutter, and chatter; the back-and-forth swish of Sel's skirts; the watermelon-sticky hands of the children; Elizabeth's sweetness that I no longer trust. His absent smile. When the mail comes, he flips through the stack of envelopes until he finds the one he's looking for and pockets it.

One hot afternoon painting in the shanty, I strip off my clothes. Sweat rises on my skin as I paint off a sketch of one of my skulls with two white cloth roses—those deathless flowers they use out in the Southwest to decorate the graves. It's oddly in balance, the severe whiteness of the bone and the pale calico of the flowers.

A chirp by the window. I glance up. Through the haze of light, giggling voices, then little hands on the sill. The younger one's head pokes up, her hair in two braids, paint on her face decorated in some very lopsided way, peering in. With three strides I'm across the room. I throw open the door, so angry I don't care that I'm naked, chasing after them with a paintbrush as they stumble away, dressed up as Indians in ridiculous fringed chintz leggings.

Back in the shanty, I latch the door. The heat is unbearable, everything just feels so impossible to do or undo. I shut my eyes and turn inward. Even my mind seems airless.

THAT EVENING AT supper, Elizabeth apologizes profusely for the children's interruption, then remarks with a coy Elizabeth smile that her daughters and their cousins talked for the rest of the day about how I was as magnificent as a goddess swooping after them, black hair streaming out, brandishing a paintbrush.

"They're quite sneaky," I say lightly. "It seems they've been well trained." I see her face flush. The phone rings. Stieglitz springs from the room. "Oh, you!" Then he turns the corner, lower tones, the words indistinct.

A wave of disgust sweeps through me. It's one thing to live in the thick of his foolishness, but another thing to be made a public fool. The others look away, all except Elizabeth—her eyes are back on me now, level, knowing everything. I want to smack that look right off her face. I get up, drop my napkin near my plate, and walk outside.

I CONFRONT HIM later upstairs.

"I'm sick of this lie, Stieglitz."

"What?"

"And how you make such a show of it—your stupid business with that stupid woman."

"You're talking about Mrs. Norman."

"No. About how you lie and deny it and rub my nose in it all at the same time."

"She is our gallery manager."

"*Your* gallery."

"Where your work is sold."

"Maybe there's another place I should think about selling it."

Silence then. The bedroom—our bedroom—feels tight and small, the twin beds pushed apart now. Paint chipped on the windowsill.

He sighs. "I need you to listen."

"I don't want to listen anymore."

"Georgia, you must try to see things from my viewpoint. If I did not have Mrs. Norman's help with the gallery, the gallery could not exist. I am not young, and the world cares little for art, and has less than that to spend on it. We've been fortunate, you and I, and we have worked hard, but I no longer have the energy to manage every detail on my own. If it were not for Mrs. Norman, we would not have a gallery for your art, and worse, I would hang on you every minute. I would try to keep you from your Southwest, your solitude, your work, everything you need."

Through the window behind him, the dusk streams over the trees. My fault again. That's what he is saying.

"You think you know what I need?" I say.

"You consider Mrs. Norman trivial. You've never extended an ounce of kindness or consideration toward her."

"Why should I?"

"Because she, her presence and fundraising, the work she does, supports your art."

"I don't need her support."

"She's integrally important to the day-to-day management of the gallery."

"And personally important to you."

"The way some things are important to you."

"It's not the same."

"When you imply I do a terrible thing because of my affection for Mrs. Norman, you do not include the fact that you have many desires. There's much you want to see and do, places you want to go. And you *must* do these things. You must be free to go away and I try to encourage your going, as hard as it is for me to have you gone, because I know that when you are happy and free, you are radiant.

You are clear and sure of self, in your person and your art. No one is more radiant. And I want that for you. And I will be here always when you return. I'll miss you when you're gone, but it is bearable."

I look at him squarely. "Don't pretend it's the same. You could go with me to Maine, or to New Mexico. You could take part in what matters to me. What part do *I* play in your affection for that woman? You've chosen something designed to run me down—"

"There's no design," he interrupts.

I look at him. His eyes meet mine, blank. Not cold. Not anything. He goes on, "I'm only trying to tell you how I see this. Lately, there's been so little honest conversation between us."

"Honest? What a strange word to use." He stares at me, and I suddenly realize he thinks that *she* is what's happened to us. "It's the lie that I hate."

"There is no lie."

"The lies and the backhanded scheming—I can't live in it."

His face crumples. "I don't want this hardness."

"This isn't my doing."

"You don't understand, Georgia, what your leaving does to me and you don't understand how much I want for you. I want the best for you. I've always wanted that."

I say nothing, and we just stand there on opposite sides of the room.

"Lie down with me," he says.

It's an awful feeling—the feeling I have in my heart, the dark soaked inside, that ache, not for him, but for what was beautiful once.

"Please," he says, and I cross the room and lie down with him in his little bed. He holds me, his mouth in my hair, promising that no matter what, from this point on there will be no more hardness.

"Don't say it," I say.

"Why?"

"Because there will be."

"No."

"When you lie to me, I don't know who you are."

I feel him shrink. "Our marriage——" he starts to say.

"I don't want to hear it." This is not, and has never been, an everyday marriage. Still, I wonder how it can happen—how there is no one else who can make me feel so much, hurt me so much or fill me so much, crack me open and make me feel so intensely and terribly alive, and sometimes when I see it like that, I can almost believe that in some separate and essential place, everything good between us—art, soul, a passion so vast—might still exist.

He touches my waist. Tentative now, almost wistful—the way he runs his hand along my body. "So beautiful," he says, that old wonder in his voice. He looks at me then, his dark eyes meeting mine, and I know what he is asking.

I almost say no, but I want to remember. I want to be in that kind of moment again, that way, only a body under his eyes—no matter how altered our life is from what it was once.

It will be beautiful. I know this even as the shutter clicks. It will be an image that I love. Down to the faint galaxy of scars on my breast. She is a country, the woman in the photographs, she is neither young nor old to him. Solely and inimitably female.

He goes back to New York to open the gallery. I stay on at the Lake to prepare for my show.

Everyone else has left. I knock out the wall between my bedroom and the closet to expand the space. I paint the floor a dark pine green and throw down my Navajo rugs. I set my bones around the house. I call them my trash, and I move other things, vases, china knick-knacks, to make room for them.

Late September, I give Margaret the day off. There's something I want to do, I tell her, and I need to be alone. I set a pair of brightly colored pajamas on a chair and prop a cow's skull against them, tinkering until the placement is right.

I begin to sketch out the shapes, abstracting the folds of cloth into the vertical plunge of a canyon. This will be my answer to the men who are always setting out to make the Great American Novel or the Great American Photograph. This will be my joke on them. Lines of red, white, and blue, and that mythic, imperfect cow skull—that piece of country—floating there through the center, the stripped cold strength of that bone that lasts and lasts, rising out of the blue like some crazy American dream. It will be unsalable—who would hang a thing like this? I don't care. They may not like it, but they'll notice. Whether they get it or not. They don't make the country like I do. They don't see that what is most magical and lush exists where you would never think to look. The bones are not what you imagine. I told Beck this once. Not death. But the life that is left over.

When I finish the painting, I study it. It isn't pretty, but it's what I want it to be.

I STRETCH NEW canvases until my fingers ache. I walk up to Flat Rock almost all the way to the birches and, when I think of Stieglitz, an unexpected warmth surges through me—something I've not felt in a very long time. This is the first fall I've stayed on alone at the Lake without him. I am working, and am pleased with the things I've made. He calls on the phone every evening. He misses me, he says. He's developing the photographs he took, and they are beautiful, extraordinary even, but not exactly what he was after. Only one or two that capture what he feels about me, that true feeling underneath all other temporary things.

I ASK MARGARET to drive down with me to the city. There are two sweaters I need to pick up at the Shelton. Then we'll go by the gallery to surprise Stieglitz, and see the new prints he's made.

In the Shelton lobby, I give a brief nod to the ridiculous life-sized wooden Indian and take the lift upstairs. I hear a woman laugh softly as the door swings open. Even before I get my mind around the sound, I tell Margaret, "Go." She steps back into the hallway with the force of my voice. I shut the door on her. Silence from the bedroom now. Then Stieglitz appears, the camera in his hand.

"What are you doing here?" he says.

I push past him, and she is there, wrapped in the bedsheets, her shoulders bare, hair loose, everything smattered with that telltale sexual disarray. The tripod is set up at the end of the bed with its black cloth, awful and familiar, not her in that bed, but me, in a different wife's room.

I turn and face him. "Get her out." I walk to the window. Behind me, I hear her scurry off the bed, a fumbling of shoes, the clatter of steps. I look out across the city as he walks her to the front door, exchanging words I can't make out and don't want to. It's ended. It could not have ended any other way. What surprises me is the flood of relief I feel, as if space has opened. At some level, I knew this was coming and I can be done waiting for it. Whatever lie he takes up next—it doesn't matter now. There's nothing here worth being honest for.

He comes back in. I tell him I want separate rooms at the Shelton.

He shakes his head. "No."

"Separate rooms," I say.

"Please, don't do this."

"You're telling me, *Don't do this?*"

He takes a step toward me. The walls tighten. I hold up my hand. "Don't."

"Georgia." Another step. "I realize you're upset."

"You realize nothing."

He reaches out. I raise my hand to strike his away, then don't. He touches my face. "I love you," he says, "no matter what you think of me, no matter what you will never believe or understand, that does not change."

I don't look at him. How small he's grown. His actions so pathetically ordinary. This guttered life. It could be anyone's.

"You are a fool," I say.

His hand drops. "If I were you, I would act differently."

"If you were me, Stieglitz, you wouldn't have done what you've done."

ON THE RIDE back to the Lake, Margaret and I don't speak. I miss the exit to Troy, an extra hour out of our way. We get caught in traffic

over the bridge in Rensselaer. The fields stare back, blank as we follow the road toward the break in the mountains. Silent, we unpack
the car. She fixes supper while I build a fire. We have not spoken more
than thirty words.

THE FIRST TIME, I let the phone ring. The second time, after nine
rings, I pick up.

"I'm going to bed," I say into the receiver.

"I don't want a separation."

"We'll talk about it later."

"That's not what I want."

"I just need to get back to work, Stieglitz. My work is what matters
right now."

The neighbors' dogs are fighting—a terrible racket, their barking
noises and snarls.

"Georgia."

"Not tonight," I say. "I'm not going to do this tonight."

HE WRITES THE following day, then again the day after. He asks when
I am coming back to New York. Margaret brings the mail. It stares at
me from the table. I wish there were no letters.

I work hard. I paint and lose myself to the smooth flow of color
filling the pores of the canvas. I work until my head is light, and the
work is good, but I don't sleep well.

I drive at dusk to the garage to get some alcohol in the car radiator
so it won't freeze. I take back the pair of Texas steer horns the me-
chanic lent to me, and he tells me a story of someone getting killed.
He is always telling those kinds of stories. The leaves are gone. All is
flat and colorless. Cold.

VIII

I ONLY COME back to the Shelton when he's done what I asked. Our things have been moved into a new, larger suite—three full bedrooms, one for him, one for me. The third I claim for my studio. I'm still not sleeping well—the noise of the city grates on me.

My December show goes up and comes down. My crosses and skulls spark all sorts of conversation and lively conjecture. Words like *mystery, cabalism, surrealism* get flung around. It all just makes me tired—having to explain what I paint or want to paint. I have nothing to say to Stieglitz or anyone else. Mrs. Norman's name does not come up. When I am planning to go by the gallery, I inform him in advance, and when I arrive she is not there. As far as I know, she's still managing things, the rent fund and whatnot. I don't care, and I don't ask. He must sense it, though, because her name has been scrubbed right out of our lives.

The marriage continues. Money, art, logistics, these are the terms that bind us now although he would never admit to seeing it this way. That's what's left.

Silence. More and more silence.

I do my work, he goes to the gallery, and the winter flows quietly by until I refuse to let him hang the nudes he took of me last fall in his February retrospective.

He demands a reason and is annoyed when I won't give one.

"Aren't they beautiful?" he says.

"Yes."

"Then why not show them?"

"I don't want them linked to my work."

"This is my work."

"You know what I mean."

His face is lit with a sudden rage, but when he sees I'm not saying it to pick a fight, only saying that, for me, something is finished and I won't relent, his eyes cool.

"You can take one of the other portraits," I say, "the one with my Navajo blanket. That one's good. But not the nudes."

HIS SHOW GOES up on February 15. He's not shown his own work since 1925. There are 127 photographs, spanning forty years. A handwritten announcement boldly stating that the gallery will be open day and night.

In the main room are seventeen images in the series of older New York: early pictures, dreamlike, elegiac, his iconic images of *The Terminal, Winter Fifth Avenue, The Flatiron,* made back near the turn of the century when the city still held that washed romantic air. There's a new series as well shot from the windows of the Shelton that documents the changing Midtown skyline. It's an artful but scathing indictment of what the city has become. The old buildings cower against the graven soulless rise of the new.

In the second gallery are his Equivalents: his clouds pictures, his landscapes of Lake George, and two pictures of Dorothy Norman. In the last room are the rest of the portraits: Marin, Demuth, Anderson, Rosenfeld, me.

One afternoon, late February, when he is going with Rosenfeld to a performance of Wagner's *Tristan and Isolde,* he asks if I would mind the gallery while he is gone.

In the lull between visitors, I walk the length of the rooms and look at each print. The sharp focus of silver tones on the new paper stand in contrast with the graduated shadows of his early pictorial work. Such severe beauty, though. In all of it. Such clarity of feeling, line, and tone. As though a breath were caught. Livingness, we called it once.

The rooms are empty. I am alone in this place that is not my place. The frosted-glass doors are closed, still, and it feels very sad—not the aloneness, but how much I once believed in what a room like this could be.

As a man, he is so impossible. Manipulative, demanding, self-absorbed. But, at the same time, he is also this. Print-to-print, I feel it like a shiver. Curiously transcendent, the incantatory power of his art. How, in a simple image, he can transform grass into water, water into the bark of a tree, the side of a building into sunlight. How he can say something about our flawed, impermanent selves in a raindrop or a cloud. This is what drew me to him. This is what I have always loved—the promise of his vision and his relentless faith in art. And even now, after all that's been undone between us, this remains.

That night after supper, I write Marie Garland to tell her I'm planning to come to New Mexico early this year. I ask if she knows anyone who might have a cottage for rent northwest of Alcalde, closer to Abiquiu.

I seal the envelope and put it with the mail to go out.

IX

TWO WEEKS BEFORE I am planning to leave for New Mexico, the noted designer Donald Deskey approaches me. He asks if I would consider a commission to create a permanent mural for the powder room on the second mezzanine of the new Radio City Music Hall at Rockefeller Center. He saw my triptych *Manhattan* in the May exhibition at the new Museum of Modern Art. He's spoken with the architect. They feel my work would be a perfect fit. They are planning to use the interior spaces and foyers to exhibit contemporary art.

It's an intriguing idea. I've always wanted to make a painting that fills an entire room. I tell Deskey I'd be interested in learning more. He enlists the dealer Edith Halpert to take it further with me. He knows whose toes he's stepping on, and he has conveniently decided to step around Stieglitz and deal directly with me. Over lunch, Edith tells me that Deskey is elated I'm considering the work—and how perfect my large flowers will be for the powder room.

When I mention it to Stieglitz, he's not pleased. He despises murals. He calls them that Mexican Disease and he's not yet forgiven the Modern for holding Diego Rivera's one-man show last fall.

"Besides," he says, "working for Radio City would be a grave mistake."

"I've accepted it."

"Only in words."

"My word is my word," I say.

"You don't know what you're agreeing to with a commission like that. When, for example, are you planning to paint this powder room?"

"Over the summer."

"What about your trip?"

"I'm going to stay and do the work instead; I'll leave when it's done."

"And if the construction's not finished by summer?"

"Then the fall."

"During the same weeks you are also painting for your show at the gallery?"

I am silent. He is making this a war.

"Industrial design is not the same as art, Georgia. Their objectives and yours are not the same."

"It's a project I want to do, Stieglitz."

"And what have they said they'll pay?"

"That's not quite settled." The wrong answer, I know, the moment it slips from my mouth.

"What figure was discussed?"

"Every artist hired will be paid the same."

"What was the figure?"

I meet his eyes. "Fifteen hundred."

He snorts. "Unthinkable!"

"I want to do this project, Stieglitz."

"You are an artist. This is not an artistic decision. Your sales control the value of your art."

I feel the space collapse. His nerve-bending logic.

"I work tirelessly, Georgia, tirelessly, to build the value of your art. I won't sell a painting for less than it's worth. I've finally agreed to let the Whitney buy one of your canvases for almost five thousand dollars, and now you've agreed to paint an entire room for less than a third of that."

"I told you the figure isn't settled."

"And you're naïve enough to believe that once they've given you a figure, and you've given them your word, they'll go higher?" The disdain in his voice is palpable.

I meet his eyes. "I'm going to do this work."

"I do not agree."

"You don't have to," I say calmly. "Because I see it now. This isn't about my decision at all, is it, Stieglitz? It's because I made the decision without you."

He turns and walks out of the room. That's the end of it. The last word. And for the first time, I wonder if I've made a mistake. Not by what I've said or felt or done, but years ago. Where would I be now if I had never stepped foot into the hot fire of the shoe-box room? If I had not come to him, who would I be?

IN JUNE, I go up to the Lake to open the house. We do not discuss Radio City. But he has voluble conversations with Elizabeth and Rosenfeld about "the whole mural business."

One night I dream of my mother—I wake with a start, the sense of her fills me, the craving I once felt for her to break out of the sternness she held herself to, and love me, notice me. *Beautiful.* Just the word shivering in the half-light of the dawn. *You are beautiful.* Words she never said.

I get out of bed and go downstairs. Stieglitz is already awake, fixing his cocoa. We say little. I pour my tea. The liquid steeps, wafts of brown leaking into the clear.

"Milk?" he says, nodding to the bottle.

"No, thank you."

He places the bottle back into the ice chest and leaves the room.

I walk for hours that morning. Walk straight and fast, thighs burning up the hill through the tall grass into the shade. There's a grief in my chest so deep and sharp. I can't shake the image of my mother's face, the intensity of her dark eyes, her unused life.

I'M EXHAUSTED, DARK loopy shadows under my eyes. Still no word about the powder room. Time feels all cut up. Just waiting. What a waste of a summer.

"You've lost weight, Georgia," Rosenfeld remarks one evening when we're all reading in the front room after supper. "Are you feeling all right?"

I smile at him. "I'll be fine once fall rolls around."

"It's that Radio City," Stieglitz cuts in, "doing a job on her nerves."

"That's not what it is, Alfred."

"I've known from the start it would."

"I'm not going to talk about this."

"You should reconsider."

"I won't."

"You don't know what you're getting into."

I lose it then. It just snaps right out—"You think you know what's right for me, Stieglitz—you've always thought every decision was yours to make about what I could do, should do, and every time I've wanted something else, or struck out on my own, you've found some way to get me back underfoot and stamp me down. Radio City's a job I want to do. And it's a job I can do. Paint on canvas. It's as simple as that. And I need you to stay out of it, or I'll be on that train heading west with no return ticket."

He says nothing then, after that. Nothing at all. No one does. He only looks down and shakes his head. I glance at Rosenfeld whose face is red, his drooping eyes, sad features sliding away.

"I'm sorry, Pudge," I say. I go upstairs to my bedroom and close the door.

———

In September, I phone Deskey and arrange for a meeting to discuss the contract. I go down to New York. We take a tour of the powder room. Construction is running well behind schedule; there's scaffolding everywhere.

"It's going to be hard for me to paint a room that's not finished," I say.

"I assure you it will be finished soon, Miss O'Keeffe."

"When, precisely?"

"By the end of the month."

"This month?"

"Yes."

We quibble over canvas. He knows little about art and wants me to paint directly onto the plaster. I refuse and explain I'll need the canvas applied to the walls and the vaulted dome of the ceiling.

"That will be difficult," he says, "given the curves of the room and the mirrors. There will be eight round mirrors."

"Mr. Deskey, this is either a commercial project or an artistic one. There are dozens of painters skilled in advertisement boards if that's what you want, but if you want me, it has to be done my way. The surface has to be right. It must be canvas and it must go all the way through the room so the perspective is continuous."

"You know exactly what you want," he says. "I'm impressed. Very well, Miss O'Keeffe, we are so looking forward to having your art on these walls. I'll be sure to have the canvas applied to your specifications."

We walk back to his office to look over the contract.

"My one concern is the time frame," I say.

"I've heard you paint quickly."

"But if the room's not ready—"

"It will be."

"I see."

"We'd like your work completed by November first."

"My work will be completed if the room is ready by the end of this month. I'll need four weeks. The plaster must be entirely dry before the canvas is applied, and the canvas itself must be perfectly smooth."

"I assure you, it will be."

"Fine then."

"*You* are a pleasure to work with, Miss O'Keeffe."

We both know what he is not saying—that Stieglitz is far from that. I sign and slip the contract across the desk. I am aware I should be apprehensive. The close time frame. The scale of the project. Doing it against Stieglitz's will. But in my mind's eye, I can see the powder room already finished—the curved ceiling's corners, enormous flowers blooming from the walls.

"Very well, then," Deskey says, standing, "so it is done!"

A firm handshake.

It is done.

STIEGLITZ IS ENRAGED when I return to the Lake to tell him the contract is signed. Beyond enraged when I acknowledge the terms. It is Rosenfeld—dear Pudge—who talks him down, pointing out in his kind voice that now that the agreement is finalized, there's no reason to oppose it.

"Besides," Rosenfeld says, "I've just heard Stuart Davis is doing the murals for the men's lounge." This gives Stieglitz pause. Davis is an artist in the Ashcan School. Never one of the circle, but his cubist landscapes are bold. Even if his brash imagery—gas pumps and jazz—aren't to Stieglitz's taste, no one can deny his prowess.

"Let Georgia do this with your blessing," Rosenfeld says gently. "You'll find a way to make it right." And it occurs to me then that Rosenfeld is perhaps the one person in our world who's always wanted us to succeed. Even now when I am so wrung out with all the machinations and fight over this job, here is Rosenfeld contending in his calm way that there is good that can still come of this. It lifts me.

Stieglitz clatters around for another few days, still irascible, but the gears of his mind have shifted. I can feel it. He knows Rosenfeld is right. If he wants to continue to manage my career, he might as well get on board. He starts to allude to some of the advantages of taking the commission. Not directly to me. He won't straight-out admit I was right. But he starts to consider the upsides. Stuart Davis for one. My giant flowers in a place every rich modern woman with her grand-daughter will pass through. But he's still not pleased with the money. "That's no good as it stands," I hear him say one day to Rosenfeld. "There has to be a way to redress that to our favor." Finally, at the end of the month, I agree to let Stieglitz meet with Deskey on my behalf to discuss the terms of the contract.

"Ask him to shift the date back," I say.

"I'm going to discuss the money as well."

"Focus on the date, Stieglitz. It's a huge project, and I want to do it, but November first may not give me as much time as I'd like if the construction continues to drag."

"I'll insist it's pushed back," he says. "It's an impossible date. Several points need to be revised. You'll do the work for free. They can reimburse us for materials, but if it's for free, as Pudge suggested so brilliantly, there's no dollar amount to smear your value."

"I don't care what you do about the money," I say, "as long as I get to do the work. But focus on the date. I want more time."

HE SWEEPS DOWN to New York, meets with Deskey and the architect, and returns to say that all is squared away. They've accepted his revisions. Everything is settled, the date has shifted from November 1st to the 15th. I'll do the work unpaid. And now we can all move forward.

To my relief, dinner-table conversation shifts to whether Governor Roosevelt will, in fact, win the presidential election. Every time the radio's turned on, his voice seems to be there, promising that the federal government will regulate industry to create new jobs. Not one of us knows how that will work. But the newness of it instigates all sorts of vociferous debate that spills from the dining room into the living room and soaks up the long evening hours.

The Lake feels odd. A kind of weightlessness to things now that the battle about Radio City is over. I've won. I know that, but all the fight has worn me down. My mind feels flayed. It's all been such a struggle and, really, for what? To get my art on some bathroom walls? Sometimes it seems just that inane.

I think about New Mexico. Sometimes it's all I think about— leaving here, going back. How long would I stay? Four weeks? Three months? Forever? I miss it. And I hold that sense of missing it close to me at night when I can't sleep. I remember once, driving out in Taos, I hit a patch of loose gravel. I wasn't expecting it. There was nothing as far as the eye could see and I was looking at the sky, my eyes following a raven, when the road changed, suddenly uneven under the tires. The car started to slide. I cut the wheel back to straighten it. I remember hearing the sound of low free laughter and realizing that laughter was mine, as I pressed my boot down hard on the pedal and drove it toward the floor, speeding faster, into that endless pellucid distance that flowed into me and around me, as godlike and intimate as breath.

In the shanty, on a massive canvas, I paint from memory. Jimsonweed—those white trumpet shapes that grow everywhere along the arroyos, opening after dusk, their fragrance strong through the night. Every part of the plant is poisonous. Once cut, the bloom will last only hours. I paint the flower cropped, right to the edge of the canvas, the curls of the blue-green leaves like an echo behind. At one point, I close my eyes and see the shape against my lids—the grace as it falls, more alive than if it were in front of me. I feather thin layers of paint into edges—edge after edge. I want to lift the essence out of every intricate detail, each crease in the leaves, each naked line—so much larger than life, this flower, the eye can't pull away. I want to lose myself in the pale throat of that flower, its mystery, surfaces softened to such a degree you will not see my hand, the petals so smooth you can almost feel them against your cheek. There is no play here. There is rigor and balance and clarity. This is a story of edges. This is a story of how something as unstable as a petal or a wave can become a definitive edge.

When the picture is done, I paint another, but the composition is off from the start. My hands, the color, the form, nothing seems to be working. An upper petal distorts, like dolphin lips. Unfixable. I quit and cut it off the frame.

IN MID-NOVEMBER, FINALLY, Deskey phones to say the powder room is ready. I pack my things and go down. Radio City is a madhouse. Workmen streaming everywhere, plaster, sawdust, half-finished light fixtures, wires popping out, ladders leading sky-high to holes in the wall. A chandelier lies in the center of the dark-red carpet in the lobby, a massive X and circle marked on the ceiling directly above. I step carefully around it, following Deskey and an assistant. We thread our way through the chaos up to the second mezzanine, and walk through a space in the framing. The powder room is pristine. A gleaming whiteness. Everything as we agreed. Canvas, perfectly smooth, wraps the walls, the gentle dome of the ceiling, and each curved corner. The eight mirrors wink back at us. I skim my fingertips over the walls, and feel a quick joy. This is what I wanted. This is what I went to war with Stieglitz over. A vast landscape. A fresh start.

I turn to Deskey and smile.

"You are pleased, Miss O'Keeffe."

"Yes."

He leaves his assistant with me. As I am unpacking my things, I notice the smell—that light sweet stink of wet. Moisture in the air. I can feel it on my face and hands. I hadn't noticed at first. My heart sinks. This room is not ready. I glance at the assistant, but she has sat down on a box and is busy writing a few things into a stenograph notebook. I scan the walls. My eyes fall on a slight shadow in the corner—a raised point in the surface. I walk over to it and run my hand along the canvas below that corner. It's dry in spots, but not everywhere; there are distinct places where I can feel the damp of wet plaster underneath. My fingers come to a lump near a seam. With a fingernail, I puncture it. White goo seeps out.

I turn to the girl. "Get him."

"Mr. Deskey's in a meeting until noon."

"Just get him."

She hurries off. I continue walking around the room. I can see it now, feel it—this whole room is a disaster—nothing's what it seems. There's nothing pristine about this. Nothing dry or clear or beautiful. Nothing brave or bold or real. I feel a wave of fury. Here I am again. Held down, held back, in a power struggle with some arrogant man, his ego and incompetence that has nothing to do with my art. It's like they're all together in some maddening conspiracy to make me good enough but not good enough to topple them. A deranged thought. I know it. And yet. My fists clench. I notice then a light-brown stain on the floor. I bend and sweep my fingers through it. Kerosene.

What a mess. This room. This project. This decision I made. A ruin.

I'm putting my things away when Deskey comes in.

"You put canvas up on wet plaster," I say, trying to keep my voice even.

"Miss O'Keeffe, please."

I continue packing away sketchbook, charcoals, paints, the few brushes I took out. I replace them now in their long beds, everything neatly arranged. My hands burn—all the shame and frustration and rage has gone to my hands.

"Miss O'Keeffe?"

I look at him. "I can't work on this surface."

"We'll fix it."

I want to laugh, or slap him.

"I give you my word."

"Mr. Deskey," I say coldly. "I told you from the start, I won't work under these circumstances. You were not honest with me and you know it. When was this room plastered? Two, three days ago? Then canvas slapped up, and a kerosene heater to force it dry? Do you think I'm that stupid?"

"This can all be redressed. I assure you. We'll fix it."

"You can't fix this. This whole room will have to be stripped and redone, and even if you do that by the day after tomorrow, it's still going to take another three weeks to dry in."

"We'll extend the contract."

I hear the assistant gasp. A huge piece of canvas has begun to sag from one of the opposite ceiling corners. It goes down in slow motion, a slow loosening wave away from the curve of the wall.

I turn to Deskey. "I won't do this work."

"We have a contract."

"I'm not going to do it."

I leave the room and walk out into the street. The blaze of the concrete, the brash black shine of the cars, things seem outrageous, overloud, my mind barely hanging together.

AT THE SHELTON, I tell Stieglitz the job is over. Done. He's had his way. This mural business, what a failure it's turned out to be—just as he so prophetically claimed—the walls literally falling apart.

"Say it. Say: *I told you so.*"

"I wouldn't say that, Georgia. Ever."

Lie. I sink into the sofa, head in my hands, nerves shot. So absurd. Imagining I needed to do something like this to make a point, for no other reason than because it was work I thought I wanted.

"I'll take care of it tomorrow," he says. "Tell me what you want. I'll make it happen."

"Just get me out. It's done. I'm done."

I break down into tears. The cushion bends as he sits beside me.

The calm pressure of his hand on my back. My chest tightens. I don't want his hand near me.

"I'll fix it tomorrow, Love." His voice is awful and gentle, sweet of course, because this is how he needs things to be. He can love me this way—when I'm weak and in pieces, when he can play the hero. The whole thing is just so damning. All I wanted was the work.

X

I DON'T GO out. I don't want to see anyone.

No ambition. No impulse moving in me. Only the deadness of feeling I seem to be trapped under. Scraped up by the failure of everything.

I think about New Mexico—the hills, the distance, the space, the sky. I need to go there. I need to be in it. I've never gone in winter. I don't know who is out there in winter, though someone must be. I need a plan. I make a mental list. Write Marie Garland. Or Frieda Lawrence. Call Brett. I can't call Mabel. The whole public debacle of Radio City is just the kind of gossip she delights in. How she'd lord that over me.

Just go. Pack. Find a train. Go west to Catherine's. Stay a few weeks. Keep going.

It hardens into resolve, but then feels like too much, all those machinations, conversations. Too much to explain.

I sew and fix my canvases. I try to paint. All I want is to work, to get back to what I know. I want the freedom again to be alone in the room. I put the brush to the paper, but it just slips around. No shapes. No burn. Nothing.

STIEGLITZ CALLS THE Shelton twice a day from the gallery to check on me. Once at ten. Again at two.

His voice on the phone urges me to paint. "It will make you feel better," he says.

"I don't feel anything."

"You're so fragile right now, aren't you? Oh, my Love."

Is that what you're telling them? I think. That I'm *fragile*. That Radio City has ground me right down? That I am *your Love* and it's all such a shame. Bastard. The word echoes in my head.

"I'll be fine," I say, but my voice rings flat and he says so.

"Georgia, please try to be well."

Which feels like somewhat senseless advice given the box of a life I live in.

A HORSE'S SKULL, I decide, only because my eyes happen to fall on that when I'm hanging up the phone one morning. I make a few sketches, then set a canvas on the easel in my studio. I squeeze out the colors into their discrete piles on the palette, sit there and wait. I don't seem to know what comes next. Everything is gray compared with the colors on the glass palette. The floor, my dress, my shoes.

I dip the very tip of my brush into the blue. I want to taste it. I want the thrill of color moving inside me again. The brush floats near the canvas. Where to start? Where to start? A stroke there, but the moment I've made it, it's wrong. Everything I've done, what I've let happen, all wrong. In that ruined stroke on the canvas, I see: It makes no difference. What I do or don't do. Where I go. I'm so far from that girl who was once so full of passion it poured out into shapes on paper. Now it seems I have no passion. No clear vision. Now I have nothing. I'm weak in a way I despise. Weak, in a way I never dreamed I could be.

This isn't just him, and what he's done to me. It's what I've let him do.

I walked in with my eyes wide open. I was the one who reached out on that train platform, drew his face to mine, and kissed him that first time. I knew who he was from the start. I knew what he was capable of, and I knew what I'd become for him—artist, lover, muse. I knew where that sled going downhill was headed, and I knew what I'd get out of it. What I did not know is what I'd give up.

I run my fingertip from the ferrule down the handle to its end, dig the point into my palm, press deeper until the pain spikes, a funny white burst in my head—an exploding star.

"You'll be all right," he says one morning on his way out the door to the Place. Such a ridiculous thing to say, I am going to point out, but then he turns and darts over to the table, looking for something he must have set down, in the wrong place evidently because he can't find it now, a promise to phone, then gone, the apartment empty. Out the window, a very far distance down, umbrellas knock around like small black flowers on a gray moving stream. I step back, startled.

Lying in bed, I walk the rooms of the house where I grew up, the kitchen where my mother peels potatoes, past the room where my father's brother lies dying from TB. I walk back and forth, looking for the door, which is not in its proper place. I slip through the walls, outside. In the distance, I can see my father. His back is always to me, his tall form always moving away. Two of my sisters are in the garden, their heads bent close together; their dresses glimmer in the sun, their hands touch, and they hold a creature between them, an injured bird cupped between their joined fingers. Then one—Claudia?—glances up and sees me. "Georgia, come!" she cries, and I feel a surge of joy. The trees ring with her voice. The moment shatters, so beautiful and precious, the shed pieces of one moment giving way to the next, and I understand that this is where life dwells—in the unregistered time between moments when you are filled with no thought, no awareness, just a garden, ancient sunlight, your sister's voice.

I knew it then. As children, we are oracles. We are flesh, hunger, eyes. As a child, I could hear the stir and groan of clouds. I could feel the shift in the grass, blades parting under the wind, the yawn and stretch of a bud, opening—

The memory snaps.

I CRY UNTIL I am an ocean, until the walls slip down. The bed does not feel safe. I get out of it and into a corner, where the walls come together like I could press myself right through that line.

He finds me in the evening when he arrives home, crying at the teetered edge of everything. Hands over my ears to keep out the sound in my head. My knees shoved in tight, to keep it all held together, to keep some inkling of myself in myself, my body pressed as hard as I can get it into that seam of the wall.

What have we done? I start to ask him, open my mouth to ask, but the words don't come. He kneels beside me.

HE CALLS MY sister Anita, who comes. She helps me pack a few things and brings me to her apartment. I spend Christmas there, in a room that is my own, luxurious and large, but not, in the end, enough to hold the avalanche falling down inside me.

Noises everywhere. And a stabbing fear of water. I can't even run a bath. Stieglitz comes to see me nearly every day. There's nowhere safe. He sits by my bed in a chair. I can't bear it, and finally I whisper to Anita, *Tell him to go.* Can't bear to see him, can't bear to think, because of all that I remember of what I was and dreamed and wanted.

XI

EIGHTY-EIGHTH AND EAST End. Doctors Hospital. In the white room where they've placed me for safekeeping, my ears fill with voices. Loud, bright, a million unknown tongues.

For most of the day, I am alone. The nurses come through with cool efficient hands. They change the bedpan, bring meals I barely touch, and check my pulse. Once a day, the doctor glides in on his rounds. Then they are all gone, the door sealed shut, and I am alone again. My mind drains out. The dead come from far away, looking not as they should. My mother. My father. My dear brother Alexius. And the ceiling is there in the corner, and my soul, if there is a name for that transparent part of me that comes and goes, has gone to do its business elsewhere.

I hear the sound of water—the roar of the sea at night in Maine, the black underwater sound of the Lake that night in the storm, so many years ago, when the boy tipped over out of his canoe, the beautiful youth of that boy a casualty, perhaps the first casualty, of our petty arguing, our discontent.

I can feel the weight of a body in the bed. Head. Buttocks. Legs. Arms. A strange body in a stranger's bed.

And I ask Stieglitz, who is not here: "Is this my comeuppance? You always said it was the blazing hunger in me that you loved, but is this what I get? For being a woman who wanted too much—too much feeling, too much freedom, too much sky?"

How guilty I have been of that wanting.

I am not the woman you mistook me for. I was never whiteness. I was never pure. I was never the woman with the unpocked skin and the beautiful hands in the photographs.

I am thinking these things when the wall opens, and his head comes through—then the whole of him appears in the sliding wall that I suddenly realize is the door. Dressed in black, a stricken concern on his face—a grief so torqued, fraudulent, with that treacherous loden cape.

He takes a step toward the bed, and there is screaming. A woman screaming in my head, and I see in his face he hears her, too.

Nurses appear, clothed in their whites, scrubbed hands take him by the arm and draw him quickly, firmly, back through the hall.

The door shuts. The screaming stops. I can still hear, faintly, the grain of his voice in the hallway. *She is my wife.*

HIS LETTERS COME to me in the white room. The everyday details and abstract wonderings it's his luxury to have. I do not answer. I have nothing to say. They have given me paper, and it sits in a neat short stack, eyeing me blankly on the table by the bed, a pen beside it. Anita comes with Ida. They bring me books and magazines to read. My mind spools back somewhat while they are there, then weakens when they leave. I take short walks in the hallway. I write to Beck, but the handwriting is someone else's handwriting—crumpled, frail.

After four weeks, I am well enough that the doctors permit him to visit for ten minutes. We meet each other like strangers.

"Won't you sit down?" I point to the visitor's chair. The air in the room is polite.

"How are you?" he asks.

That is a rotten question. He should know by now.

"What have you brought?" I point to the slim packet under his arm.

Photographs, it turns out, of my exhibition titled *Paintings—New & Some Old*. There is my trumpet flower; a slim cross; barns and shells.

Art on the little hospital table between us. After all, this is what we know how to do—this calm, almost habitual practice we are proficient at—studying a few pieces of art no matter how roiling the world around us is. It is after all what first bound us together, then saved us—if one would call it that—again and again.

"Tasty food here," I say. "Eggs this morning."

"I've wanted you to see your show."

I touch the edge of a print.

"I think it would be good for you to see it, Georgia."

"Yes, I do see. Thank you for thinking of me and bringing these."

"No, I mean I think you should see them on the walls of the Place."

His voice has that urgency—that dark push in it I once loved. It fritters me now.

"I don't believe they'll let me out," I say carefully. "I'll discuss it, though, with the doctor when he comes."

"I've already asked," he says.

"Of course you have," I murmur.

"He said if you are willing . . ." Again the pleading look. I feel my heart sink. Walls everywhere. "Please, Georgia." I notice an uneven patch of white scruff at his chin where the razor skipped a spot. "Please," he says, again.

Of course I will go. I should want to. To see my things, my show that he's put up for me. This is what a good wife would do, I think to myself. Which is not the reason I will go. Just to be clear. But right now it's too much work to argue.

———

ANITA BRINGS ME to the Place. Stieglitz is in the back room, reading the paper, a letter drying on the desk. He leaps to his feet as we come in, so youthful, bounding across the room toward me. I try not to shrink.

"I wanted sunlight for you," he says, a sweeping gesture toward the window and the scud of clouds through it. "It was here an hour ago, I begged it to stay. Alas." He smiles.

Alas.

The floor spins. I feel a little sick to my stomach. He has taken my hand, a firm pressure. It should be comforting, his hand. I can only manage to stay for twenty minutes. Even that feels too long. The Place, I notice, is empty apart from us.

"Just last week, Elizabeth Arden bought one of the earlier flower paintings," he reports.

"And from this show—has anything sold?"

He shakes his head. "Not yet."

Because the new work's no good, I think. The lines are very nicely done—all that—but you can't put the bold back in when it's gone.

He glances away. He clears his throat. He seems to be waiting.

Let him wait.

AT THE END of the month, when I am released from the white room, I can't bear to go back to the Shelton. That vertiginous view, too intense.

We pack our things and speed north. The countryside is familiar—like a ride I took once. I do not tell him this is how it feels to me. Then I would have to explain it.

After two days, he leaves me in Margaret's charge. For weeks, I am boneless, drifting. I do nothing but sleep until late morning, lie in the sun, and eat until my underwear no longer fits, and I have to wear Stieglitz's undershorts. I can't get back into myself. My insides are a scrap bag, full of limp mismatched things. I take the new roadster convertible up to flat ground so I can walk. The hills feel like too much effort. I keep the top down and drive very slowly, not quite trusting myself.

A stray cat has begun to come around the house. I name her Long Tail and watch her little pink tongue lap cream off the inside surface of the bowl. She is one long feathery gesture, like a stroke in charcoal I might have made once in another life when every day was a different color.

When Stieglitz arrives for the summer, he banishes the cat. He's always despised them. I dissolve into tears, and she stays.

IT'S ODD HAVING him around, going through the motions of a husband and wife, as if that still had relevance. It does seem to, though, to him. He is attentive, aware of me moment-to-moment, where I am in the house, what I might need, my happiness, my mood. Almost as if he believes this will be our life again, reconstituted. As if I've only temporarily stepped away.

At one point when things feel nice between us, I try to explain that something in me is broken, more than broken, and that thing is the very part of me that drew him in the first place. He looks at me sadly. The sunlight through the trellis tattoos one side of his face.

"You'll get well," he insists. "You must rest. You *will* get well."

I wonder who he is trying to convince.

HE WRITES LETTERS to those who cannot come to visit because of my "illness." He knows they cannot come without my having to say anything. All I have to do is turn into myself and go silent when he brings up the possibility of inviting so-and-so. The silence frightens him, although at times I sense a trace of irritation, perhaps because he is helpless to fix it and he knows the last thing he can do is get angry.

He works on drafts of the essays for the new book. *America and Alfred Stieglitz: A Collective Portrait.* Waldo Frank is editing it. My art will be featured, though I am not submitting a written piece. Everyone else is: Marin, Strand, Dove, Anderson, William Carlos Williams, Gertrude Stein—all have written some glowing laudatory piece about Stieglitz.

The Hill is quiet. My heart has begun to settle. Some days, it seems so still I wonder if it's stopped.

Beck writes from Taos. She and Paul have separated. She has gone back out west to be with a man who runs a trading post there. Stieglitz and I don't discuss it, like we've tacitly agreed it's better that way. *You'll manage, dear Beck,* I write to her. *Someday, this will seem a small thing.*

I haven't painted since last fall. One day I am surprised to see the goldenrod in bloom. A year since I saw it last. Is that possible? I walk out to the shanty, sit in the meadow, and wait for myself to come back.

STIEGLITZ STARTS TO go back and forth to New York to prepare for the Marin exhibit.

One weekend when he comes up to visit we lie in bed together before breakfast. He kisses me gently, peels the clothes from my body, and makes love to me. It is slow and sad, like a leave-taking. He holds me afterward—how tender it feels, lying together like this.

"It should have always been like this," I say.

"I know," he answers, but I can see he really doesn't, he only says it to please me. My eyes fill—such a rotten betrayal, those hot tears I crumple into. He whispers my name and pulls me closer, and I let him, a part of me wishing I could lose myself there all over again.

Later that morning, we take a walk up Hubble Lane. He tells me the news from the city. How Rosenfeld stopped by the gallery with the artist Cady Wells who asserted that my *Black Iris* is arguably the greatest painting in the world. And the young poet Cary Ross lost a drinking contest against Scott Fitzgerald, whose wife, Zelda, does watercolors and drawings. Apparently, about a year ago, she raved to Cary about some things of mine she saw—but now she's locked up in her own white room. We talk about this, and other things that have to do more with other people, and only obliquely with us. So many names to keep track of. All these names prop something up in him. Funny, how clearly I see it all now.

As we come back around to the house, we linger under the old chestnut trees. The leaves a swath of purple, yellow, scarlet at our feet.

"There was an owl in these trees just three days ago," I say. "Such a great big thing, that bird."

He tells me how last week, back in the city, he was going through some things in storage, and found a batch of photographs he had taken so many years ago when I first came to him. Platinum prints and early Palladios.

I don't want to hear about this.

"Look at the yellow leaves," I say, reaching to one still on a branch. Unthinkably bright. I touch it—that's all it takes—it falls.

"Those photographs of you were so beautiful," he continues.

"Why did you come this weekend, Alfred?"

"To see you."

"Sometimes it feels you come to see me, call and write and all the rest, because you feel you ought to."

"I come because I want to."

"It doesn't quite seem so." I don't mean to be unkind when I say it. It's just a fact. But he is hurt.

"Sometimes," he says, "I wonder if I'd not run across you, if you would have been better off."

A pointless question, now, for either of us.

I change the subject. "How is Dove? I keep meaning to ask you."

Over the past few months, I have begun to see all too clearly what is true: what we did and failed to do, what we believed and wanted and destroyed.

I don't say this. There's a split now between what I will tell him, and this other stirring thing in me—a tiny, keen life that moves like a little plant in its own black soil with its separate thinkings.

———

I PACK HIM a sandwich for the train, cut celery and cake.

"Don't forget to have your buttonholes fixed." I point to where they have loosened, threads spitting out. It kicks in me—a funny sadness—that his coat doesn't fasten properly because he doesn't have the time, or take the time, to have something so everyday and essential mended.

"I could fix them for you," I say.

"No, no, Love," he says absently. "I'll have it done."

I STRIP THE sheets from his bed to wash. I fold the blankets and place them in the closet. Leaving the room, I pause by the window. Grass strung through with wet dusk, the poplar like some unearthly sentinel against the sky. He claimed this bedroom, years ago, for the view. Every time he arrives at the Lake, the first thing he'll do is come upstairs to see it. This matters to him, so deeply, to know that everything is as it has been and as he expects it to be.

The kitchen is empty, a bowl of eggs on the counter Margaret must have brought. Her coat gone from the peg. She must be outside somewhere. I fix my tea and write to him. How hard a letter is now. I force myself to fill a page. I write about the cat, about the house. I inquire about his day. So much work, it seems, to come up with this litany of news that sounds like something but amounts to nothing. I put the pen down. I remember when he first wrote to me about the Lake, he and his life only the gauze of a dream. I was still in Texas, my body already filling with his faith: in my talent, my art, in what I wanted, the risks I'd only just begun to take. I poured my entire self into my letters to him.

Through the kitchen window, the shapes of the sky—a zigzag of spindly treetops. Light echoes in the glass. Just a small quiver. But something moves in me, watching it.

XII

SNOW BEGINS TO fall. A light dusting of white on the ground, the last burnished leaves. I move a cot into the front room downstairs. Everything sits, my rocks and bones on the shelves. Easel, paints, brushes, still waiting for me.

Jean Toomer writes from Chicago, looking to see if I've kept any letters I might have received from his dead wife, Margery Latimer. Margery died in childbirth—she began to hemorrhage, but she was a Christian Scientist, and so no doctor was called. She delivered the baby and, several moments later, lapsed into a coma and died.

In his letter, Toomer says he's coming east to gather Margery's correspondence for a memorial collection. I write back. *Yes, I believe I do have one she sent to me, a lovely letter—she was a beautiful soul, your wife. I'll be in the city later this month. I'll find that letter for you then.*

I had not in fact planned a trip down to New York, but now there it is. So funny—that little intent inside me working away on its own, leaving aside my daylight mind.

———

"I DON'T SEE why you won't stay at the Shelton," Stieglitz says when I tell him I'm coming to the city.

"I'm going to stay at Anita's."

I can feel his uncomprehending sadness, a crinkle in the silence on the phone line.

IN NEW YORK, I go to the Brancusi exhibit, and visit with my sisters. I ask Claudia to stop by the Shelton with me so I can hunt up that letter for Toomer. I keep my arm tucked through hers as we make our way down Fifth. "It's somewhat thrilling," I say, "that I can walk in the streets again without losing my mind."

After lunch with Rosenfeld on Thursday, I stop in at the Place to see Marin's new landscapes. As I'm studying one, the slightly cubist thing he's doing with planes of space and color, I sense a presence behind me, and turn. For a moment, I don't recognize him. Then I realize that it's Jean.

"So good to see you!" I say.

"And you as well." He presses my hand, his fingers warm.

"I couldn't find that letter," I say. "I'm sorry. It seems I've misplaced it. It was an extraordinary piece of writing, and I'll keep looking."

"How long are you in the city?" he says.

"Too long already."

He tells me he's working on his essay for the Stieglitz portrait. He needs a quiet place to finish it and is going to talk with a friend who has a house on Long Island.

"Come to the Hill," I say. "If you're writing about Stieglitz, isn't that where you should be?"

"I never thought of it."

"Nothing but quiet this time of year. The house is drafty, but if you don't mind a few sweaters along with some mice to share the kitchen with, consider it."

"I think I could brave that." A pause. "All right," he says. "I'll come."

AFTERWARD, I WILL see my invitation as strange, as it must have seemed to him. Stieglitz, however, is ecstatic that I'm feeling well enough to suggest a visitor.

"You'll be yourself again," he says. I almost smile. He has a new Picasso drawing in the office—a standing nude. I want it for the upstairs hall at the Lake. He gives it to me happily, and I leave the Place.

I think of Jean again on the train back up to Lake George, the drained fields rushing by. Through the window, a light snow has begun to fall. The sky breaks up into soft flakes floating down.

THE FIRST WEEK he is there, I spend the better part of every day closed up in my bedroom with a miserable cold. I hear him moving through the house, talking to Margaret. He makes her laugh, and laughs with her. A good strong sound, the way he laughs. Then long hours of silence, only the tap-tapping of his fingers on the typewriter keys. He works all day, then goes out and does our errands. He gets the mail no matter the weather. He starts my car to make sure the engine doesn't freeze.

"It's quite nice," I remark to him one evening at supper, "to have you around. Very useful."

He looks at me across the roast beef in the center of the table, unsure of the tone in my voice—if I am teasing.

"You've been quite taken by that head cold of yours since I arrived."

"That doesn't mean it hasn't been nice."

And it has been. Unexpectedly nice. Having someone here preoccupied with his own thoughts, work, and silence.

THE TEMPERATURE OUTSIDE plunges to eight below. The lake skims over with a layer of ice.

That afternoon, I make up my little cot downstairs by the window, add two more blankets, and crawl under them to read from the new Jung book Stieglitz gave me down in the city. From some far-off corner of the house comes the soft tapping of his typewriter, his fingers on the keys, a pause between thoughts, then the uneven sound taken up again, tap-tap-tapping. A drawer closes above, a door opens, footsteps on the stairs, coming down. He walks into the living room, and stops, surprised to see me there.

"Could you get me some water?" I ask.

He goes out and returns with a glass. "So, at last, she has surfaced to the world," he says.

"Barely."

"Stieglitz wrote a few days ago to say how he worries after you."

I nod. "Give it one more day, he'll catch the cold. My sister Ida puts it in this way: One of us sneezes and we both get sick."

Toomer laughs.

I take a sip of water. "Next life, I think I'll come back as a blond soprano."

"Spare us."

"No," I say. "A blond soprano who can sing very high, clear notes that shatter the glass."

"You'd break all the windows."

"That's exactly what I'd do. And I'd be living in a place where there was not this kind of winter, and one could afford to lose a window now and then."

"Taos, perhaps?"

"Taos is awfully incestuous—lots of high drama."

"Too much for your taste?"

"By tenfold."

His eyes slide over my face to my throat. It is only a moment. Then he gets up and says he needs to refill the wood box before dark.

———

THE NEXT MORNING we have frozen pipes. Putnam comes up from Bolton's Landing.

"They can be thawed," I say.

"Not with this kind of cold, Miss O'Keeffe."

"You're wrong, Putnam." I give him succinct instructions and pack him off to the cellar and, when his head pokes up, I banish him back down again until he has done what I told him to do and realized I am right.

It snows and snows. I love winter up here, in this house that was never built for it. I love the hardship, the bitter cold. I love the minor mishaps—frozen pipes, for example, which are, unlike other things, fixable.

When the snow finally ends, Jean goes out to shovel.

I wear my slippers to the back door. "See how useful!" I call out to him.

He quits shoveling and smiles at me. "It's a hard life I've got up here."

"Such trouble."

"Go back in. You'll catch cold."

"I can't catch worse than I've got."

He laughs and shifts his grip on the shovel handle. "Go on, Georgia," he says. Again, his eyes rest on my face, then he turns away and digs the blade into the next drift. I close the door, a quiet thrill in my chest. The phone starts to ring as I climb the stairs. Stieglitz more than likely. Who else would it be? I should answer. I should let him hear my voice to give him assurance. The steps are cold through my socks, the phone echoing. I let it ring.

JEAN. I AM beginning to know him. How he sits, speaks, moves, how when he is working at his typewriter, he leans slightly forward, his weight on his elbows. He gives me things to read—sections of the novel-in-progress he is writing, and a copy of his first book, *Cane*. After supper, we listen to music—Bach, Mozart, the spirituals. We talk late into the night, disconnected abstract conversations about his dead wife, writing, art, politics, the race issue. His father was born into slavery, he tells me, then became a prosperous farmer. His mother was the daughter of a governor. He went to segregated schools—all-white, as well as all-black. He is mixed race—half Negro, the other half Dutch, Welsh, German Jewish.

"Does it matter, Georgia, really? Negro, white, mulatto, what does it all amount to? I am none of those things and all of those things. I'm no more or less than the man I am."

His eyes have a strangely risen quality; they seem to float near the surface of his skin. Inexpressibly beautiful. Light coming through water.

I tell him about New Mexico, and Abiquiu, that small village that seems cut right out of the hills. "It is such a particular point of earth," I say. "Light like nowhere else. Even the dust there is different." Powdered adobe, walls crumbling to mix back into the earth they came from. That dust is different from the dust of any other place.

"I don't believe that."

"That's only because you've not been."

"I've been to Taos."

"It's not the same."

There is a wrinkle then in the silence between us. My voice came out stronger than I intended.

"You should stay," I say abruptly.

"What?"

"I invited you for two weeks."

"Yes."

"It's been nearly two."

He doesn't answer.

"You don't have to," I say.

"I know that."

"But you are welcome to. If you want."

The edges of his mouth turn up. "Because I am useful?"

"Exactly. You are useful, and everything is humming along here quite nicely. Don't you think?"

"Yes," he says slowly. "I do."

The cat comes up to me and jumps onto the pillow of the cot. I stroke her head. She tolerates it for a while, then leaps down and circles his chair.

BY THE TIME Stieglitz comes up for Christmas, the air feels almost warm, and I can get outside again. The grass sheathed in frost glitters in the sunlight.

When he walks through the door and sees me, his face lights. "Look at you!" he says happily, touching my chin with his hand. "You look so well!"

I feel something in me twist, and resist the urge to turn my face away.

THE THREE OF us exchange simple gifts. My gift to Toomer is a bright-red scarf. "It looks dashing on you," I say.

"That's your teasing voice, isn't it?"

I laugh. "Stieglitz, tell him how fine that scarf looks."

"Indeed," Stieglitz says. "A glorious red."

"There," I say. "Now, you'll believe me, won't you?" Jean shoots me a quick look, then presses the tissue back into the box. Stieglitz is saying how he's always wanted a Christmas at the Hill, and now it's here—a few perfect days with snow everywhere—and how heartening it is to see me looking so well, looking almost like I did fifteen years ago. I feel my breath catch. Has it been that long?

WE HAVE A big dinner. Bellies stuffed, we roll into the kitchen. Stieglitz builds up the fire, then sits down at the table as Toomer and I start on the dishes. We are laughing. So much food, so many plates to wash. My arms are plunged into the warm soapy water, suds on my sleeves, I've pushed them back, but they keep sliding down.

"Give them here, Georgia," Toomer says.

I hold my dripping sudsy hands toward him and he folds the cuffs back from the wrist, until they are tight against my elbow.

"You do that very neatly," I say. A quick flash of light breaks across his face.

"Do I?" He picks up a rinsed dish from the rack and runs the drying cloth over the moon-white center.

When the kitchen is clean, we move into the living room, and Jean reads us his essay on Stieglitz. He has written about the Hill—how it was an old farm, now with a new world set into its borders, how every window is uncurtained, each with a searing capacity to perceive and feel and know. He speaks about my presence here, how I've molded the house to my austere vision: the lack of ornaments, the pale-gray walls, the uncovered lights. He continues reading about Stieglitz's genius, his generosity, his commitment to the livingness of art. He talks about the artists Stieglitz saw before the world did, and his uncanny gift to render in his photographs *the treeness of a tree, the stoneness of stone . . . what a face is . . . what a hand, an arm, a limb is . . . the amazing beauty of a human being . . .*

Under his hands, the papers shine in the light off the fire, and I know. Even before he has come to the end, before his eyes lift from the last page and meet mine, I feel the rise of desire in his face, how he wants me, and has, I see now, for some time.

STIEGLITZ STAYS UP late with me. He sits in the chair by my bed. When he starts to fall asleep, I nudge him, but he claims he doesn't want to go up to his room. I am well again, and he doesn't want to wake up tomorrow and find anything changed. He clutches my hand, so happy I've begun to rouse again as the woman he knew, the woman he loves.

His pleasure seeing what he calls this sea-change in me is genuine. He sees the light moving through my face. He hears my laughter, the same kind of laughter he and I fell into fifteen years ago, that first summer in our refuge. That time in his life when he discovered me was the time when he was most certain, virile, and alive, and he will always love me for that reason. And when he hears my laughter now, it reminds him of who he was when he heard it then—

His eyes have closed. I feel a rush of warmth toward him. He looks his age tonight, white hair around the sweet pale of his face. He is almost seventy, and despite whatever foolish mess he gets himself worked up in, despite the fact that he can still make me so angry, in the end he is just a man whose sunlight is behind him.

I reach for his hand. He stirs, startled for an instant, then he sees me.

"You are glorious," he whispers, his eyes sleepy through his glasses.

I lean over, balancing my weight on the arm of his chair. My lips graze his cheek.

HE LEAVES TO go back to the city. A letter arrives. One of those letters that spans his day—an entry at 11:27 A.M. from Fort Edward, in his seat on the train, 2:10 P.M. from Albany, passing the stand of birch trees, the same route we've taken season after season, year after year. Three more entries—8 P.M. from the Place, then 8:23, then 8:38. Ending with his plan to take a bath.

It strikes me as the last letter. I know it isn't. There will be thousands more, exchanged over years, west to east, east to west, his country to mine, and back again. Nowhere near the last and yet, in a way, it is.

I used to think the letters told the story of our life together, the truth of that strange beautiful love. But the letters were never who we were. They were who we wanted to be.

JEAN AND I walk out onto the frozen lake over ripples in the surface where the water has rushed over and gotten trapped. Light winks off the snow. We find a smooth spot out toward the center, and skate in our boots. We slide over the ice and laugh, moving more quickly, sliding, running, almost racing. When I slip and almost fall, he catches my arm. I look up and smile. He is looking down at me, not smiling. Then, neither of us laughs, and there is only the ring of the silence and the white frozen world, drops of thaw like crystal on the trees. The scarf I gave him hangs loose on his neck, the dazzling red of that scarf, and his eyes unending, except for a simple hunger I recognize. His grip on my arm tightens, and I feel it move through me like a current.

We continue walking across the frozen lake back toward the house. We pass children on the road, breaking icicles off the trees, sucking on them, hurling them into the sunlight.

THAT EVENING, I bump into him as I step from my room into the hall. I close the door, my hand on the knob behind my back.

"Looking for me?" I say.

"Always."

It's a narrow space, that upstairs hallway.

WHEN MARGARET LEAVES after supper, Jean and I go into the living room as usual, but the silence feels new. We are reading, apparently. I have the Jung book open on my lap.

"What *is* this?" he asks, looking at me now, and that seems as far as things are able to go. I want to touch him, taste him in my throat. I want his skin on mine, his mouth. I can barely make sense of the wanting.

Once Stieglitz and I were talking about a painting I had done: one of my flowers he wanted to hang. I wasn't happy with it, though, and didn't want it in my show. I explained it to him this way: That painting was done with my head, before my heart and my body were ready, and while it may be beautiful, it does not have the sense of fire or breath that is life.

I remember this now. I have not answered Jean. He looks back down again at the book—he seems irritated, perhaps because I did not answer.

I AM WAKENED by a monstrous low growl. The house seems to shake. I slip out of my bed in my socks and pull a heavy cardigan around me. Jean is by the back window.

"The snowplow," he says. It's the strangest-looking thing—half boat, half devil, circling the yard, cutting paths through the moonlight, heaping up layers of snow.

"It's cold," I murmur. He takes my hand, his fingers weave through mine. I glance at him, but he is staring out into the night.

The plow moves off, its light swinging over the trees, the sound of the engine fades down the road. He pulls me toward him, holding my face, and kisses me. A long kiss.

"You should go back to bed," I say.

"I am going to put you to bed first," he answers, and we laugh at how teeny it is, the little bed. He tucks me in, then bends to kiss me good night. I grasp his neck and pull him down with me.

My cheek rests against the pillow facing him, his eyes are dark and still they seem to glow in the strange bluish night of the room. I put my palm on the narrow space between us, that thin strip that separates us. We are apart by the span of my fingers.

"This space is the bundling board," I say.

"Really?"

"Yes."

"Will that be adequate?"

"If it wants to be."

"So if I reach across it like this . . ."

I strike his arm away. "It can be effective," I say with a smile.

"Does it want to be so effective?"

"Hmm. Not sure."

"What does it want?"

He traces my fingers. I can smell his skin. He reaches across the space I've marked out and draws open my sweater, his fingers undo the top button on the V of my nightgown.

"I'd steal you," he whispers, his eyes shining. "Beg you to come with me, leave here, go to your Abiquiu. I'll take you there—"

"Stop," I say sharply. And he laughs. Catching my fingers, he brings them to his lips. He draws me to him and kisses me hard on the mouth.

Later, I will remember a vague light through the window, the moon perhaps, or the blue itself, how it fell across my thigh.

AFTERWARD HE LIES near me, his face near my face.

"Why do you hold back," he says. "It's like you don't want anything I could give you because you'd have to give me something in return."

"That's not it."

"I think it is."

I am silent, remembering what he said earlier. *I'll take you there.* How easy it is for a man to say a thing like that. *I'll take you.*

"It won't work," I say.

He looks at me for a moment before he gets up. His hand lingers near my face—again that slight electric tremble in the air between us.

Then he's gone, the doorway empty, footsteps fading up the stairs, fainter, fainter. Gone. And the room is not the room it was. The night is brightly framed in the window. Things are in their places: the pictures on the mantel, the lamp, a short pile of books, the kindling and fire tools. It is all familiar, and it is not the same. The room has left as well—part of some distant, slowly disappearing world.

Years from now, I will understand that this is the moment my life became wholly mine, more mine than it ever was before because I will never again let it be anything less. I will go back to New Mexico. I will walk out into the dry nothingness of the country that I love and paint: sharp-edged flowers, desert abstractions, cow skulls—images of Thanatos. I will title my work and that is what they will see: the subject that fills space and the words that define it. They will not notice that what I am really after—all I was ever really after—is that raw desire of the sky pouring through the windowed socket of a bone.

After

WE STAY MARRIED. I realize it would make no sense to dissolve the business end of things, which works so well. He manages the logistical details I am not interested in. He doesn't notice the seismic shift that's taken place. He sees what he wants to believe. And I get what I need.

I divide the year in two. I spend every summer in New Mexico. Every fall, I return to him in New York. I buy a house at Ghost Ranch, north of Santa Fe, and then, in 1943, a second house in the small village of Abiquiu—the ruin of a house with the door I've always known was meant to be mine. I build out the Abiquiu house from the inner central courtyard. I make a studio and bedroom out of the old stables and carriage barn, setting plate-glass windows into one wall of the studio and long tables down the length of the room where I paint. I have the walls rebuilt in the traditional way, the adobe smoothed by local women's hands.

The house has water rights. Unlike Ghost Ranch, it's a place I can live year-round. I plant gardens. Vegetables. Fruit trees. Flowers timed to bloom throughout the year. I paint and make tomato jelly and walk the ridge toward the high sheer cliffs where the colors tumble down in waves. It is a gorgeous mad-looking country, more merciless and spare than the land around Taos. The sun hits the earth and burns deep into it, so even at night when I sleep under the stars, I can still feel the warmth of the day stored in the ground.

Every morning, I drink my coffee in the cold silence of the house. As the light gnaws at the edge of things, I feel a quiet joy. There is nothing in this new day that is not mine.

WHEN SWEENEY FIRST calls from the Museum of Modern Art to offer me a retrospective, I refuse. Then, because it is Sweeney, I call back to accept. At the opening on May 14, 1946, Stieglitz sits on the stairs with Marin, surveying the crowd. They seem oddly out of place, the two of them, as if the tide has passed them by. I catch Stieglitz's eye, and he smiles.

The day before I leave to return to New Mexico, he and I walk together through the exhibition halls. I hold his arm. "This is what we are," he says quietly, his eyes sweeping over my paintings on the walls. "This is what we made. This is you." Back at the apartment, while he rests, I sit at the table and write notes to him on small slips of paper. *I love you. You are my sweetestheart. A kiss to you. Take care, my love.* As always before I leave, I will tuck them through the house, into a drawer, on a shelf in the medicine cabinet, I will fold one and place it into a book he is reading. He likes to find them when I am gone. He has said it makes him feel I am still with him.

He calls me into the bedroom. I draw a chair over and sit by his side.

He has his glasses off, and his eyes look small. "I would like you to stay please, Georgia."

I press his hand, his palm is cool and slack. "I know."

"Just awhile longer, please?" he says.

I shake my head. "Maybe next time."

———

HE PHONES TO tell me that a brilliant review of my retrospective has appeared written by James Thrall Soby, a modernist critic who has never especially liked my work. Stieglitz is elated. He reads passages aloud to me over the phone: "'She is the greatest of living women painters . . . Hers is a world of bones and flowers, hills and the city . . . She created this world; it was not there before and there is nothing like it anywhere.'"

Silence hangs between us on the line.

"I'll send it to you," he says.

"You don't have to," I say. "Just send me McBride's piece. I always look forward to reading what witty things he's got to say."

"No," he insists. "You must read this one as well. It is true, my darling. There is nothing like your world anywhere. This is what I've wanted for you, always."

He is tired—his voice dwindles, fading in and out, as he tells me that yesterday, he had the pains in his chest again and had to lie down on the cot in the back room of the Place, and he was resting there when our friends the Newhalls stopped in. They had brought him an ice cream cone, chocolate, because they knew that was his favorite.

"It was already dripping everywhere, I couldn't lick it fast enough. It made quite a stain on my shirt, I'm afraid."

I tell him about a new painting I am doing: another sky through the hole in a pelvis bone—the same blue oval of the other pelvis paintings, edged by whiteness, completely abstract but, in this one, I am making a fold of reddish-orange dusk along the top.

"I suppose that's just how it goes," I say to him now on the phone, "when one has more sky than earth around."

HIS DOCTOR TELEPHONES a few days later and suggests I fly back to New York. His heart is not behaving well. But there have been many other calls like this, and I put it off. By early July, he's faring better.

Soon I'll be as good as new, he writes. *Nothing for you to worry about. Today I found another of your notes. I remind myself that in only a few months, you'll be home again.*

On July 10, his assistant finds him unconscious, lying on the floor halfway between his bedroom and mine. His pen near his hand. A letter to me unfinished on the writing desk.

I am shopping in Española when I receive the telegram. I go straight to the airport. I can feel the heat working through my red cotton dress, and as we rise through the clouds, and the earth below us falls away to simple shapes, I think of how he did not want me to go this time. He never does. Not really, but maybe this time I could have noticed it was different: the sadness in his eyes, the way he held my hand, the last touch between us before my fingers, cold, left his.

My ears pop as the altitude changes. I close my eyes. Under the hum of the engines, the echo of his voice. *Just a little longer, Georgia, please this time. Stay.*

A SIMPLE UNLINED coffin. No eulogy. No music. Only a few flowers. Time passes as though underwater.

THE DAY AFTER the funeral, I phone Dorothy Norman and explain that I will assume control of the gallery, including the rent fund. She must remove her things. When she begins to cry, I tell her that she was one of those people Stieglitz was quite foolish about. The affair between them was disgusting, and I will have no more to do with it. I hang up. I clasp my fingers together, holding them tightly in my lap, until I can feel every bone.

I throw out his medicines, his clothes, his shirts. Some in perfectly good condition, almost new. I should give them to someone, I think, but that thought lasts only an instant. There's one with a dark stain, the chocolate ice cream, ruined. I rip it before it goes to the trash. I rip it slowly, that horrible sound of a thing torn apart from itself all the way through.

I drive to Lake George and bury his ashes deep near the root of a tree and cover the spot with leaves. For years, the rest of his family will push me to reveal the spot.

"I put him where he can hear the water" is as much as I will say.

IT WILL TAKE me three years to go through his things. Sorting archives, art, letters, personal items, photographs, books. Relatively speaking, I save little, but that is only because he kept so much. Handwritten copies of every letter he wrote, the letters he received. I winnow it down to fifty thousand pages or so. There is the art, of course, works of Dove, Marin, Picasso, Cézanne, and others. I leave the bulk of his collection—around six hundred pieces—to the Metropolitan Museum of Art.

Nancy Newhall tells me that Stieglitz told her once I would probably destroy the nude portraits he made of me. She says this casually one night when we are at a party. She's holding a glass, a stain of lipstick already on the rim, and I watch the glass tilt thoughtlessly in her hand, wine sloshing gently back and forth.

Is that what you really thought? That I would destroy them? Damn you, Stieglitz.

I KEEP ONLY the finest ones. I go through thousands of his prints, and distill them to a master set of sixteen hundred. I want to give them to the Metropolitan, but the rather snitty head of the print department informs me that the mats are too large.

"They'll have to be cut down," he says.

"No, I won't do that. He sized his mats very specifically to fit each print."

"As they are, they will not fit in the museum's solander boxes. They'll have to be trimmed. This is what we do to store the Rembrandts."

"Well, Mrs. Rembrandt isn't exactly around to contest it, is she?"

In the end, all sixteen hundred photographs go to the National

Gallery in Washington. I include multiple prints of the same image that he'd printed in silver, platinum, and copper tones. How many times he touched her face, her body, reworking shadow and light so it clung, each time slightly different, print after print. I look through them until it breaks my heart.

Then it is done. Everything is done. Leaving New York, I determine that when anyone asks, I will say I took nothing. I purged it all. A woman who keeps nothing. A woman who has stripped her world down to tomorrow. It's only up to me now: what I give them to construct their understanding of who I am.

WHEN I COME back to New Mexico, it is fall. The earth seems barely tethered to the sky. I wake in the morning and the floor seems unstable, as if the edges of the world are crinkling.

I paint my mountain and the river valley. I paint snow. Red hills cloaked in whiteness. As I put in a blue wash of sky, crows rise past my window. My brush pauses midair. I follow them with my eyes until they disappear. I draw in a single crow above my hills, long wings outstretched. A black bird flying—always there, always going away.

I loved you once. How I loved you.

A wrenching thought when I let it in.

Now

LOOKING BACK, IT often seems it happened overnight. I became the old woman I was meant to be. Fiercely alone.

On the long tables in my studio, we are looking over my paintings. Years of work spread out, all the way back to the charcoals. It is 1970. There will be a show at the Whitney. It will be the first major showing of my art in New York since he died. I am eighty-three years old. I have traveled all over the world, to Peru, Egypt, Austria, Greece, the Near East. Two years ago, I was featured on the cover of *Life* magazine. They call me the Pioneer Painter. They are enthralled by the woman artist who has chosen to live in the desert, who wakes in the dark before dawn, drinks her coffee, and walks out with her chows toward the horizon. I have become that horizon, unreachable and absolute. They call me mysterious, because I turn strangers, especially famous ones, away. I allow only certain photographers to take certain kinds of pictures of me: in my black and white clothes, my kimonos, my shawls, poised with my cow skulls, my wizened face and wrinkled hands. A symbol of the American West, reclusive, self-reliant, I can no longer quite see the mountains in the distance, but I still love them beyond reason.

We do not talk about my eyes. I have worked hard to do this right. To give the world just enough so they will still want more. In every interview, I play up very precise details of my artistic career. When I am asked about Stieglitz and his influence, I find ways to sidestep the question. New York was a different life. The woman I was, a different person. It isn't always easy—looking back across the vast distances of time. I see it clearly. Sometimes more clearly than I could see it when my sight was still unchanged. My life with him. My life before. I have begun to buy back some of my paintings at auction to drive their values higher. One must protect oneself. I've gone through my artwork from time to time, culled out a few pieces, ripped them up, then walked outside to burn them in the can. I've marked the best works with a star on the back and my initials in a circle. Over the years, I have often chosen not to exhibit my abstractions. I have continued to paint them, and I keep them, along with my early works, in my own collection. I am no longer known as an abstract artist. I am known for my New Mexico landscapes, my bones, my sharp-edged flowers, my sky holes, and my clouds. This is, after all, what I learned from him: to keep what I want to myself. To reveal only what I want to be seen.

I have worked hard to build a legend to replace the one he fashioned for me.

I am not expecting to feel what I do that day in the studio when I am sitting there with my manager and my assistant reviewing my early work spread out on the long tables—the charcoal drawings, the abstract watercolors from 1915, and 1916, those pieces I did before I came to him—*Blue No. 1, Blue No. 5,* the spiral, the canyon, two lines. I feel my heart turn over. They are so fresh, even now more than half a century later.

"Well," I say flatly. "We don't really need to have this show after all. I never did better."

They miss my point—they often do—and Doris, the manager, says firmly, "We will arrange the paintings thematically. That way they will see how those early forms are reflected in your later work."

I look at her. "You're trying to bolster the credibility of my later work."

"No," she says, in that glorious no-nonsense way she has. "This is just the alphabet you've used throughout your career."

I am not so easily fooled. She doesn't want me to stumble into the thought that I might have abandoned my best work, my vision, for him. I can't say I haven't asked myself that question. What would I have done with those early abstract forms if I had just continued working on my own? What kind of artist would I have become if I had not gone to him that day in 1917 and the obsession between us began?

He once called our relationship a mixing of souls. But then again, he called it a love story. And it was far more—and less—than that.

I sigh. They are like ashes—thoughts like this.

The Whitney show is a tremendous success. It travels to Chicago and San Francisco. By the time I come back home, piles of letters and invitations have already streamed in. Letters from museums all over the country, phone calls from magazines and newspapers. Letters from women who see me as a symbol for the feminist movement, which I want nothing to do with. Letters from young artists seeking guidance. I read through a number of them, then lose interest. There is only one piece of advice to give: "You want to be an artist? Go home and work."

I CONTINUE TO paint, and my eyes continue to fail. My central vision slowly clouds, until only tiny holes remain at the edges of my seeing. There is no cure, they tell me, and at a certain point I will also lose my peripheral sight.

I refuse to authorize a biography of my life. I write two memoirs instead. My form of memoir. The first a series of drawings with small paragraphs of text to accompany them. The second is more complete, told exactly as I want it told, at arm's length—moments of a life strung together, each like an arrow in flight hurtling toward some center. I mention Stieglitz three times, and even that seems a little excessive.

Every day, Candelaria comes in to do the housekeeping and Estiben builds my fires. He has a zen for building fires. He shaves out kindling with his knife, and arranges the wood in three or four graduated vertical layers, the smaller pieces toward the front. You can light his fires with one match. A girl comes every day to help me with my paperwork. We dry apricots off the fruit trees in the garden. We make Irish soda bread and grind homemade flour in my small mill. We organize the shelves in the book room, and she rubs oil into my back and legs to soothe the ache. She drives me in my white Lincoln Continental between Ghost Ranch and Abiquiu and to my weekly appointments with the eye doctor in town. She looks away discreetly when I drop my head into my hands to hide the tears. And then there is Juan, who has become my primary companion. He showed up one day at my back door, a tall long-haired artist looking for work. He has been with me since. It was hardly altruistic, my taking him on. I loved his lanky handsomeness from the get-go. I love the way he laughs. He is good with me. He knows when to nudge and when to leave me alone. He knows how to talk back to me, how to flirt like a younger lover, and how to let me fuss over him as a mother would over her beloved son. He takes me to the opera in Santa Fe, and he knows just how to hold my arm as we walk the sidewalk to keep me from the low edge of the curb I can no longer distinguish.

After supper in the evenings, I listen for the village children playing outside in the street in front of the cantina, their laughter clatters with the fading sunlight off the walls, their voices sparkling like music. From time to time, I call them in. Through the housekeeper, I learn which child belongs to which family. I send them to the movies sometimes in Española. The ones who are too poor, I pay for them to go to school.

After dark, when the children are gone back to their own lives, I ask the girl to read to me from Blyth's books of haiku. As she reads, I run my fingers over the pot on the bench shelf. The clay is smooth and cool under my hand, raised flecks of dirt strung through it. Mino, the gardener, helps me with my pots. We work on them together. When a pot is done, I feel it with my hands. If it's not what I want, we rework it. If the clay is too dry, we smash it with a certain glee, and start again.

MY SISTER CATHERINE's grandson, Ray, is coming to visit. He came here once when he was thirteen. He has not been here since. His sister was named Georgia after me. I paid her way through college and offered to pay his as well if he went to Harvard, but he preferred to pay his own way and chose a different school. He's a lawyer now, in his early thirties, about to be married. He has a legal case down here, and will come to visit for the weekend.

The morning he is to arrive, I rise early. The girl comes into my bedroom, lets out the chows, and lights the fire in the small kiva in the corner, then she goes to make my coffee. When she comes back, she helps me dress and we go out to walk. I make my laps around the courtyard, setting a small rock down for every lap to keep track. I feel the blood pulse in my neck, the slight push of life under my fingers when I press them there. Afterward, I rest in the sun by the old well. The door is across the patio. I can only see the darker uneven stain of where I know it is on the wall. The light hits that one spot differently. Sometimes in the dry air and the smell of sage, I swear I sense him in that door.

I have my coffee and yogurt with a handful of raspberries from the garden. I tie up my hair in a scarf. I smooth cream into my hands, working around each knob of my gnarled fingers. My skin is cracked, like the desert floor.

The morning is very white today. I can feel it on my face. It will be a hot day.

When Ray arrives, I take his hand and show him through the house. I tell him that since he was here last, there have been many changes—white carpet now in the studio and in the bedroom.

"The chows were black, you see, and when I could no longer tell dog from floor, those black tiles had to go." In the studio, I point out two paintings. I cannot see them, of course. "That one by the little sitting area is *Above the Clouds*, and this one here on the long wall is *A Day with Juan*." I point to the small stovetop next to the sink. "That little thing clicks on from time to time without anyone hitting the switch. It has a mind of its own."

"Like other denizens here?" he asks lightly.

I laugh. "Oh, maybe. Speaking of which, where is Juan? I want you to meet him." But he is nowhere to be found. Candelaria knows nothing. Neither does Mino. Juan does this sometimes: disappears when a member of my family comes or an old friend who belongs to a life I lived before. Perhaps he is afraid someone will judge him. Or perhaps he just needs a few hours on his own to be free. "He'll be back," I say to Ray now. "Come let me show you the rest of the house." We cross the inner courtyard and walk through the short passageway. I show him the dining room with dark floors and bright-white walls, daffodils I placed this morning on the table surrounded by wooden captain's chairs, Mexican weavings draped over their backs. I show him the pantry, where I keep my kettles, my spice jars, my refrigerator, pots and pans hung on nails against the wall. I tell him that the other girl I used to have would argue with me all the time about the proper way to preserve ginger. He asks me who was right. I shrug. "Well, she's no longer here." I take his hand, young and soft, not an artist's hand—the skin is smooth, and reminds me of my sister Catherine's hands. We walk through the kitchen. I feel along the worktable with its red-and-white-checked plastic tablecloth set near the sink and the stove.

"It's a Chambers stove," I say, "very dependable. Older things tend to be that way, though I did finally break down and get a modern dishwasher."

I lead him through the small hallway, then into the long sitting room, with the three-paneled window at one end and my tamarisk tree. "It's like having a three-paneled painting that changes through the seasons," I tell him. "I used to love to watch that tree."

"Is the Porter rock here?" he asks.

I laugh. "Oh, everyone knows the story of that rock."

"It was in the *New Yorker* piece about you."

"Yes, but the reporter got it wrong."

"What do you mean he got it wrong?"

As we walk back through the maze of small hallways and across the inner courtyard to my bedroom, I tell him how the part about the rafting trip was true. "I went with Eliot Porter, his wife, and some others, and Eliot found that rock, an astonishing small dark rock that had been rinsed by the creek, worn down to a perfect gleaming shape. You'll have to see." We have reached my bedroom. I feel along the shelf until my fingers find it.

"Here." I hand it to him. "I asked Porter to let me hold it, and it fit so neatly in my hand, I told him he should give it to me so I could add it to my collection. But he refused and took it back."

"And then gave it to you several months later," Ray says.

"No." I laugh. "See that was the not-true part. The Porters invited me for supper, and I stole it."

"Stole it?"

"It was right there on a coffee table among some other things." I shake my head. "That rock belonged in my hand, and I knew it."

I take it back from Ray now and rub my thumb slowly back and forth across the soft curved indentation my thumb has made. It is still my favorite. That rock. It is mine. Certain encounters in a life are meant to happen. As Stieglitz perhaps was mine. Long before we met, the space for him existed in me, unmade, unspoken for.

"Did you make these pots on the shelf here?"

"Yes. It's not painting, but it's what I've got."

"And what is this?"

I feel a tiny shudder inside me, because I don't know what he is looking at. He must realize, because he quickly adds, "This hand, here on the wall."

The Buddha's hand. A mudra. The palm is held up, turned outward, the fingers straight—it is a gesture of fearlessness. Also called the gesture of renunciation.

"It was a gift," I explain to Ray. "But then one of the fingers broke off, and I sent it to be fixed, and it was fixed, perfectly. You couldn't see the seam where it had broken. But there was nothing left in it afterward. No power. Just those long and graceful fingers on the wall, signifying nothing."

There is a brief uneasy silence, and I can tell he does not understand. There are no hiding places here.

THAT EVENING, WE have roasted leg of lamb with garlic and honey mint sauce, bread and salad. There is salad with every noon meal, and also with supper. Always in the same shallow white bowls, salt cellars in the white footed sake cups with shell spoons. I explain to him that the only way to wash certain greens, spinach for example, is with the leaves down, stems up.

"It makes a difference, you know, in the taste when food is planted and prepared a certain way."

"The lamb is delicious," he says.

"It is delicious because it took a ridiculous amount of time to prepare. To make it taste like this, you have to make slits all along the meaty part of the lamb. In each slit, less than half an inch deep, you stuff a garlic slice."

"Well thank you for taking the time," he says.

"I did it for myself as well," I say. "Though I suppose I would not have gone through the trouble if you were not here."

The fire snaps, the tines of his fork graze his plate. In the silence after, I hear him smile.

After supper, we listen to records. I play a few of the Beethoven sonatas for him, and then one of my favorites, by Monteverdi. When the record stops, I get up and feel my way to the stereo, lift the needle from the groove. I turn the knob until it clicks off, and sit back down. I tell him that I remember when his mother last came to visit, she came with my sisters Claudia and Catherine, we talked late into the evening after supper. "Your mother asked me if they had tired me out."

"And had they?" he asks.

"Certainly not. I felt like the evening star."

We talk for a while about his plans for the future, his job, his passion for the environment. We talk about the girl he's planning to marry.

"The law makes marriage a very long thing," I tell him, "sometimes it's best just to be tied to someone in your heart."

He gently changes the subject, and tells me that when he first came to see me, back in 1960, it was the landscape that impressed him.

"Even more than me?" I ask.

I hear him laugh. "That first visit, yes."

"Well, thank goodness we are having a second visit."

At one point, as we are talking, I ask him casually if my sisters have recovered yet from the shock of Stieglitz's photographs of me that I allowed to be published as a book last year. What a flurry of letters and phone calls—they were so horrified by the scandal of my naked selves gracing coffee tables everywhere.

"Are they over it yet?"

"I suppose," he says.

I laugh. "And we can't blame it on their being a different generation and all that, now, can we?"

"You're different from most women your age," he says gently. "I'm sure you know that."

There is a goodness about him—my sister Catherine's goodness. Sometimes that kind of goodness lends a quality of greatness to a life. I never had that kind of life.

I could tell him this now. I could tell him that the past is so much lighter than we can imagine, flakes of snow falling that melt in an instant and are gone. All that happened then and since. Stieglitz and me. My art. Our letters that I have sealed. That girl in the photographs.

"It's all so long ago," I say to Ray now. "I can't imagine it would matter."

THE FOLLOWING DAY, we drive out to Ghost Ranch and walk from the house to the cliffs. I hear the ravens calling as they soar on the updrafts. I hear the soft whoosh of the wind through the piñon trees. "It reminds me of the sea," I tell him, "that sound." I lean a little on his arm as we walk.

Halfway out, we stop at my chair that I have left in the shade of the trees, so I can sit and take a rest. I tell him about the trip I took earlier this year to Costa Rica and Guatemala. Then we continue on. "I know the way," I say, "and I'll lead you. But you'll have to be the one to watch for rattlesnakes."

THAT EVENING WHEN he leaves, I walk with him to the door. I touch his sleeve.

"Let me see your face." I feel his hesitation, unsure what I am asking.

"Nearer into the light," I say, "let me see you."

He takes a small step closer. We are less than an arm's length away. I can feel how the air shifts as the space between us shrinks, his shadow falls across my sight. I reach up my hands and trace his features. I touch his face the way I will touch a bone and feel the humming of the sky through it. I read my sister in his face, my mother, my father, the fierce dreams they each once held, this torn beauty of a moment we've come to.

There are things I wish I could tell him. Things I wish I could somehow leak from my heart into his. It feels so strange that these lives I've lived, these things I've known and done and seen, the vastness and the beauty, the risk and joy and devastated wonder—all of this will go with me. There's an odd weight in my chest. So unusual, to feel this kind of sorrow.

"You are very fine, Ray," I say.

He leaves. I stand at the door and, without seeing, watch him go.

THE NEXT MORNING, after breakfast, I walk outside. The garden floats, a blaze of light.

I hear the sound of the hoe against the earth. I call Mino's name softly. The hoe stops, and he comes. "I want you to help me with something," I say, taking his arm. We walk together through the house out across the patio and into the studio. I tell him to take down the thick rough wove paper, the watercolor paints, and the brushes, I ask him to tape several sheets of paper to the table, and knob the tape, so I can know where one sheet ends. I run my fingers over each brush until I find the one I am looking for.

"Just one color to start," I say.

I ask him to lead my left hand onto the first sheet of paper. "The center please." I move the brush toward it and feel his hand on mine, guiding slightly left. He smells like the garden, like earth.

"Thank you," I say. He leaves and I am alone. I paint shapes— a wave, a circle—the color slides like grace over the page. I make forms that echo those early abstract forms I made when I was no one, and it occurs to me that art is a separate country, outside the body, outside time, like death or desire, an element beyond our physical selves we are traveling toward.

My hand shakes. Small drops of paint have spilled. So human, so flawed and imprecise, and beautiful for that.

ACKNOWLEDGMENTS

I would like to acknowledge the work of O'Keeffe biographers, curators, and scholars, whose interpretations and writings about O'Keeffe's life and art provided the building blocks of the structure underlying my novel. In particular, I would like to acknowledge the work of Barbara Rose, Sarah Greenough, Barbara Haskell, Laurie Lisle, Benita Eisler, Hunter Drohojowska-Philp, Roxana Robinson, and Barbara Buhler Lynes. The scholarship of these women guided my creative journey through O'Keeffe's life.

For reading earlier drafts and giving invaluable feedback: Barbara Shapiro, Holly LeCraw, Kim Wiley, Caroline Leavitt, Elizabeth Lane. William Callahan's detailed edits markedly strengthened this book. Gratitude to Millicent Bennett for her friendship; to Sarah Barnum for her perceptive observations about O'Keeffe's work; to the Madden family and Lucy and Amy White for time at Lake George, which was critical to my understanding of that place. Endless gratitude to my mother and father for instilling in me a faith in the power of art, and to Karen Lustig, who lived with me in the world of this novel.

My agent, Kim Witherspoon, is like no other—passionate, incisive, clear. I am fortunate to have her as a trusted advocate and friend. At Random House, inestimable thanks to Derrill Hagood, Anna Pitoniak, Sally Marvin, Michelle Jasmine, Leigh Marchant, Alaina Waagner, and Avideh Bashirrad for their dedication to Georgia's story as one that is relevant to women and art today. Thanks also to Sandra Sjursen, Benjamin Dreyer, Joe Perez, Simon Sullivan, Tom McKeveny, and artist Robert Hunt, who created gorgeous artwork for this novel. Special thanks to Carolyn Foley, wise and thoughtful guide, and to my wonderful production editor and friend, Vincent La Scala, who understands how the slightest edits throughout a manuscript can transform the weight and impact of a story.

Georgia would not have been possible without the bold vision of Kate Medina, who worked with me to shape this novel from the start. Her brilliant editorial guidance, warmth, and commitment have been a singular gift—not only to this book but to my life.

Above all and always, gratitude to my husband, Steve, who reads every word of every draft and whose fierce intelligence and insights make the difference. And, finally, to our boys—heart, soul, sky, ground. You are all that.

Georgia

DAWN TRIPP

A Reader's Guide

A CONVERSATION WITH DAWN TRIPP

RANDOM HOUSE READER'S CIRCLE: Why did you choose to write a novel about Georgia O'Keeffe?

DAWN TRIPP: It's a gut impulse, always, that drives me into a story. I came to O'Keeffe through her art, specifically a show of her abstractions at the Whitney Museum in New York. In that show, O'Keeffe's art was paired with Alfred Stieglitz's photographs of her—clothed and nude—along with excerpts of their letters, and I was struck by the realization: Here is a woman that most people know of but barely know at all. Growing up, I'd always admired O'Keeffe's flowers and landscapes, but that day at the Whitney, I fell in love with her abstractions. As early as 1915, Georgia O'Keeffe—not even thirty years old—was creating radically new abstract forms. And I wanted to know: Who was the woman, the artist, who made these shapes? What did she think, feel, want? What was happening in her life? And why have I never seen the full range and power of her abstract work before? Why isn't she known for *this*?

There are many stellar, insightful nonfiction works that have been written about O'Keeffe, but I believe that fiction can get at a different kind of truth, an experiential truth that allows us to enter a character's story and be transformed. Facts and the historical record are always incomplete. Truth is kaleidoscopic, continually changing and evolving according to our perspective. To me, fiction is another means of cutting past the surface to reshape our understanding of what is true, to cast new light on the weight and impact of a life.

In *Georgia*, I wanted to write a first-person account from O'Keeffe's point of view, in her voice, as I imagined it. I wanted to get into her head—into the sweeping and intimate world between her and Stieglitz. I wanted to get right up against what she might have felt and thought and questioned, what she loved and feared and ached for, what she fought, remembered, dreamed. I wanted to bring that internal world to life.

RHRC: What intrigued you about the relationship between O'Keeffe and Alfred Stieglitz?

DT: Their love affair was a loaded one: Ambition. Desire. Sex. Love. Fame. Betrayal. A search for artistic freedom. The more I learned, the more I wanted to know. The stormy passion that characterized their marriage was intriguing, but the politics of that relationship, and how those politics impacted the work of both artists, even more so. Here was a young woman—intelligent and independent—with a ferocious artistic talent and a revolutionary vision years ahead of her time, and here was a man—famed art promoter and the father of modern photography—nearly twice her age and at the tail end of his own artistic career. He fell so deeply in love with her, had faith in her greatness, but needed to orchestrate every element of the world around him, blind to the risk of losing what he wanted most.

O'Keeffe was a strong woman who recognized that passion, sexual and otherwise, can be a key inspiration for creative work. That said, she refused to allow her art to be described in the eroticized language first assigned to it—language born out of Stieglitz's photographs of her and cultivated by the primarily male modernist New York art world of the

1920s. O'Keeffe balked at the feminization of her work. She had no interest in being a great *female* artist. She wanted her work viewed simply as art. She began to take clear, methodical steps to create a new lens and language to frame her artistic vision.

RHRC: *Georgia* is a highly researched historical novel. What was that experience like?

DT: Research is always a process of discovery. There is so much you learn about a person, a world, an era. You see the underside of things and it sparks your imagination. That process itself is thrilling. One thing that did strike me—and continues to strike me—is that O'Keeffe has been a powerful force in the consciousness of many women over time—artists, writers, feminists, curators, scholars—who have consistently dedicated themselves to holding her and her life up in a way that has ultimately precipitated a meaningful reassessment of her work and influence on twentieth-century American Art.

Georgia is a novel grounded in the actual events of O'Keeffe's life during the years she lived with Stieglitz in New York. Those years were a crucible for her. Those were the years when her art was first recognized. Those were the years when she fell in love, craved a child, had her heart broken, became famous, nearly lost what mattered to her most, and resolved never to compromise again. Those were the years when she made unthinkable sacrifices in her life and key innovations in her art. To my sense, those years forged her greatness. Not because of what Stieglitz, or anyone else, did for her, or to her, but for how she met and overcame the challenges and the gender bias that she faced; and for how she went on to shape the direction of her art and career on her own terms.

RHRC: What was your primary goal in writing this novel? Why did you decide to take on the story of a key American figure and explore—through fiction—a part of her life that is less well known?

DT: Vladimir Nabokov once called the art of fiction "a shimmering go-between" and that's the space I wanted to write into—the space between what happened and what could have. I wanted to craft a story about true events and circumstances to explore how O'Keeffe might have met and experienced those events, and also to reveal how our perception of her—even to this day—has been shadowed by the gendered language assigned to her early work. I believe in O'Keeffe's strength, her genius, and the creative innovations she made. The abstract art she was creating as early as 1915—and the abstractions she continued to create throughout her lifetime—gave rise to some of the most important artistic movements of the twentieth century. My hope is that *Georgia* gives readers a glimpse into that. And I hope it brings people to her art.

RHRC: What was the greatest challenge for you writing *Georgia?*

DT: The voice. It took me over a year to find the voice of this novel. I did research, filled notebooks (I still write my early drafts longhand). I studied her paintings and the evolution of her art over time. I looked at Stieglitz's portraits of her and portraits made by other photographers taken later in her life. I wrote pieces of scene, fragments of thought and dialogue, but most of those early pages felt like cardboard, and I tore them up. Throughout that first year of work, I'd catch glimpses of what I thought the voice would be, but I couldn't quite nail it.

I was not at my desk when it hit me. I was outside, down at the river with my two boys. It was a warm afternoon in April. They had their jeans rolled up and were playing in the water. I was lying on the dock in the sun, and the words came: "I no longer love you as I once did, in the dazzling rush of those early days. Time itself was feverish then, our bodies filled with fire. . . ."

I sat up and looked around and the world was different. I started writing the following day.

RHRC: Do you think O'Keeffe would have become the American icon she is today if she had stayed with Stieglitz?

DT: She might have been an iconic figure, but she would have been a different kind of icon if she had not removed herself from New York and the confines of that landscape and that life. That said, O'Keeffe is only just beginning to get her fair share of recognition in the art world. Last summer the Tate Modern in the UK held its first major retrospective of O'Keeffe's work and stated its goal to: "review O'Keeffe's work in depth and reassess her place in the canon of twentieth-century art, situating her within artistic circles of her own generation and indicating her influence on artists of subsequent generations." O'Keeffe has been known as one of the most famous figures of American art, but she has—often and incorrectly—been considered simply a "popular artist." Nothing could be further from the truth. The range of her work is stunning. Her abstractions are masterful—visceral, glowing, cerebral, strikingly original and precise.

RHRC: This novel took six years to write. What was it like to be engaged so deeply in Georgia O'Keeffe's life for that length of time?

DT: For me, writing is a kind of soul-excavation that is personal and, at the same time, transcends the personal. O'Keeffe's fierce spirit, her determination to build a life on her own terms, and the sacrifices she made for the sake of her art, remain the most inspiring aspects of her story.

Growing older, I've come to understand that a key part of a creative life—whether you are a working artist or not—is recognizing that every day is a choice. You choose to dedicate more or less time to a given endeavor. You develop ways to balance your work with your personal life. To me, that awareness of everyday choices is exhilarating, and there is also an attendant sadness. Every choice comes with a sacrifice. That's not a reason not to make it, or to apologize for a choice you've made. Choices made at one point in your life may change as the parameters of your life change. I believe in staying open to that. O'Keeffe was a strong, innovative woman who achieved fame and success in an art world dominated by men—male painters, critics, gallery owners. She did not apologize for the choices she made, and she continued to make bold choices, again and again, as she aged. That alone makes her story intensely relevant to women and artists today. It will make her story relevant years from now.

QUESTIONS AND TOPICS FOR DISCUSSION

1. Georgia O'Keeffe is a woman many people know of, but her life as a young woman in New York is a chapter that is less well known. How did your understanding of O'Keeffe and her art change as you were reading *Georgia*?

2. O'Keeffe was a groundbreaking female artist at a time when the art world was dominated by men. O'Keeffe had to navigate this world—of male artists, critics, and gallery owners—to build a successful career without sacrificing her unique artistic vision and her sense of herself as a woman. Discuss some of the challenges O'Keeffe faces in *Georgia*. Discuss how those challenges as well as the risks she took—as a woman and as an artist—feel relevant today.

3. Think about O'Keeffe's childhood. Do you feel that the lessons she learned growing up shaped her early relationship with Stieglitz and the

choices she would make later? Although O'Keeffe's mother died from tuberculosis a year before O'Keeffe traveled to New York to see her first show at 291, O'Keeffe is haunted by her mother, and by the choices that her mother made. Why were these choices significant, and what was their impact on O'Keeffe?

4. O'Keeffe's passion for the landscape is a powerful engine for her art. At one point, early in the novel, O'Keeffe thinks to herself that Stieglitz and his faith in her art are "like that open space, vast like these plains, this night, vast enough it seems sometimes to hold me." Do you agree with this? In what ways is this perception true when O'Keeffe first meets Stieglitz, and in what ways does it change as she matures? Do you feel her experience is one common to women as they evolve and change in the course of their lives?

5. In the opening chapter of the book, O'Keeffe contends: "This is not a love story. If it were, we would have the same story. But he has his, and I have mine." What do you think O'Keeffe means when she says this? In what ways is *Georgia* a love story? How does O'Keeffe's understanding of the word *love* change in the course of the novel?

6. The relationship between O'Keeffe and Stieglitz begins as an exchange of letters and art—her abstract charcoals, her paintings, and his photographs of her. At first O'Keeffe is fascinated by the woman she sees in the photographs, the "low defiant heat in her eyes that looks directly into the camera, poised, almost insolent. She seems absolute. No past. No future. She belongs strictly to herself, alone." What are your first impressions of this statement? How does Georgia's relationship to the woman in the photographs evolve over the course of the story?

7. Discuss O'Keeffe's breakdown. Why do you think she falls apart? Discuss what it means to her when she feels she is unable to paint, and thinks to herself: "This isn't just him, and what he's done to me. It's what I've let him do." Do you agree? At several points in the novel, Georgia reflects on the transactional nature of her relationship with Stieglitz. Do you

believe that every relationship—no matter how passionate or spiritual—is a kind of transaction?

8. Desire is a powerful force for O'Keeffe—artistic desire; desire for place, connection, and solitude; desire between two people. How does O'Keeffe's relationship to desire change? What does her exchange with Toomer toward the end of the book say about what she has learned? Discuss the ways in which love and desire overlap and diverge. Which is more vital to O'Keeffe? Which do you believe is more vital in your own life?

9. Georgia's relationship with Stieglitz was complex and controversial—it was a source of artistic growth for both artists, but it was also restricting. Discuss the dynamics in the relationship. Do they remind you of relationships in your own life—either relationships you have observed or relationships you have experienced? How have those relationships impacted your life? What have you learned from them?

10. Reflect on O'Keeffe's relationships with other women in the novel. How do those differ from the relationships she has with men—including Stieglitz, Strand, Toomer, Steichen, Rosenfeld, and others?

11. In the final sections of the novel, O'Keeffe becomes the legendary artist that we know. What sacrifices does she make as a result? Do you feel these were sacrifices she had to make in order to live and work on her own terms? Do you think those choices are unique to her? In what ways do you feel they are common choices that all women face?

12. If you could have one O'Keeffe painting in your home, which one would it be? Before reading this novel, would you have chosen a different O'Keeffe painting? How has your understanding of O'Keeffe and her art changed as a result of reading *Georgia*?

13. What do you think it means to be an icon? What did it mean to O'Keeffe during the time she was with Stieglitz? How did her identity and portrayal as an American icon change over the course of her life?

14. O'Keeffe is known for being fiercely independent, and she is often seen as a key figure of the feminist movement. O'Keeffe herself, however, publicly eschewed any "–ism," including feminism. Consider the gender dynamics in *Georgia*. Do you feel it was the politics of O'Keeffe's relationship with Stieglitz, her upbringing and the hardship of her young adult life, or her unique creative vision that shaped her resolute unwillingness to be associated with any movement, artistic or otherwise? Why do you feel that was so important to her? Discuss.

DAWN TRIPP's fourth novel, *Georgia*, is a national bestseller and finalist for the New England Book Award. Tripp is the author of three previous novels, *Moon Tide*, *The Season of Open Water*, which won the Massachusetts Book Award for Fiction, and *Game of Secrets*, a *Boston Globe* bestseller. Her essays have appeared in *The Virginia Quarterly Review*, *The Believer*, *The Rumpus*, *Psychology Today*, and NPR. She lives in Massachusetts with her family.

dawntripp.com

ABOUT THE TYPE

This book was set in Fournier, a typeface named for Pierre-Simon Fournier (1712–68), the youngest son of a French printing family. He started out engraving woodblocks and large capitals, then moved on to fonts of type. In 1736 he began his own foundry and made several important contributions in the field of type design; he is said to have cut 147 alphabets of his own creation. Fournier is probably best remembered as the designer of St. Augustine Ordinaire, a face that served as the model for the Monotype Corporation's Fournier, which was released in 1925.